Sins as Red as Scarlet
a Devon town in turmoil

Sins as Red

as Scarlet

a Devon town in turmoil

by Janet Few

Cover art by Robin Paul facebook.com/thebranchline
Published by Blue Poppy Publishing 2020
info@bluepoppypublishing.co.uk
Printed by Severn - Gloucester

ISBN 13 : 978-1-911438-73-1

Acknowledgements

As always, when a project such as this comes to fruition, there are people to thank. In particular, I would like to mention my daughter, the real Martha, who might resemble the Martha of this book in some ways but who is emphatically not the same as the fictional Martha. Her copy-editing skills are unparalleled. Any errors that remain will be because I went back and tweaked things after the text had passed her scrutiny. I would like to thank the members of my authors' group for their encouragement during the two years whilst *Sins as Red as Scarlet* was gestating. I pay tribute to my colleagues at Swords and Spindles and my former colleagues at the now demised Torrington 1646, without whom my understanding of seventeenth century life would be the poorer. The talented Dan Britton *chrisconway.org/dan.html* has composed a compelling companion song for *Sins as Red as Scarlet*. Thank you, Dan for achieving this, despite the added complications of recording during lockdown. The words of Dan's powerful song have been reproduced at the end of this book. I would also like to thank Dr Cheryl Hayden for sharing her extensive research on the Winslade family. My publisher, Olli, who single-handedly manages Blue Poppy Publishing, has been brilliant, as ever. Robin Paul of The Branch Line *facebook.com/thebranchline* has created an amazing cover from my vague suggestions and scribbles that were the first 'art' I had produced since failing art O level not once but twice. Finally, I thank my nearest and dearest, who put up with me and made sure that I did eat occasionally during my preoccupation with *Sins as Red as Scarlet*.

A Note About Martha's Version of 2020

In some ways, Martha's experience of the year 2020 does not reflect reality. Although the modern strand of this novel is set between June and September 2020, the writing was completed by April of that year. The narrative contains references to actual events that took place at the end of 2019 and during the early months of 2020 but the more serious ramifications of the COVID-19 pandemic were not compatible with the plot. After much consideration, I decided that Martha should inhabit an alternative version of the year 2020. Although the seventeenth century portion of the book is based on fact, this is, after all, a novel. So, COVID-19 does exist in Martha's world but its effects are far less severe. I hope that readers do not feel that this trivialises the situation that engulfed the world in the spring and summer of 2020.

Janet Few 2020

This story is dedicated to all victims of intolerance, past and present.

The Folk you will Meet
In Seventeenth Century Byddeforde

The seventeenth century characters in this novel are all based on real people. In a few cases, their Christian names have been changed to avoid confusion between the many Marys, Elizabeths, Williams and Anns.

Bess Gard - a daughter
Susanna Edwards – a soldier's wife
Davy Edwards – Susanna's husband
Rachel Wynslade – Susanna's mother
Henry Ravening – a barber surgeon
The family of Hugh and Julianna Cadwell – plague victims
John Strange – one-time mayor of Byddforde
'Goody' Temperance Lloyd – a seaman's widow and sometime healer
William Bartlett – a preacher of Independent thought
Reverend Arthur Gifford – a sorely tried rector

Mistress Ellyott – a woman accused of witchcraft

Walter Herbert – a old man who believed himself bewitched

Will and Margaret Herbert – a blacksmith and his wife

Lydia Burman – a self-righteous accuser

Reverend Nathaniel Eaton – a maverick rector

John Harvard – the founder of a college

William Ames – a Calvinist

John Davie – a creditor and wealthy merchant of Byddeforde

Dorcas Lidstone – a young woman seeking attention

Jack Coleman – the object of her affections

Jane Dallyn – a woman afflicted

Ann Fellow – an Excise Officer's daughter

Reverend Michael Ogilvy – a rector with a fondness for strong liquor

Mary Trembles – a woman lost

Grace Thomas – a woman who believed herself bewitched

Eliza Eastchurch née Thomas – Grace's sister

Tom Eastchurch – Grace's brother-in law

Annie Wakely – a friend to Grace Thomas

John Hill – a town clerk

Master Hann – an erstwhile curate

Doctor Beare – a physician

Joseph Barnes – an accuser

Charity Barnes – his wife, who believed herself bewitched

Mistress Jones – an accuser

Anthony Jones – her husband, a man taken in a fit

Benedict Dunscome, Philip Weekes, Edmund Smale and Robert Wren – four lads in search of a witch
Elizabeth Caddy – a respectable matron
Mistress Weekes – an accuser
Robert Weekes – her husband
Polly Beare – a woman betrothed
Henry Paul – a man reluctant to take a wife
Moll Fry – a downtrodden companion
Francis North – a compassionate man of the law
Roger North – his brother, a recorder
Thomas Raymond – a sycophantic man of the law

The Characters In 2020

Martha
Hebe – Martha's mother
Gran
Calliope – Martha's dog
Mr Mortimer – an inspirational teacher
Tyrone, Alfie, Jeremy, Poppy, Lucie, Hunter, Kayleigh, Skye and Zainab – Martha's fellow students
Lynn – a re-enactor
Joan – a Devon Family History Society volunteer

Prologue
Bess' Story
25 August 1682

I watch them die, these three. Their bodies twisting and gyrating in a parody of dance, as their bladders and bowels betray them. For those around me it is but a jaunt, a spectacle that will be on their lips for a space and then forgotten. For me though, for me, it cuts to the heart. I stand close, close enough to hear their last words. She speaks of sin, she does, she who is tied to me by invisible cords. She who is the first to swing. Sins as red as scarlet and yes, I know. I know sin stains many souls.

***

We'd arrived early, whilst the dew-scent still sullied the grass. The children became restive as we waited; young Nathaniel grew heavy in my arms. A sickly child, I dared not let him run free with his brothers. Had I kin to whom I could have entrusted my precious babe, I would not have brought him on such a journey. There was no one. My brothers, long since gone for sailors; narry a word I've had from them for many a year. Most like they've minded to settle in the New World, as my father-in-law has done. We might have joined them, my good Master and I but we are content to bide in Byddeforde and we prosper in some small way. He is a good man my Richard. Folk whispered when he took me to wife, murmured that I was not of his rank, prated that my sisters were whores and that my blood carried a papist stain. Yet he looked to ignore them Richard did and now I am Mistress Gard, respectable matron. I have given him five sons and we bear the sadness that two lie within the churchyard's shade. 'Tis rare now that folk remember that I am sister to Kathryn and to Unis, who both brought forth babes afore they were wed. Few call to mind that I am my mother's daughter and on a day such as this, 'tis a blessing.

The whispers of mist burned away as the sun climbed above the shimmering horizon; another day of heat and gathering storms. Undeterred, the bystanders gathered. Restless we stood, nameless within the crush of the crowd. They came to gawp, to exclaim, they came to tremble in anticipation. For them, the frisson of voyeurism. For them the comfortable relief that those who were to die were naught to them but mere players in a show put on for their gratification. The time drew nigh. They were all there, the accusers, the arresters, those who had come for the pleasure of it and in amongst them stood I, feigning indifference. The press of people on Magdalen Street parted as the women were led forward; women who knew that they would never see another sunrise. My eyes were drawn to the first. She looked slatternly, diminished. When did she become so very old? When did her vigour leave her and the years begin to weigh her down? I bowed my head lest I should be recognised by the one whose last breath I had come to witness.

An updraught caught a dandelion clock, which fluttered in the sunbeams, out of reach of a chasing child. A simple thing, yet it brought to mind days long past. Days when a motherly hand clasped mine as we wandered, carefree in the fields; brothers, sisters, kin I know no more. The crowd quietened. Even the food-sellers ceased calling their wares. They led her forward, that poor dame, who bore only some small resemblance to she whom I had known in the fullness of her life. She asked that they should sing a psalm. A strange final request for one who eschewed the church. The ragged strains were taken up by the crowd. My tongue stumbled across the fitting words.

"For innumerable evils have compassed me about: mine iniquities have taken hold upon me, so that I am not able to look up; they are more than the hairs of mine head: therefore my heart faileth me."

What brought that psalm to mind? What long-buried remembrance prompted her to desire those words within her ears as her heart stilled? I wanted to avert my gaze. I dreaded the death throes, the moment when it would be done. Yet I could not look away. I knew that I must behold the end. How did it come to this? I feel I should know. I should know what tangled web of circumstances steered her upon this path. Why was it she who stood sobbing, with the rope above her swinging gently in the breeze? She spoke of scarlet sins, sins that have stained so many lives. Yet the sins are not hers alone, others too must bear the burden of blame.

Martha's Story
Autumn 2020

Martha pressed 'save' with a satisfied smile. Her project was finished. Over the past couple of months, the inhabitants of seventeenth century Bideford, their hardships, their foibles and their intolerances, had become more familiar to Martha than the people around her. Nothing changes, she thought sadly, there were always those who were too quick to judge, to ridicule others for their differences and to condemn. Martha bore her own hidden scars and anxieties; insecurities that were the legacy of taunts, of snide remarks, of careless posts on social media. She'd long since abandoned the attempt to understand why she was the bullies' target but she was beginning to unravel the many factors that contributed to those three women from her home town climbing the gallows on that sultry August day in 1682.

Three Months Earlier

Martha's feet scuffled in the dust as she waited for the school bus. If she pretended to look at her phone, perhaps she would be left in peace. Why was she even on her way to school? Her exams were over and Martha had been anticipating a long holiday, respite from the anguish of the classroom. Everything about Martha was ammunition for her tormentors. She was bright, expected to get top marks in the GCSE exams that she had just completed. For a spell in year eight Martha had tried doing deliberately badly but that had only served to incur the wrath of the teachers and took away the one positive side to school, the chance to learn and to do well. She hated sport, she wasn't interested in boys; to be truthful, Martha didn't really like people. She preferred books and writing and taking her dog on long, solitary rambles. She no longer tried to fit in, to make friends; whatever she attempted backfired.

The bus halted with a screech and a sigh on the edge of the village green opposite Martha's home. She lived with her mother in a seventeenth century cottage that was just too far from town for Martha to be able to walk to school, so the daily bus ride was another gauntlet that had to be run. Her mother, Hebe, was an additional cause for derisory comments. She attracted the contempt of those whose narrow lives were circumscribed by the need to belong, by all being conventionally the same, by mocking anyone who was not like them. No one else had a mother with dreadlocks and rainbow-striped leg warmers, a mother who brewed herbal potions and went on protest marches, a mother who insisted on a vegan diet and avoided the use of plastic.

The crowd of unheeding students pushed past her, the weight of the bag across Martha's back swung her round, as a boy collided heavily with her shoulder. Was it deliberate? Hard to tell. There were a few sniggers as Martha stumbled in an attempt to maintain her footing. The last to board the bus, Martha gingerly lowered herself on the extreme edge of the seat, next to the least-worst person, anxious to avoid body contact, eye contact, any sort of contact really.

***

The classroom had an abandoned air, as if it had already settled into its dusty, summer holiday mode, even though there were still four weeks left of term. Martha was the first to arrive, she chose her seat with care. It was essential to avoid the tables furthest from the front, those were for the popular, for the accepted. Not too near the teacher either, or that would give the impression that she was a keen student, another sure way to get noticed and not in a good way. Pupils bundled through the door, crashing bags on tables, pulling headphones from their ears, calling to friends, ignoring Martha. Mr Mortimer swept in and perched on the teacher's desk. Martha pushed her glasses back up her nose, it was a nervous habit rather than an essential manoeuvre. Why had her mother insisted on her returning to school for a month for the pre-sixth form enrichment course? The only consolation was that there was no way her main persecutors would be taking part. They were full of plans for beach barbecues on the dunes, or summer jobs in the local holiday camp. Martha sighed. Here she was, consigned to four weeks incarcerated with the other misfits in the humanities group.

Dave Mortimer, not long out of training college, was keen to have something to boost his CV. He could make a success of this. It was a teacher's dream. A class of students who had opted to be there, devoid, he hoped, of all the troublemakers. Such freedom to let his pupils learn without the constraints of an exam syllabus and target grades was rare.

"Right guys," he said with a hearty attempt at enthusiasm. "You have all chosen Arts subjects in the sixth form. We are going to build on that and encourage the sort of independent study that will stand you in good stead next year and when you go to uni'."

Mr Mortimer looked at the dozen not-so-eager faces in front of him, wondering whether agreeing to run this course was such a good idea after all. His examination classes had finished; he could have been enjoying the luxury of the free lessons instead. He was losing them; he could feel that he was losing them before he had even started.

"You can work alone, or in twos or threes," he began.

Martha shuddered, working with others was the worst possible thing. Either she ended up doing everything herself, in order to get a good mark, or she remained silent whilst others mucked about and did it all wrong. She refocussed on what Mr Mortimer was saying.

"You will research your chosen topic and present it however you like. We are thinking interdisciplinary here guys."

Several students exchanged puzzled glances.

"You can focus on whatever subject areas interest you most. At the end of this four weeks, you will have created an art installation, a video, a piece of drama," Martha looked bleak, "or a short story, or an epic poem," he went on.

That might be better, Martha thought. Much as she didn't want to be like her mother, who fancied herself a poet, amongst other things, secretly, Martha did enjoy putting her thoughts on to paper.

"The only restriction is that your work must somehow be connected to Bideford."

The students looked at their teacher uncomprehendingly, such a free rein was something that they were not used to. How on earth could you pick a topic when you could pretty much choose anything?

"Ok," said Mr Mortimer, "ideas?"

There was an eerie silence broken only by the sound of the caretaker strimming the parched grass outside the window.

Finally, a response, "Like what sir?"

"Yes sir, we can't think anything."

Dave Mortimer hesitated, if he started making suggestions, the kids would stick with what he said, they needed to think outside the box.

"Right," he said, "let's take Martha here."

Please, thought Martha, reddening, please just let's not but Mortimer was gaining in confidence now.

"What options have you chosen for sixth-form, Martha? I know you are down to study history with me."

"Yes, sir," mumbled Martha, "and English and psychology."

"Ideal," enthused Mr Mortimer. "So, you choose an incident or legend from Bideford's history. You can research it in the library and I'll explain to you about going up to the Record Office in Barnstaple. You don't have to do all this in the classroom, the idea is to get you out and about. We will be studying the Stuarts next term, so I recommend that you perhaps look at what was going on in the town in the seventeenth century and then you can pick something that catches your interest and write it up as a short story, a poem or a play, which brings in your English."

"How's that linked to psychology then sir?"

There had to be one smart-arse, thought Mr Mortimer, as he eyed up the speaker, a hefty lad who was slumped in his chair, flicking his pen between his fingers.

"History is about people, Tyrone, people and how they behave. So, Martha can try to understand why particular things happened. She can investigate what there was about the people involved and their backgrounds that made them make certain choices, or act in a specific way, what motivated them. There's your psychology."

Tyrone rocked his chair onto its back legs and wished he'd agreed to help his father on the farm instead of coming along to these stupid lessons. He had thought he could wing this project lark, that it would be less hard graft than the early morning milking but it seemed that he couldn't even have the fun of baiting Mortimer.

"Do you see Martha?"

"Yes, I think so," replied Martha hesitantly. "How do I know what was happening in Bideford in the 1600s?"

"I can give you a couple of websites for a brief overview and then you can concentrate on whatever appeals," said Mr Mortimer. "There was plenty going on here then. Bideford was booming."

A few of the students looked incredulous at this, Bideford was a backwater, nothing ever happened. There was nowhere to go, nothing to do, the best they got was the fireworks at New Year; even the carnival was rubbish unless you were a kid.

"Merchants were making their fortunes from tobacco, ships were sailing back and forth to the New World. Prosperous inhabitants were building the town. Who's spotted the date on one of the houses in Bridgeland Street?"

No one had. Why did kids never look up from their phones for five minutes and see the town where they lived? thought Mortimer.

"Well they were built at the end of the seventeenth century. Then there was the plague and the Civil War and the Bideford witches."

"I'n't there summat about them on a plaque thingy by the library sir?"

Hallelujah, at least someone paid attention to their surroundings but Alfie's mother worked at the library, so if he hadn't noticed, what chance was there for the rest of them?

"Ok sir," said Martha, "can I use one of the tablets and start Googling?"

"Yes, of course," said Mr Mortimer. One down, eleven recalcitrant students to motivate.

Martha scrolled through the websites Mr Mortimer had recommended, trying to get a feel for the key events in Bideford's seventeenth century past, searching for something that could be a starting point for her project. The Civil War. That might be interesting. When Martha was about seven or eight, Hebe had briefly belonged to a group of Civil War re-enactors, attracted by the chance to exploit her knowledge of herbal medicine as part of their living history team. For one long summer, Martha had been dragged from field to field dressed in a scratchy, woollen outfit, that was deemed suitably

11

authentic. Her memories were of the smells rather than precise details. The open fire smoking when someone threw on a green log, the pungent drying herbs, the musty aroma of the shady canvas tent, the acrid stench of the black powder when the musketeers fired a volley. Already, words were forming patterns in Martha's head; she could see how the Civil War might form part of her story. She wasn't sure she could write from the standpoint of one of the soldiers, that was too far from her experience but one of the women, perhaps.

***

Mr Mortimer had put Martha in touch with a living history group who specialised in the English Civil War period. Fortunately, it wasn't the one that Hebe had been involved with as there had, Martha vaguely recalled, been an acrimonious parting of the ways. So, dressed once again in borrowed period costume, Martha found herself self-consciously accompanying Lynn to a nearby recreation of a Civil War battle. Lynn was a diminutive figure, approaching sixty, who clearly took her re-enacting very seriously. Martha had been worried that she might not be welcome but Lynn but was patently very enthusiastic about sharing her extensive knowledge.

"It's lucky that the battle anniversary has fallen just right for you timewise," said Lynn as they lugged baskets of props on to the area that was doing duty as a battlefield for the day. "We don't go out every week, so you could easily have had a long wait before there was an event like this."

Mallets rattled as tents were erected and an arena was roped off, ready for the battle to take place. Martha stayed on the side-lines, watching, learning, absorbing the atmosphere. She was stationed with Lynn and a small group of middle-aged ladies, in the tent dedicated to textiles. So, Lynn sat spinning, whilst others were weaving, carding or dying wool. Spinning looked unbelievably complicated to Martha, rather like patting your head and rubbing your tummy at the same time, she thought. Under Lynn's deft fingers the carded fleece swiftly transformed into evenly spun yarn. When a member of the public approached, Martha shrunk back, dreading that someone would expect her to speak, to have knowledge that she didn't possess. At least there was no danger of being recognised by anyone she knew; this was the last place people from school would come. Between spells of chatting to those who stopped by the tent, Lynn unleashed a torrent of facts about daily life in the seventeenth century. The tricky part was taking notes. Martha's anachronistic, rapidly filling, spiral-bound notebook and purple plastic pen had to be concealed from the public.

Outside, the drumbeats grew louder and Lynn suggested that they went to watch the battle. Hiding in a tent was one thing, being seen dressed like an idiot amongst the crowds was another. As she left the cool tent, Martha tugged her coif down over her ears and took a deep breath, hoping to quell her rising panic. Her eyes took a moment to adjust to the sunlight. In the arena, two opposing armies faced each other. Flags furled and unfurled in the wind, insults were hurled, swords were drawn, pikemen marched unerringly forward. Then the musket-fire that was so firmly etched in Martha's memory. A layer of smoke hung momentarily above the onlookers, before dispersing in the breeze. Martha's anxiety faded as she became absorbed in the sights and sounds that surrounded her. Patiently, Lynn talked Martha through every stage of the battle re-enactment. Martha itched to get back to her notebook before all the impressions were lost. She could do this. Now she could visualise how her project might develop. She had her notes, she had some books that Lynn had loaned her but most importantly, in her head, were the words that she needed to begin her story.

Chapter 1
Susanna's Story
1642-1643

"Charge for Horse!", the captain's rasping shout sunk beneath the battle-noise.

The quaking drummer, scarce more than a boy, rolled the required tattoo. Reluctant pikemen, exhausted beyond measure, fixed their weapons. A forest of metal-tipped wood lowered; deathly spikes trained upon the oncoming enemy. Sweat-flecked horses, eyes rolling, nostrils flaring, thundered across the heathland. Then, swirling, screaming, spinning, rearing, to avoid the impenetrable iron barbs of the defending pike-block. Riders sawed at bits, struggling for control, fighting to stay astride their terrified mounts. Those who failed were trampled beneath pounding, churning hooves, their death-screams obliterated by the crack of musket and the clash of sword. A veil of smoke rose and fell.

The sulphur stench caught at the throats of man and beast without discrimination. A momentary lull, all too brief, as the second rank of musketeers moved forward, their fellows falling back to reload for the next assault.

Boots slipped and soldiers cursed as they struggled to keep their foothold on the squelching mud. What was war but interminable marching, punctuated by gut-wrenching fear such as this, when their opponents were in range? Who indeed was a comrade, who an adversary? Who were these enemies that they sought to kill, lest they themselves be killed? Somewhere in that whirling mire of mud and bloodshed, somewhere in that hostile army, might be friend, neighbour, brother, a man you'd shared a yarn with, or a draught of March beer. A man like yourself, who thought of family, fretted over fields un-ploughed and dreamed of home. And all for what? For king? For country? For some inexplicable cause that their betters deemed worthy of such slaughter? Yet, here they were, pikes discarded once the first push was over, wielding swords now, dodging, lunging, thrusting, ducking to escape the iron-clad butt of a musket swung by one who had no time to pour powder and ball down a still-warm barrel. Here they were fighting. Crying. Dying.

***

Daybreak's weak light reflected in the remnants of the past week's rain. Threads of gauzy mist hovered over the puddles and the mud. Endless mud. It spattered and seeped, clinging to clothing and caking boots, impeding every step. The once lush grass had fallen victim to the buffeting of the horses' hooves. On the edges of the battlefield, moisture dripped from the browning bracken. Strewn carelessly across hastily-constructed, wooden frames, sodden blankets steamed. Moisture beaded on the canvas slopes and gently gathered to form rivulets that fell from the tents' sides. The sky was streaked with ochre and grey but finally, mercifully, the rain had ceased. Rain dampened skin and spirits in equal measure. It leached into shoes, soaked bedding and firewood, jacket and shawl, depriving folk of every fragment of comfort.

The tethered horses nodded their heads, bits jangling, their breath escaping in hissing clouds. Early risers squelched across the ravaged earth and fanned the flames of the dying fires. Damp wood spluttered and smoked, making eyes stream and throats constrict. Morale was low and not just because of the weather. The anticipated swift victory had not been forthcoming. The enemy had shown surprising resilience; rumours of Royalist unpreparedness had been greatly exaggerated. Desultorily, soldiers rolled from their tents. After yesterday's inconclusive skirmish surely today they could oust their adversaries from this benighted valley and move on.

Briefly, Susanna Edwards wondered whether abandoning life in the relative security of Byddeforde had been a wise decision. She might have remained behind whilst Davy went to war. Yet she had thrown in her lot with the driggle-draggle throng of women who followed their menfolk from one bloody battlefield to another. Had she really had a choice? In times of conflict passions were inflamed, differences heightened and the marginalised, the outsiders, provoked not just indifference but alarm. There had seemed little option but to leave. She had needed to get away from the taunts and the gibes and the occasional hurled missile.

Eleven Months Earlier

Late on a Friday night, with frost sheening the rutted lanes, Parliament's soldiers marched into Byddeforde. An army on the move is never silent. Nailed boots clashed on the stony road, horses threw back their heads and whinnied, armour clanked and men called to each other across the darkness. It had been but a short march from Barnstaple and the troops' nervous enthusiasm was not yet dimmed. The three companies of foot set up camp on the edge of the town, eager to swell their ranks with local men on the morrow.

Davy Edwards, sluggish from a surfeit of ale, saw them arrive. The night-air's sharpness cleared his befuddled brain as he lurked on the edges of the encampment, hoping to learn something to his advantage. Byddeforde had not treated him well of late. He wondered if it had been prudent to leave his life working a barque, criss-crossing the Bristol channel, bringing culm from the South Wales coast. At the time, it had seemed shrewd to settle on the banks of the Torridge. He had been reassured by the familiarity of a town that he'd visited often. He'd wed a local girl, not pondering on what she might bring him beyond a willing body and a flashing smile. It was the turbulence of recent times that had made him uneasy and it was Susanna who had brought trouble to their door. Mayhap 'twould be in their favour to get away for a space. There were worse things than the life of a soldier and he cared not whether he fought for king or parliament.

At first, Susanna had remonstrated when he took work building Chudleigh's fort, a scar upon the hillside on the Torridge's eastern shore and a permanent reminder of Parliamentarian power. Yet she'd buried her reservations, ignored her instinctive sympathy for the discredited king and been grateful for the coin he'd earned. The money had been more than welcome, they'd nought left for bread nor ale. Fallen so low they had, that, for the sake of the babe, they'd swallowed their pride and gone as supplicants to the church. They left empty-handed. "Not deserving", they'd said. Davy could still see the gleam in the overseer's eyes as he refused them, as if the man derived some salacious enjoyment from their plight. It was Chudleigh's call for labourers that had saved them. In any case, whatever conscience might dictate, 'twas ever wise to be the pragmatist, to side with those who looked set to be the victor.

Unobtrusively, Davy wound his way between the groups of soldiers, as fires were lit and tents pitched. Huddles of men stamped their feet and swung their arms against the cold, oblivious to the presence of an interloper. Davy was used to blending in with a crowd, watching, listening, gleaning invaluable information that might trip from careless lips. Snatched conversations overheard told him that this band, under Sergeant Major Benson, were seeking volunteers to march upon the Royalist troops. The adversaries were thought to be not far distant in Torryngtowne, a town that was staunch for the king.

Though it was but a few miles hence, Torryngtowne was very different from Byddeforde. In Byddeforde, the likes of preacher Bartlett stirred up support for the Parliamentarian cause with their vehemence and their rhetoric, speaking out against pomp and popery at every opportunity. No matter that the lords of the manor had been in high favour with the monarchy for generations past. Just last year the corporation had seen fit to appoint Bartlett as lecturer to assist the rector. Bartlett upheld the views of those who had engaged him, proving to be a thoroughgoing puritan, who could find sin in the most innocent of actions. Lewis Stucley too, a well-connected man of ancient lineage, with considerable influence in the town, was firm set against the king and Byddeforde folk were swift to ape their betters, to be swayed by what they heard. No matter that these men, who proclaimed piety, used righteousness as a cloak for self-interest. There were few who would reason for themselves, who would dare to swim against the puritanical tide. In truth, most were like Davy Edwards, keen to remain unnoticed, unremarked, out of trouble, leaving the posturing, the speechifying, the decision-making, to those of rank.

He'd heard enough. Davy slipped away through the darkness, resolving to offer as a volunteer at daybreak. As for Susanna, she could do as she wished, come along or stay and shift for herself. Like as not she'd follow the army at a distance with the baggage train and the other womenfolk. Some, respectable goodwives who were reluctant to leave their men to face the privations of war alone. Others, women of a more disreputable kind, who sought to give solace to soldiers in return for a share of the vittals and the warmth of a rough blanket as night fell.

The next day, Davy presented himself, along with some two hundred other men from the town and the nearby villages of Appledore and Northam. Many were seamen by trade, as Davy himself had been, with little knowledge of warfare beyond haphazard attendance at pike drill after morning service on the Lord's Day. It mattered not to those in charge. Men were what they needed. Men to cow the enemy with the sheer force of numbers. Dispensable men, men who could face musket-fire and sword and little matter if they survived or fell, as long as there was victory for the cause.

The new recruits crowded together on the rough ground beyond the town, unsure of what to do. A heaving mass of horses added to the confusion. They were led by soldiers who had been sent out to local farms to commandeer shires and cobs, scarce caring that these were the livelihood of their former owners. The confused beasts, their legs encrusted with winter mud, showed the whites of their eyes and shivered, as much from fear as from the cold. Occasionally, one reared from the mass of its fellows, pulling its halter taught, thrashing hooves threatening nearby man and beast alike. Soon, clumsily-erected hurdles contained the tightly-packed bodies of the animals and they, like the men, awaited their fate.

Susanna Edwards tightened the shawl that bound her squirming infant to her back. She could scarce let her daughter roam in this press of people. She was pleased that Davy had volunteered, there was nothing for them in Byddeforde whilst war raged and folk sought papists under every stone. Mayhap later when this was over, whatever over might mean, surely then she could return to the town of her birth without fear of persecution.

***

Many months had passed since then. They had seen out the seasons following the fortunes of the Parliamentarian army as it criss-crossed the county. It had begun with the encounter at Torryngtowne. Then the winter's campaign in Plymouth, when Chudleigh's men had been sent to aid the relief of the besieged city. That had sorely tried the soldiers and the women had suffered alongside. The men had been ill-prepared, with too few muskets and foot-soldiers who were reduced to wielding pitchforks in place of swords. Nigh on a hundred and fifty men were captured by the king's forces and they'd led away some thirty poorly guarded pack animals loaded with ammunition and vital supplies. Ofttimes they were gut-foundered; hunger was ever a part of the campaign trail. The dull ache of an empty belly was commonplace.

Susanna scanned the sky, clouds were amassing; like as not the rain would return afore long. Regardless of the weather, the enemy must be driven back. In the clearing beyond the camp, the men formed ranks, preparing for another futile battle. For Susanna, one skirmish was much like any other, soul-chilling, devastating, purposeless. Few encounters distinguished themselves from the never-ending blur of marching, of struggling, of worrying but the prospect of yet more rain brought their time at Sourton to Susanna's mind. In the spring that was and they'd been camped on Dartmoor's peaty edge. The talk was of insufficient ordnance. The men feared defeat and their womenfolk widowhood. It had been difficult to commandeer dray horses to drag falconet or cannon. Word was that the locals, hearing that the army were short of horse-flesh, had secreted their animals away before the soldiers came. The Royalists had looked fair set for victory until heavy bursts of stinging droplets blurred the view and threatened to dampen the powder, rendering muskets useless.

Susanna and the other women had huddled in tents that proved inadequate protection against the onslaught of the storm. Thunder roared. Lightning cracked the sky. The men returned with stories of how it had ignited the bandoliers and powder flasks of the king's musketeers. The pious saw it as a portent, a sign that God was on their side. The downpour had put an end to that particular encounter, yet there'd been so many more. They'd been at Stratton when Chudleigh was captured, turned his coat, they said and in truth the news had but late come that Chudleigh had fallen, defending Dartmouth against Fairfax and the men he had once led. Susanna felt a pang of regret, Davy had respected Chudleigh as a fair commander, even though he drove his men hard.

In the early days, Susanna had attempted to maintain some semblance of normality, laundering shirts and shifts in the stream, striving to prepare nourishing food, garnering the bounty that might be found in woodland and in hedgerow. She was not the only mother amongst the camp followers. Children were kept well away from

23

the fighting but they were there, lurking in the shelter of the trees, corralled by anxious mothers as the battle-sounds reverberated and fear stalked. Now, hampered by advancing pregnancy and the presence of two-year-old Unis, Susanna was struggling. She dreaded the prospect of another winter. Time was that campaigning ceased when days were short and temperatures plummeted but it seemed that there was always just one more interminable march, one more siege to be relieved, one more battle to be fought.

As Susanna thought back, she acknowledged that, even before the war, Byddeforde had shunned her. Indeed, if truth be told, it had been ever thus. Her deepest childhood memories were of being shamed in the street. Her mother, Rachel Wynslade, had tried to shield Susanna and her sister from the sneers, the glances, the backs that turned when they walked the town's lanes. It was as if, inexplicably, passers-by feared that their mere presence might contaminate.

A single incident stood out in Susanna's mind. She'd been but a small child of perhaps seven summers, walking with her mother, when a stout woman in a blue cape, strange that Susanna could still recall that cape, had stepped in front of them blocking their path. As Rachel had side-stepped to avoid her, dragging Susanna roughly by the arm, the woman too had moved across, impeding their progress down the narrow alley. Although she could visualise the dull blue of the cape, memories of the incident were a blur of anger, of fear and of perplexity. Why was this goodwife so cross? What had Susanna done to so enrage her? Still, the shame and the guilt haunted Susanna. She had blamed herself for the stranger's wrath. It must be her fault, she'd thought; it could not have been her mother's. Surely all must love her mother who was good and perfect and quietly-spoken.

The child that was Susanna had tried to recall recent misdemeanours. Was it because she had failed to darn her shift sufficiently neatly, or because she had been less than fervent at her prayers? Why was her mother motionless, scarlet-faced and silent, as this threatening harridan, blue cape swirling, shouted ever louder? Words poured from the woman's mouth, unstoppable, irretrievable. Much of the invective Susanna's childish brain had not understood but some phrases were still etched in her mind, perhaps because, as they were uttered, Rachel's whitening knuckles had tightened their grip on Susanna's hand. Although she had held her head high, Rachel's anguish and her embarrassment were palpable. Susanna, tainted by her mother's torment, took on the mantle of humiliation.

"Strumpet steeped in whoredom," the woman screamed, waving an accusatory finger in Rachel's face.

Susanna had later asked Rachel the meaning of these strange words. Rachel, usually so patient with her daughter's constant questions, had failed to answer. That in itself had been concerning. It was not until she was near grown that Susanna understood that many deemed the papist ceremony her mother had gone through to be no true marriage. A shadowy, insubstantial figure, the man she must call father, a man she seldom saw, a man whose name she did not share. Yet Rachel had considered herself wed, in the eyes of the church at least and surely that was what mattered.

For others though it was the wrong sort of church, certainly the wrong sort of priest and perhaps even the wrong sort of god that had borne witness to the joining of hands of Rachel and her man. They had plighted their troth against the wishes of their families. The Wynslades had long been followers of the old ways, the papist ways and had suffered in the upheavals of the current regime, the Church of England as they must call it. Well, it was not the church of the Wynslades, nor was it the way of worship of Rachel's upbringing.

Susanna knew that she had wealthy kinfolk in Byddeforde still. Time was, she'd heard tell, the Wynslades had had a big estate out Putford way. Gentry those Wynslades had been, until staying true to the ancient manner of worship had brought them low. Not that Susanna was known to those whom she might call cousin. Rachel strove to avoid them, shrinking back in doorways when she glimpsed them in the street; attempting to remain unnoticed by those whose blood she shared, yet who had disowned her.

Many was the time that Susanna had been railed at for popery, yet she was indifferent to the ranging and ever-changing shades of worship. She had learned to be non-committal, to keep her religious observance restrained and beneath the notice of the authorities. Yet there were those in Byddeforde whose memories were long, those who knew that Susanna was tainted by the dual stain of bastardy and Catholicism. When boredom struck, they would revive those half-forgotten thoughts for the sport of baiting one who discomforted others by her difference. In these tumultuous times, folk cleaved to their own. Harsh though life was following the army, 'twas prudent that Susanna kept away until suspicions settled and folk looked to their own affairs once more.

***

Two soldiers sweated and strained as they struggled to the wooded edge of the battlefield, bearing their wounded comrade between them. There on the periphery Susanna and the other womenfolk stood, sheltering from the rain, watching, fearful, guiltily relieved when the latest casualty proved not to be their man. A fresh-faced boy this last, with no trace of a man's beard-growth. His blue jerkin was blackening as the blood oozed from a wound in the lad's side. He moaned softly as Susanna gently removed the louse-ridden woollen coat. If he survived this hurt like as not the typhus would get him, thought Susanna, when she saw the crusts of blood on the boy's neck, a legacy of the lice's presence. Yet try she must, try to bring some meaning from this senseless slaughter. She sought her bag containing her precious herbs; remedies she'd carried with her from the outset. No amulet for her but the hessian sack was a talisman nonetheless, her best defence against harm that might befall her, or Davy, or their child.

Susanna lifted the lad's shirt to better see the damage that the musket ball had inflicted. She wondered at the binding on his chest. An old wound perhaps, yet the linen showed no stain of blood or pus. The other women crowded round.

"Send for the surgeon, mistress there's naught that we can do to treat such a wound."

"If the ball is still within his body the poison will spread. Best we leave it to the surgeon."

No one had laid eyes upon the lackadaisical surgeon since daybreak. He trailed behind the army with the womenfolk, reluctant and habitually in drink. Ofttimes, when he was most needed, he would be inexplicably absent.

"I think the ball has passed through," Susanna said as she probed the wound.

She had followed the army long enough, aiding those who had fallen victim to enemy fire. She knew that even if the ball was not within, an injury fouled with dirt from the black powder, or fragments of clothing, might be equally deadly. The boy flinched and groaned again.

"There be no cause to seek the surgeon," Susanna went on. "I must staunch the wound afore any more blood is lost."

The young soldier began to shake uncontrollably, his eyes closed in his whitening face, as his life-blood leaked on to the unforgiving ground.

"Is he taken in a fit mistress? Have a care, the devil might be abroad."

"'Tis often thus with those that are grievous hurt," Susanna responded.

She had seen this afore when soldiers had taken a battle wound.

"I need to deaden the pain, to quieten him at little," said Susanna, stroking the boy's brow soothingly.

"Opiates, mistress, surely not! 'Tis against the good book's teaching."

Susanna looked up, exasperated. Many of the women were of a puritanical bent, encumbered by heavy Bibles that they had painstakingly learned to read in order to quote the scripture at every turn.

One such pious goodwife nodded sagely, "'Twill be God's will if he lives or dies."

Sending the interfering onlookers to seek cobweb and moss to pack the wound, Susanna reached for a small vial containing a concoction of poppy, valerian and willow-bark. Oh so precious but how could she deny the boy in front of her his chance? A maggoty-pie alighted on the oak overhead, its long tail tilting as it gained its balance. Raindrops showered as the twig bent under the bird's weight. Susanna glanced up at the tree, the blue-black feathers, chequered with white, were bright against the foliage. 'Twas strange to see but the one. Folk said it was a sign that sorrow would befall. Briefly, Susanna's thoughts turned to her husband, out there in the carnage, sucked into the vortex that was the futility of war.

She addressed the bird, "You'll not say aught ter those interfering crones, will ee?"

With beak agape, the bird cocked its head in comprehension, as Susanna held the vial to the boy's lips and administered the draught. Gradually, his palsy ceased. The bird flew away, it's rough cry drowned by the battle sounds.

Susanna was skilled in herbal lore. Meticulously, Rachel had imparted the ancient wisdom, teaching the young Susanna where to seek out each plant that she might need. Mother and child had searched beyond the town, as dictated by the moon's phases, gathering when the plants were fresh. The pervading aroma of drying herbs had scented their Byddeforde home. Always there were poultices and plaisters, pillules and decoctions, in preparation for any ailment.

Thoughts of Rachel saddened Susanna. The resentment she had felt when Rachel abandoned her had abated, leaving only deep sorrow. She recalled the day when she realised that Rachel had gone. Susanna was no longer living at home, having had secured a place as a serving maid in a household prepared to overlook her family circumstances. After a month away, snatching a few spare minutes, she'd returned to visit her mother. As she approached, she had been alarmed by the absence of smoke from the chimney. Drawing nearer, it was clear that the door had been barred, the cottage abandoned. Neighbours came running as Susanna, sobbing, fruitlessly pummelled her fists against the wood. Neighbours indeed, so designated because of the proximity of their cottages but there was nothing neighbourly about their barbed remarks.

"Likely she's taken ship," one observed. "There's plenty hereabouts, who'd suffer a woman on board if the payment was right, for all the ill luck it might bring. Gone for the New World I shouldn't wonder."

"Taken up with a sailor most like," another had offered. "Once a whore …."

Anxious questions revealed that Rachel and little Jane had not been seen since Susanna left. For months, for years, Susanna made enquiries. Where could they have gone and why? Had the taunts become too much to bear, driving Rachel from her birthplace? But why had she not sent word to Susanna?

Though her thoughts had been wandering, Susanna was not distracted from tending the soldier before her.

No one had returned with aught to pack the wound. Too many times during this campaign, Susanna had torn a strip from her shift to do service as a bandage. Mayhap she could use the strapping that circled the boy's chest. As Susanna removed the twisted linen she fell back in shock. She glanced round furtively but no one else was near enough to see the soft breasts that fell from their restrictive bindings. There'd been rumours of course, tales of women who feigned manhood to be able to exchange cooking pot and laundry bat for musket and sword but Susanna had not thought to encounter one such and never like this. Hastily, Susanna took the bloodied jacket from where she had placed it, under the youngster's head and used it to shield the tell-tale signs.

***

Wearily, Susanna stroked her swollen belly as she rested on the narrow bench that ran round the walls of the church. During divine service, this was the prerogative of the elderly, the infirm, those too weak to stand but today there was no one to gainsay her. She breathed heavily. There was something indefinable about the atmosphere that reminded Susanna of her childhood. A faint whiff of the old ways, the hidden ways. Infrequently, as she was growing up, Susanna had been led by her mother to some secret, furtive place. Even as a small child, Susanna knew that it was imperative that her loose tongue made no mention of their visit. Yet there was peace on those occasions. It was a time when sonorous words were spoken in the ancient language, the forbidden language. Hocus pocus they'd labelled it,

now faith had turned men one against another and all
popery was regarded as evil. Ways of worship that had
sufficed for centuries had become a mark of insurgency.

The women who had sought refuge in the church
hushed their children. The fighting raged on the open
common. There was little shelter for those who waited
whilst their menfolk flourished swords to defend a cause
that, for the most part, they neither believed in nor
understood. Susanna shifted a sleeping Unis from one
shoulder to another. It was the smell of the church that
brought the memories tumbling back. The damp stone,
yes but overlaid by a sweetish odour that had penetrated
deep into the very fabric of the walls. The swinging of
the censor, with its papist taint, was frowned upon now
of course. Yet the building still retained deep reflections
of generations of worshippers and their ways. It
remembered, even if folk were forced to forget.

The saints' statues too remained; no one had thought
to remove them now that saints could no longer be the
recipients of prayers; prayers urgently, desperately
offered up by those in crisis and in fear. Some of the
woman were praying now, falling to their knees in
supplication but praying to an acceptable deity. Susanna
did not set much store by prayer. Her man would be
kept safe by his own cunning, by being vigilant and by
luck. No words muttered in piety would save him. The
muffled sounds of musket-fire were intermittent now.
An indication perhaps that one side or another was
acknowledging defeat. Victors or vanquished? Susanna
cared little, providing Davy was safe. It was time that
they returned to Byddeforde. Like an animal, her instinct
was to find a nest before her child was due. She had

helped at birthings on the campaign trail; the infants rarely thrived. No matter that Byddeforde was an uncomfortable place to be, it was all she had to call home and that is where she needed to go. After these long months following the flag, surely Davy could slip away unnoticed, as so many men had done. Men were expendable. Little heed was paid to who had fallen in battle or who had survived to endure yet another bout of pointless slaughter.

Just this one last battle, she thought. Just let Davy dodge musket ball and sword cut this final time and we will go home. Susanna scarce acknowledged that her thoughts were as much a prayer as the words uttered by the kneeling women around her. He'll see the sense to it. There's no shame; he is as weary of this as I and 'tis no place for Unis as she gets more venturesome.

A commotion. The door swung back. The women started, hearts pounding. In the dim church, their eyes strained for the all-important sign, the sprig of gorse or the white cockade, field symbols that would distinguish whether these rattlesome incomers were friend or foe. Children, sensing their mothers' alarm, rushed to clutch at knees or to bury their faces in comforting petticoats. Susanna dodged back into the deepest shadows behind a chamfered pillar. It little mattered if these men were for the king or Parliament, they might still regard the women as the spoils of war. Surely, they would not be taken against their will in a place of sanctuary, in a house of God, thought Susanna. Though there were tales told of rough soldiers, deprived of a woman for many a week, who were not respecters of person, nor of place. This time though, it seemed that it was not the cowering women who were the target. To cries of "no popery", iron-shod butts of muskets were brought down upon the statues that had stood in their niches for centuries past. Heavy stones, garnered from who knew where, were ground into the placid features of the Blessed Virgin, of St Michael and of our Lord himself. Burnished brass candlesticks were swept from the high table and crashed to the floor. Coloured shards fell from the shattered windows. These were men who liked their worship unadorned. The resourceful preserved the lead that had contained the glass. Lead was scarce and musket balls needed to be fashioned in deadly quantity.

The soldiers were snarling now, frenzied in their hatred of symbols that they had been taught to abhor.

"Graven images be damned."

"An end to idolatory."

One climbed the pulpit, better to reach the intricately carved rood screen, lovingly worked by some anonymous craftsman, in the days before the world went mad. Even though she did not consider herself devout, Susanna was shocked by the desecration, flinching at every blow.

She'd go home, bear this child and maybe others in the years to come. Children who would be a delight, who would love their mother as she had loved her own. Sons who would grow up strong and proud and who'd not become counters in a rich man's game of war. More daughters perhaps, whom she could teach as Rachel had taught her. She would prepare her simples and her remedies from the safety of a cob cottage, not a roughly-erected, canvas shelter. Mayhap she would set up as a midwife. She do naught to offend, naught to cause alarm. No one would bother her. Townsfolk had more grievous matters to concern themselves with now, she could be safe.

Martha's Story
2020

"Dinner's ready," called Hebe.

Martha closed the webpage that she had been reading and reluctantly, refocussed on the present. Entranced by the emerging stories, her engagement with the bygone inhabitants of Bideford was all-consuming. With a start, Martha realised that it was days since she had logged on to her social media accounts. Normally, despite her dread of finding that she had, yet again, been ridiculed on one platform or another, an insidious obsession led her to scroll fanatically through the posts of her classmates with unfailing regularity. Martha knew that, for her own sanity, she should block those who disparaged her, yet, somehow, she could not bring herself to do so; a masochistic fascination drew her back again and again. Since starting on her project though, flicking through photographs of smirking girls, or tentatively pressing 'like' on videos from so-called celebrities, just because her contacts had re-posted them, was no longer quite such a compulsion. So what if she wasn't aware of all the parties from which she was excluded; it wasn't as if she actually wanted to be invited. Striving to belong to a world which held little attraction was so much effort. The desire to fit into the alien environment of her peers was gradually waning. If there was time, maybe she would look later, thought Martha, as she bounced down the stairs to the kitchen, although she did just need to check a few of the local history websites first.

The embryonic psychologist in Martha fuelled her preoccupation with the individuals who were gradually materialising from the obscurity of the seventeenth century. She had immersed herself in every aspect of their lives, where they came from, how old they were, if they had families and crucially, what might have made them behave as they had done, for good, or for ill. This, for her, had been the most interesting aspect of her research into the Civil War story. How could political quarrels escalate to such an extent? she thought. Although, looking at the present-day politicians, you soon realised that having different political opinions led to childish posturing and invective, rather than reasoned argument. And 'fake news', mused Martha, they just make stuff up and people believe anything they read in the papers or on social media. That was what was so great about history, it helped you to evaluate evidence, to understand propaganda and to realise that individual biases soon came to the fore.

***

Acting on a suggestion from Mr Mortimer, Martha had contacted the local family history society and had found out that their volunteers ran 'help-desks' in the local library. So, on Monday morning, Martha caught the bus to the library in town, relieved that she could work on her project without going into class. Two girls she knew slightly from school were giggling and shrieking on the back seat. Martha's half smile in their direction was disregarded. Martha shrugged, she was used to this and there were worse responses than being blanked.

Adjusting their sunglasses to the appropriate angle, the girls pouted into a phone, so that their acceptable image could be circulated amongst those who claimed to be their friends.

"Oooh, three likes already!" one exclaimed.

Her friend snatched the phone. "Has Ollie seen it?" she asked, "Let's take another and tag a few people."

The girls began criticising the new hairstyle of one of their classmates.

"God. I'd hide my head in a bag if I looked like her."

"Well she's not coming to my party, not looking like that, what would people say?"

"I'm unfriending her," said the other, punching at her phone, severing the link to one who might tarnish her reputation by association.

From the girls' loud conversation, Martha could tell that they were planning to spend the day on the beach at Westward Ho! and that they were hoping certain boys would be joining them. Martha had been in classes with these boys. Superficially good looking she supposed, if you liked boys with scarcely disguised acne, incipient facial hair and trousers that were continually slipping well below their hips. The chances of having anything that passed for a conversation with these self-absorbed individuals was about as likely as Martha winning a class popularity contest. Martha sighed, it was all so shallow, these lives lived on a tiny screen, revolving around having the right clothes, the right make-up, the right friends; it was all about being the same and scorning anyone who was not like them.

Martha shut out the squeals from behind her, as the 'like' count on their recent post swelled. She reviewed the information that she had gathered so far about the Bideford of four hundred years ago. Her focus today, she'd decided, would be on the time that the plague had come to the town. She had been surprised to learn, from the website that Mr Mortimer had recommended as a starting point, that this had not been in 1665. She'd done History of Medicine as part of her exams and had studied the famous plague of that year and the 1348 Black Death of course but despite this, she'd hadn't really understood that there had been plagues in between. Bideford, she'd discovered, had been infected in 1646.

How terrifying for people, thought Martha. They'd be reeling from the Civil War and then they had to contend with the horrors of the plague. With the recent corona virus scare, Martha could begin to understand just how panic-stricken the inhabitants of Bideford must have been back in 1646. They had their talismans, their stones with holes in and their posies of herbs and we have our hand sanitisers and our face masks, she thought. Perhaps they did the panic buying thing. Not toilet rolls of course but dried peas or something. Hebe had scorned those who raided the supermarket shelves for disinfectant and anti-bacterial hand-wash, who piled their trollies high, leaving nothing for the vulnerable. Martha wished she had a mother who was more, well, normal she supposed. Her classmates had parents who had fought to the front of the chemists' queue, hoping for a new delivery of gels, or creams, or wipes, that might save them from the invisible enemy at their door. Hebe merely smudged the house with sage and made her own herbal concoction, which she encouraged Martha to use.

For once though, her mother had shown an interest in Martha's schoolwork. At the mention of the plague, Hebe had dug out her reprints of old recipe books and found some ludicrous herbal 'cures'. With no understanding of the causes of this terrible disease, the people of Bideford would have been helpless, thought Martha; all the measures at their disposal would have been next to useless.

Mentally, Martha ticked off the list of characters who featured in this section of her research. John Strange the mayor was key of course, although Martha was more interested in the less well-known Bidefordians who had played a part. Henry Ravening the surgeon, I need more on him, she thought and if I have time, maybe I can find out about some of those who died.

***

Sat at the computer in the sunny library, Martha was gathering far more information than she had imagined possible. She'd had no idea that so much was available online. Joan, the Devon Family History Society volunteer, had helped her to print off copies of the actual pages from the Bideford burial register for 1646. The sheer number of names appalled Martha and fired her desire to give some of them a lasting legacy by including them in her story. She had already decided to take the local surgeon at the time as her central character for this section. The 'point of view' person, Mr Mortimer called it. It had only taken Joan a few minutes to find out a little about Henry Ravening, his wife and children.

"Look," said Joan, "here is a Henry Revening in 1626. Don't worry too much about the spelling, people weren't really bothered about how they spelled things, as long as it sounded right."

Martha leaned across to look more closely at the index entry that Joan was pointing to.

"He is in the admissions' registers of Bethlem Hospital in London," Joan continued. "It was the national lunatic asylum, what would now be an institution for the mentally ill. Your Henry was probably in his twenties then."

Joan clicked to reveal the original document. Martha looked blank, she'd had enough trouble reading the handwriting in the burial register, this was almost impossible however Joan was undaunted.

"Henry Revening," Joan read, "by warrant from Sir Thomas Middleton for incontinency, is kept at work."

Martha was not a great deal wiser. Joan's fingers were flicking over the keyboard, typing 'Sir Thomas Middleton' into a search engine.

"Looks like Thomas Middleton was mayor of London," she said. "I'm not sure but I think 'kept at work', might mean that Henry was allowed to continue his daily work, even though he was under the supervision of the asylum."

"Why would he be in the asylum?" asked Martha. She had visions of the incontinence pads that were stacked in the corner of her Gran's bathroom. It wasn't really something that she associated with a man in his twenties and why would that lead him to be admitted to a lunatic asylum?

"It wouldn't be the sort of incontinence you are thinking of," smiled Joan. "It would be promiscuity, err, sexual incontinence."

"Oh!" replied Martha, blushing.

Joan was mindful of Martha's age but also aware that the girl in front of her was striving to grasp the historical context in which her characters lived. This was rare in someone as young as Martha. In fact, the adults who came seeking advice on their family trees weren't much better, thought Joan sadly. They were all too keen to race backwards as far as possible, adding people to their pedigrees, without stopping to reflect on the lives that their ancestors led. Joan warmed to Martha and wanted to encourage her.

"You see," she said, "any kind of sex outside marriage was frowned upon. It went on, of course it did but if it was too blatant, you would be hauled up in front of the church courts. This was a time when the puritan outlook made people come down even harder on that sort of thing."

Martha was beginning to understand why the Henry Ravening that she had come to know, might have been less judgemental than some of his fellow townsfolk.

"So, do you think this is my Henry?" she asked. "Should I include this in my story?"

"Well," replied Joan, "there does only seem to be one Henry Ravening at this time but the records are very sketchy; it could be him."

"I want it to be right though," said Martha. "I don't want to accuse the poor man of something he didn't do and when I knew him in Bideford, he was a happily married man."

Joan was amused by the way Martha was referring to her characters as if she was acquainted with them personally.

"Maybe leave it out then," she said. "You've plenty of other material, too much really, this is going to be more like a book than a school project."

"Yes!" laughed Martha, thinking how easy-going Joan was and how she was enjoying spending time with her.

"Some of the others are handing theirs in in July but Mr Mortimer said I could carry on during the holidays if I liked and I can have until we go back in September. I am trying to do one person each week, that's the plan, then I should just make the deadline."

"Good luck!" said Joan. "It is certainly quiet in here today. Everyone must be out enjoying the sun; it makes a change. It means I can carry on helping you a bit though. Who's next on your list?"

Martha ran her eyes down the list of burials, "What about Hugh Cadwell?" she said. "There are so many Cadwells in the burial register, it must have been awful for the family."

More confident now, Martha typed the name into the search boxes, remembering to tick for variant spellings of the surname, as Joan had taught her. She pressed the search button and waited for the results to appear.

Chapter 2
Henry's Story
May – August 1646

Blood spurted across the sawdust-strewn floor of The Newfoundland Inn and a chilling groan emanated from the young seaman. He was lying on the scarred and sticky table, limbs inexpertly pinioned by two of his crew-mates, a leather strap held between his gritted teeth. Standing over the writhing man, Henry Ravening drew the back of his grimy hand across his sweaty brow and sniffed hard, so that the droplet of moisture did not descend from the end of his pock-marked nose. He urged his assistants to tighten their grip on the patient. One of the anxious onlookers took a black, leather flask from his belt and swilled a slug of usquebaugh down the hapless victim's throat, hoping to dull the pain as Ravening's rusty saw drew inexorably back and forth, with a rasping sound.

"Not seen a barrel make that much mess o' a foot since I left Glasgee, these two years gone, poor gille." The speaker shook his head slowly and fingered his ginger beard. "It has been a sorry time on board of late. Only last week young Saunders fell from the topmost mast. Broke 'is neck he did, there was naught to be done fer ee."

The surgeon's discarded knife-blade reflected the light from the tallow candle that guttered on the warped, oak mantel-shelf. It was not yet fully dark outside but the inn's low ceilings and tiny windows made candlelight advantageous. Henry Ravening, Byddeforde's only barber surgeon, worked swiftly, knowing that he had no more than three minutes to sever his patient's shattered foot before the boy bled to death. He'd heard tales of some new-fangled French idea, where the blood vessels were tied individually after amputation but such fanciful notions were not for the pragmatic Ravening. His cautery irons were glowing cherry red in the roaring fire and a small, iron pot of hot tar stood on the hearth stone, ready to encase the stump.

Ravening, the father of four young children and with a comely wife awaiting him, had not expected to spend the evening operating. He'd been sat comfortably on the curved, high-backed, wooden settle, woollen-encased legs apart, supping the last of his ale. A cauldron of pottage swung above the tap-room fire. Periodically, the ale-wife ladled a portion into a wooden bowl for a hungry traveller. Idle chatter drowned the noise of the horn spoons scraping across the sides of the roughened bowls. Henry, already sweating from the unusually hot May weather, had positioned himself as far as possible from the stifling fire. The shadows were lengthening as the dusk encroached on the early summer's daylight and he had been about to head homeward when the door crashed back on its hinges. Two men had hastened inside, half-carrying, half-dragging a moaning lad who had a bloodied neckerchief clumsily tied round his foot. The boy had been crushed by a falling cask, as he worked to load dried goods onto Master Strange's vessel, *The Friendship*. The proud merchantman could be seen through the scratched window glass, rolling and bobbing on the river in the stiffening breeze, ropes slapping against the mast in the wind, as it was being made ready for its voyage on the morrow. Young Glover had been in the tavern earlier, downing a mug of ale and boasting to all-comers, excited to be part of the forthcoming voyage. This would have been the lad's first time on the Virginia run. Now he lay sobbing on the table before Ravening, his dreams of adventure cruelly curtailed, his ambitions dust. If he was lucky enough to survive the surgeon's ministrations, Glover was now condemned to the life of a supplicant, dependent on parish relief.

Ravening did his best for the lad. He wished he could have administered opiates to dull the pain but the church frowned upon their use. The Bible dictated that pain was beneficial to the soul. If that was the case, young Glover had just eased his passage to heaven. His crewmates had ensured that the boy was supplied with enough alcohol to take the edge off the agony but not sufficient to render him insensible. As far as Ravening was concerned, a silent patient was a dead one. Even the hardened seamen, who had seen the consequences of such onboard mishaps before, were sobered by Glover's ashen face and unearthly scream as the cautery iron sealed the stump. The smell of burning flesh fought with the odour of pipe-smoke and boiled mutton. They rolled the still-sobbing boy onto a roughened blanket and carried him back to his mother at the top of the town. If the wound didn't turn bad, he'd stand a chance, thought Ravening. Coins skittered across the table as he paid for his ale. He bade farewell to the ale-wife, stepped outside and inhaled the familiar scents of tarred rope and rotting fish.

The quay was a dangerous place, Henry mused. Yet it held a fascination for the town's children. Chores done, they all headed to the river, despite being told to stay clear of the men working the winches and the pulleys, as goods were swung to and from the ships that lay at anchor. His own boys were no different. Only today, when Henry had been back to his Alhallonstreete home for his mid-day meal, young Harry, his eldest son, had been recounting excitedly how they had watched a Spanish three-master unload its cargo of fine merino wool. The boys had seen the bales loaded on to the backs of the patient pack-horses to begin the journey to the weaving sheds in Tiverton. It was there that the fibres would be twisted with the coarser Devon wool to make the durable perpetuana cloth, for which the area was famed.

Ravening had gone barely a yard from the inn when Hugh Cadwell hurried up to him, face flushed and breathing laboured. Cadwell was a man of middling years, running somewhat to corpulence, his neat beard tinged with silver threads. Henry was acquainted with the Cadwell family; he had tended Hugh for the gripes not long since. Hastily, Cadwell swept off his hat in greeting.

"I be mighty glad I caught ee chirgeon," he gasped, as he struggled for air. "Your goodwife said ee might be partaking of a jug o' ale afore supper and ter look for ee on t' quay. 'Tis our Jack, he be proper bad and the missus, she be in a right takin'."

Henry sighed, now it would be a while longer before he could enjoy Jane's 'umble pie. Still, a sick child was always a concern and Cadwell had already lost one son a few years earlier.

As they reached the door of the Cadwell's home, Henry could hear wailing.

"That'll be Julianna," observed Cadwell, "she be a-fretting that Jack'll be took, as his brother afore him."

"'Tis God's will," said Henry, without much conviction, "but it be mighty hard on a mother."

The wooden bedstead was set against the wall of the downstairs room. Ravening recognised the boy, who was ofttimes a playmate of his own sons. He leaned towards the child who was restless on the straw-stuffed sack upon which he lay. There was no need to stretch out a hand to the boy's forehead to know that he was running a high fever. Young Jack's face was flushed and the heat radiating from him was palpable. Ravening reached into his leather bag for a bleeding bowl.

"'Tis an excess of blood, mistress," he said as he turned to the weeping Mistress Cadwell. "I'll bleed him now and mayhap 'twill ease him some."

He lifted the boy's rough, linen shirt. Jack's eyes were glassy and he seemed unaware of his surroundings.

There was no sign of a rash, so not the pox then, thought Ravening as he freed the boy's arm and prepared to make an incision with his fleam. Most folk got the pox in the end; there was no telling who would succumb, whilst others were spared. Ravening himself had been lucky to recover from it as a child. To be a survivor was of benefit to a surgeon, as all knew that you couldn't suffer a second time. He could tend his pox-ridden patients without fear of contagion. This was not a case of the pox though, of that Ravening was convinced.

"We'll see you right chirgeon," reassured Hugh Cadwell.

Henry knew that the Cadwells were wealthier than some of the townsfolk who called upon his services. He had no doubt that payment would be forthcoming and payment in coin, rather than an embarrassed proffering of a basket of eggs or a bag of apples. Bleeding over, Ravening bound the child's arm with a scrap of linen.

"He seems quieter now mother," Cadwell addressed his wife. "Chirgeon'll soon put him to rights, you'll see."

"Send word tomorrow if he's no better," said Henry as he tossed the blood that he had drawn off on to the rushes and replaced the bowl in his bag.

"He went down with it so fast," said Julianna, whose sobbing had abated at the sight of Jack lying still at last. "He was only out playing with your Christopher this morning. Then he came home for his nammit at noontide and said his head pained him and by four of the clock he had a powerful fever."

"Are the others in health?" asked Henry, looking at Jack's four sisters who ranged from Sarah, who was barely past babyhood, to Florence, who was fast reaching her mother's shoulder. Julianna nodded in response. It looked as if Mistress Cadwell was with child again, thought Henry, as he observed the woman's profile. Woman became fanciful at such times, happen that accounted for her excessive distress.

***

It was two days later when Florence Cadwell knocked on Ravening's door, just as the sun was rising. Henry bade her enter but the girl seemed reluctant, remaining on the pathway, shifting from foot to foot.

"'Tis Jack," she said. The ends of the cord that fastened her bodice were woven between her fingers and she twisted them tighter in her agitation. "He's none the better, worse even. He's been vomiting blood an' all. Do ee need a purge do ee think? Ma's afeared he be mortal sick and says could ee come dreckley."

"I'll make haste," said the surgeon kindly, as he pulled his worn leather latchets on to his aching feet.

The stench assailed him as he entered the Cadwell's house. Death had not yet claimed young Jack but its fingers were tightening their grip. The boy lay prone, unresponsive upon the soiled palliasse. Instantly, Ravening knew that the child was barely clinging to life. As he knelt on the hardened earth floor by the bed, the reek of putrefaction overpowered that of the strewing herbs by his feet. With his pulse quickening, Henry pushed the boy's shirt aside in order to examine him, fearful of what he might find. The surgeon's throat constricted and he scarcely suppressed a gasp. The hard, purple swellings upon the boy's neck, under his arms and in his groin, left no room for doubt. Involuntarily, Ravening clasped his fingers round the Abracadabra charm that he wore on a leather cord round his neck. He was not adverse to trying to ward off the plague by any means possible.

A dead toad lay on the child's bolster. Ravening removed it gingerly.

Julianna Cadwell looked shamefaced. "I did call upon Goody Lloyd," she said. "All hereabouts tell of the power of her simples and remedies. Did I serve him poorly sir? Will it have eased him?"

Ravening sighed, mildly irritated that Mistress Cadwell had not thought his own attentions sufficient. He'd come across countless strange treatments from the likes of Goodwife Lloyd and could not say which aided recovery and which did not. There was no real harm in it though and the desperate would try anything. The plague hunted the unwary and although some claimed to know it's cause, Henry remained unconvinced. As to cures, they were many and varied. The best he could offer was to lance the buboes and hope he was in time; folk did recover but it was rare indeed.

"'Tis the pestilence baint it sir," said Julianna, scarcely daring to name the disease lest it should increase its virulence. "What's the cause, sir?"

"'Tis likely the miasmas," Henry replied, giving the theory that he found the most plausible. "The town's been stinkin' these days past. 'Tis powerful warm for May and the night-soil men have been hard pressed to keep the putrid matter from the streets. There's dung hills at the bottom of the High Road that have not been cleared this sennight and when I passed by The Shambles in the forenoon yesterday, 'twas in a terrible state."

The butchers' stalls lined the area of town known as The Shambles and the remnants of slaughtered livestock were a permanent feature of the shady lane. The burgesses really ought to enforce the regulations that prevented the butchers from leaving entrails and offal in the streets, Henry thought. It only attracted the cats and dogs and there were those who were of the opinion that they caused the plague. In a port there were bound to be cats of course, kept aboard ship to control the rats that gnawed on the rigging and chewed on the grain. Where would the rope-makers be without cats to keep the number of rodents at manageable levels? Many folk owned an earth dog for rabbiting and then there were the abandoned curs that scavenged on the streets. When these animals roamed loose about the town in such numbers, as they had of late, they were a problem.

Ravening knew that what he needed to do would distress both mother and patient but it was the only recourse that he had.

"Best take the young 'uns to the front chamber, Mistress," Ravening suggested to the weeping Julianna.

Julianna hesitated, a mother's place was with her dying son.

"You take the maids," said Hugh. "I'll bide with Jack while the chirgeon does his work."

And grim work it is too, thought Henry, as Julianna left the room with her daughters. He railed against his impotence in the face of this all-pervading disease. Reluctantly, he removed his knife from his pack and drew it several times against the whetstone. Jack had fallen into a stupor, which was a blessing, reasoned Henry, ruefully. He took a deep breath and sliced the largest of the vivid purple swellings in Jack's groin. The boy shrieked and thrashed on the vomit-stained straw. Hugh gasped as an evil-smelling pus oozed from the wound.

"'Tis the bad humours leaving him," Ravening said reassuringly. "'Tis a goodly portent."

Henry lifted the knife again.

"There's more to be done? Can ee not let the boy bide now chirgeon?" Hugh protested, feebly.

"I must lance all the buboes if he's to have a chance," said Henry, knowing, as he spoke, that any possibility of the boy regaining his health was all but gone.

Stoically, the surgeon recommenced his task. Finally, Jack fell silent, overcome by the excruciating pain.

"I'll have to inform the authorities," said Ravening, getting to his feet slowly, as might a man of twice his years.

Henry removed the worst of the blood and pus from his knife by wiping it across his heavily soiled, coarse linen shirt. Then he moved slowly towards the parlour where Julianna stood wide-eyed and trembling; the sounds of her son's agony had cut to her soul.

"Be watchful for signs of infection in the others," Henry said, "and stay within doors. If you go abroad the sickness will spread. Likely the mayor will see to it that households who are struck down remain confined, so there'll be no risk to others."

Some years ago, Henry had been working in London when this terrible disease had laid its evil hand on the population there. Then, if one in a house was afflicted, the healthy were nailed within their homes along with the sick, to fend for themselves until such time as the plague was deemed to have passed. Happen they'd all perish of course but there was naught else to be done. Brutal though this course of action was, it did at least seem to slow the plague's unerring advance.

Julianna gathered her two younger daughters to her and moaned softly. The small girls were bewildered by her behaviour but their sisters, Florence and Ann, were old enough to sense their mother's desperation and recognise the terror that had gripped their family.

Hugh Cadwell showed Henry to the door. "Is there naught to be done, chirgeon?" he asked. "How wilt I save the maids?"

"There be no sure ways," said Henry, wishing that there were. "Keep Jack apart if 'tis possible." He looked up at the looming church tower. "Mayhap a prayer or two. And for yourself, they do say a pipe of good tobacco will keep the pestilence from you. I'll call again if you've a need."

Ravening hoped that he would not be bidden to attend the family a third time. Both men knew that if Henry was again summoned to the Cadwell's house it would mean that another one of the family had sickened. Henry headed home with heavy heart and reluctant feet. He needed to tell Jane the appalling news and then he must send word to the mayor straight away. It was a vain hope but if they acted swiftly, happen they could check the contagion's spread.

***

The days passed. More folk fell sick. Henry, fatigued beyond believing, dragged himself from one stricken household to another. Jane, acutely aware of the virulence of this awful disease, feared for her husband's safety and if truth be told, for his very sanity. Henry copied an idea he had seen in London in his youth and donned a mask, which allowed him to keep strong-smelling herbs close to his nose, in an attempt to ward off the foetid air. It gave him a grotesque appearance and as he moved about the town, those children who were still on the streets regarded him with fear and ridicule in equal measure.

The pestilence scythed through family after family. They laid Jack Cadwell in the ground two days after Henry had wielded the knife, followed by Florence and her youngest sister, then their mother, struck down as much by grief as by sickness. Hugh Cadwell survived his wife by just four days. Concerned for their own safety, no relative volunteered to care for the two orphaned Cadwell girls but the parish insisted, not wanting the expense of maintaining the children, who might in any case be carrying the sickness with them. Byddeforde was in turmoil. As soon as Henry reported that there was plague in the town, the mayor saddled up his horse and left for the country. Henry had been relying on the mayor. With his departure, there was no one who might put measures in place to keep the stricken from the those who were, as yet, well. It needed a masterful presence to take the lead if they were to lessen the disease's lethal grip. To Henry's horror, pack trains still clattered across the bridge to the quay. Ships laid anchor and then set sail again; vessels that brought tales of how the plague was raging in Seville. Was that how this horror had reached Byddeforde? wondered Ravening. Had it taken passage from Spain on a merchantman, alongside the cargo of wool?

Praise be, the troops no longer traversed the town in such numbers. Byddeforde had surrendered to Black Tom and even the folk of Barnstaple no longer held out for the king. Although there were now few passing soldiers to carry the pestilence abroad, the scars of the recent conflict were all too apparent. There were those who felt that Byddeforde had escaped lightly. The poor folk of Torryngtowne had had their church and several houses raised to the ground when the Royalist gunpowder store was ignited. Rumour was that it was a young papist from northern parts, one Robert Watt, who had fired the church a-purpose, at Hopton's instigation. Well, the lad had confessed as much but folk will say aught under the not-so-gentle persuasion of an enemy interrogator. Chudleigh's new fort stood sentinel over Byddeforde, a gash in the green hill and an ever-present reminder of the struggles. Word was that the king's cause was all but lost. He had surrendered to the Scots and it was said that his stronghold in Oxford was now in the hands of General Fairfax. Those who put their faith in young Prince Charles had their hopes dashed, as it seemed that, mindful of his own safety, he had taken ship for the Scillies, before seeking refuge on the Isle of Jersey.

Now there was this new threat to engender panic and shatter lives. On his way to yet another patient, Henry pushed through a large crowd that had gathered in the marketplace. A sombrely dressed man was raised above the throng on a makeshift platform fashioned from empty wooden crates. Ravening recognised him as William Bartlett, a man of a decidedly puritan outlook, who had been foisted on the Reverend Gifford as a lecturer. Folk whispered of the antipathy between Bartlett and the rector; Gifford's more moderate stance did not sit well with Bartlett, or many of the town's leaders. Ravening watched as the red-faced preacher jumped up and down on his rickety podium, exhorting the crowd to abandon their sinful ways.

"My brothers and sisters in Christ, this plague is a judgement upon us. We must root out all licentiousness," he bellowed. "Turn to the purity of simple worship. Beware of the devil's work. Look to the sins of thy neighbours and be ever watchful, so that thou shalt not be tarnished by their ungodliness. Look too to thine own shortcomings. Fall upon thy knees and prostrate yourself before God, lest thee be damned for all eternity."

Some of those at the front, glanced at their neighbours and then did as Bartlett demanded, kneeling amongst the vegetable peelings, animal droppings and other detritus left over from the previous day's market.

Bartlett shouted even louder, spittle flecking from his mouth in his agitation. "Beg forgiveness for thy evil ways. Only then will God take this punishment from us."

"'Tis the papists amongst us that have brought this sickness to our doors," called a man from the back of the crowd.

Murmurs of agreement became increasingly raucous; fists were waved in the air and the voice of the preacher could no longer be distinguished.

"No popery!"

"Death to those who cling to the ways of Rome."

The press of bodies surged toward the man on the dais. Henry struggled to extricate himself from the melée. In his experience, hostility rapidly turned to violence in such gatherings. The friction between the hotter type of protestants, such as Bartlett and those who were less extreme, had led to many an altercation in recent times. Already some young lads at the back of the crowd were gathering stones in their caps, despite the lack of an obvious target. Turning on each other served no good purpose, thought Henry, though dread did strange things to the ways of folk and it suited some to point the finger at those who were not of a like mind. 'Twas as if they thought that their self-righteousness granted them immunity. The surgeon shrugged his shoulders. It would all be to no avail; he had tended to those from the reformed church and those who, it was rumoured, still embraced the old ways. The manner of church to which you cleaved made not a whit of difference. The plague struck at puritan and papist alike.

Terror. Insidious, chilling dread. The pestilence brought suffering and death but it also bred panic amongst those who had not yet succumbed. As the days passed and the isolated handful of victims rose inexorably, inevitably, exponentially, folk no longer believed that it would not happen to them. There was a wariness about them all. They eschewed human contact, contact that might bring this evil scourge to their door.

Folk scurried to market, scarcely daring to greet their neighbours in case they might be carrying the mark of the pestilence upon them. Sidelong glances were exchanged. Was it her? Was it him? No one lingered to gossip. The ale-house keepers bemoaned the lack of custom. Someone coughed in the street. Others leapt back in alarm. Were they afflicted? Would the contagion spread? Who would be next?

The inhabitants of Byddeforde had little with which to arm themselves against this all-powerful invader. They clutched at amulets and sought to apportion blame. It was the Spanish, the licentious livers, the ungodly, those whose way of worship was not like their own. It was the fault of those who had stood up for Parliament. No, it was those who had supported the king. It was God himself punishing them for their shortcomings. Words from the Anglican pulpit were echoed by the Independent preachers. They spoke of the last days and surely, surely, they were here. This indeed was Armageddon.

Next, the ultimate blow; Henry's own children showed signs of the sickness. Christopher first, followed by Harry and then the baby, John. Jane shrieked recriminations, accusing Henry of bringing the contagion to their door. Henry shouldered the guilt and the sadness alone. He had to forcibly restrain his wife from tending to the boys, telling her that it was her duty to keep little Eliza in health. In between his visits to those afflicted, the desperate surgeon stood by, helpless, as his sons' fever raged and the tell-tale buboes appeared. Just another patient, Henry told himself, just another patient, don't think of it as your own son.

Impossible of course. One glance at Harry's flushed cheeks, or the sweat-darkened curls plastered to Christopher's forehead and Henry's stomach heaved and his heart raced. Nonetheless, he drained the buboes and staunched the wounds with a herb-infused plaister, changing the dressings often, as he had seen his master do back in the London outbreak of 1625.

Jane spent hours on her knees, praying that her sons would be spared. Henry did not voice his thoughts, lest he be condemned for heresy but he found it hard to believe in a God who could wreak this much agony on innocent children. First, they took Christopher's body to the shady churchyard, then John's. Not allowing himself time to grieve, Henry tried to banish thoughts of his sons' torment by working ever more zealously. He rose before the June days broke and was still seeking out the sick long after night fell. In between his visits to the victims, he returned home to succour young Harry, who, incredulously, steadfastly refused to die. Henry remained convinced of his own immunity, after all, he had administered to many a victim afore this and remained in health, albeit that was some years ago. Even so, he was not impervious to the terror and the dread, which consumed him in his rare idle moments. Those hours before dawn, when he lay, wakeful, beside Harry, were the times when he could not escape from his fears. Concerns for his own safety and sorrow for his neighbours were subsumed by his overwhelming anxiety for what remained of his family. Henry kept apart from Jane and Eliza, not wanting to take the sickness to them. So he was unable to comfort his wife, who hugged her daughter to her and spilled out her gratitude to God, thankful that the six-year-old did not yet display symptoms of the disease.

It had been five agonising weeks since Jack Cadwell was first taken ill and still those in authority seemed powerless to act. Alderman Sherman's body was found washed up on the foreshore. There were folk who said that, such was Sherman's dread of the disease, he had taken his own life but Ravening thought it was probably just one of those accidents that occurred all too frequently in the town. All knew that the side-rails on the bridge needed raising and it was treacherous to cross after nightfall. That said, mayhap Sherman had cause to be troubled; the sickness was no respecter of rank. Old man Marke, who had eked out an existence by wandering the town's streets scavenging, was found dead on the roadside at Bull Hill and was laid alongside Alderman Saltryn, another of the town's hierarchy who had lost his life.

In the summer's heat, the ground was parched and strength was needed to wield the iron shovels as pit after pit was dug. It was well-known that, to keep the pestilence from escaping, they needed to bury the dead a good two yards down and that liming the pits helped to contain the sickness. Usually, there were folk who were grateful for a day's labour but as more succumbed and panic escalated, the sexton struggled to find any willing gravediggers. The few remaining men with enough vigour to dig made excuses, fearing that they too would be struck down as they tipped the shrouded corpses into the earth. Soon, it became impossible to provide individual graves and masked by the night's darkness, plague pits were dug; pits that could accommodate many bodies. Many bodies but not enough. The unburied were piled by the wall of the church. Short of space, some were laid to an uneasy rest in a nearby field, where the digging was easier. The rector forewent full burial services in favour of a muttered prayer and before long, even that was abandoned. Name after name was scrawled in the burial register. Each day, Reverend Gifford reached for his silver rimmed, glass inkwell and his quill in order to document the demise of yet more parishioners who had expired in the sickness. The inscribing of each name renewed his anguish, particularly if it was a child whose death he was noting. As the list of victims grew ever longer, the rector was aware that there were those whose passing was going unrecorded. There were just too many.

The plague swept through the streets in an unyielding flood-tide. Increasingly, the desperate turned to the cunning women, the likes of Goody Lloyd or Goody Edwards, who, for a coin or a crust, would tend to those whose frantic kinsfolk sought their services. Ravening encountered evidence of their ministrations in the homes of his despairing patients. Usually, it was only when the potions of these women failed, that folk finally summoned the surgeon. Henry found chicken feathers laid upon the buboes, more dead toads, or occasionally a rotting pigeon. Others anointed the swellings with a concoction of honey, egg yolk and rue. Still others paid good coin for plague water that required many a rare and costly ingredient, powdered unicorn horn and the like. The Crosse family were hard hit and Goody Crosse exhorted her husband to urinate upon a mixture of yarrow, tansy and feverfew that she had purchased from the apothecary. She strained the liquid and the hapless Crosse gulped it down in the vain hope that it would save him. When these measures proved futile and folk showed no improvement, Henry was expected to perform wonders where others had failed. Still they died.

***

Much to Ravening's relief, aid finally came when John Strange assumed the role of mayor. As the death toll escalated beyond anything Ravening had known, even when he was in London, the two men met by chance on the foreshore. Strange approached Henry, flourishing his hat, heavily embroidered gloves clasped in his hand. Ravening knew the man by sight, most in the town did; Strange had served as the mayor afore. Henry reviewed what he knew of this imposing man, whose home at Ford House was further up-river, on the outskirts of the town. A wealthy merchant, foremost in the Virginia trade and owner of several ships that brought tobacco to the drying sheds in Butt Garden; his boast was that he'd never lost a ship. Henry was hopeful that he might relinquish some of his responsibilities to this maverick of a man.

"Ah, chirgeon," smiled Strange, "I looked to see you these past days. You'll have heard tell I have taken up the post of mayor once more. Yes?"

Henry nodded and Strange continued, "You've been doing a wondrous job in these perilous times, my good man. We must work together. Yes?"

"Indeed," replied Henry, grateful that Master Strange was perhaps going to take long overdue action.

"Have you time to talk awhile?" asked Strange. "I have much need of your good counsel."

"I can spare a few moments sir," replied Henry, "but I am sore tried in these dark days."

Strange leaned himself back against a nearby bollard and indicated that Ravening should sit alongside him on a large coil of tarred rope. Henry looked at the rope dubiously, wary of Jane's reaction were his breeches to become stained. He lowered himself tentatively. Strange lay his hat upon the cobbles at his feet. Its feather stirred gently in the breeze. Henry waited for the mayor to speak.

"I shall be instituting a number of measures to keep this sickness contained," Strange said. "All who are in health must clean the dirt from the streets; let each be responsible for the path outside their own door. I shall call upon the watchmen and constables to guard the ways into town, to see that none enters from afar, nor leaves taking the disease with them."

Henry wondered what his role was to be in all this, he was already heavily burdened. "What do you want of me?" he asked. "I've little chance to do more than I am at present and I've a lad sick at home. His brothers have been lost but though young Harry is in a weakened state, we entertain hopes of his recovery."

"Praise the Lord for that," responded Strange. "I'd not ask more of you than thou hast given thus far my man. 'Tis not so much what you might do for me, more how I may be able to assist you in your labours. Mayhap though you could spread the word as you are abroad in the town. Help folk to see the need for such courses of action as I will be enforcing. There will be those who will be reluctant, as 'twill be disadvantageous to their trade. There will be no more pack trains nor ships allowed to tie up at the wharf until this plague is taken from us. The merchants will find it irksome but I myself will be losing profits also. We must all suffer for the common good. Yes?"

Henry found the man's habit of ending each phrase with an interrogative in this way disconcerting. Was a response expected? He settled for inclining his head once again. Strange ploughed on, obviously not requiring any reply from Henry.

"Those who trade at the market must put their coins in vinegar, money must not pass from hand to hand. Can you bring to mind goodwives who will examine those who perish, to rule if it is the sickness that has carried them off, or some other ailment? The bodies must be sooner disposed of, we cannot leave them unburied, especially as the days are growing ever hotter."

Ravening despaired; there were precious few who would risk their own lives by searching the bodies of the dead. All knew that the virulence of the plague did not die with the victim. Even the destitute would turn down the offer of fair reward for work of this nature.

"'Tis not so simple to think of those who might take on such a task, sir," Henry said slowly, giving himself a chance to ponder on the matter. "There are goodwives who've been tending the dying, so it seems they are not afeared of the sickness. They are of a lowly sort who might be persuaded if the recompense was sufficient."

"Good. Good," responded Strange, enthusiastically. "You know where to find these good dames? Yes?"

Henry thought of Goody Lloyd, who lived in a ramshackle cottage at the top of the town. Would she be one who could be prevailed upon? She normally kept her distance, despising the surgeon's cures and setting great store by her own eccentric methods. Or were they so eccentric? Henry wondered. Little that he was doing seemed to be of benefit.

"You must not think that you will be striving alone whilst the pestilence is upon us," Strange continued. "I myself can assist in some small way. I am not a medical man; nonetheless I can tend to the sick. Yes?"

"Be ee not afeared of the contagion?" Henry asked.

It was rare to find anyone who was willing to put their own health in jeopardy for the good of others.

"Fear not, chirgeon, I'll not be gainsaid. I've providence on my side," Strange said with a hint of a smile. "I have cheated death afore and I will do so again. See this?" Strange pointed to a deep scar that rent his ruddy forehead.

Again, Henry made no response, none seeming necessary.

"I was still but a young lad. Off after church, as young men did times past, to practice with my bow in the butts' garden. Of course, nowadays 'tis pike drill but the good Queen had not long since decreed that we should abandon the bow in favour of weapons of fire and folk hereabouts still clung to the old ways. So the butts it was for us, when divine service was over. A reckless youth loosed his arrow without waiting for the call and I was struck. 'Twas a blow that would have done for a man with less good fortune but I was spared."

Henry made a noise in his throat that he hoped signalled an appropriate mixture of admiration and incredulity.

Strange was warming to his theme. "Even as a child," he continued, "God afforded me protection from what might have been a certain death when I was climbing the cliffs at Abbotsham. Being lively youngsters, we were in search of eggs, all wanting to be the first to find one of some rare species perhaps. I fell that day, slipped from a goodly height, yet I suffered no harm save a winding and a few scratches."

Strange drew breath. The church clock struck noon. Henry was eager to be on his way but it was clear that the mayor had more to say.

"A few years since," Strange went on, "I was coming across the bridge." He gestured in the direction of the stone archways that spanned the Torridge. "I'd been to see Master Davie at Orleigh House and I was in haste as rain was threatening. A footpad accosted me and made as if to cut my purse from my belt. A well-muscled rogue he was, a fighting man turned to evil ways I would think. I attempted to draw my sword but he flourished his dagger and made as if to wound me. I slipped on the mud and as I fought to regain my footing, I was caught off guard and fell back. The low parapet was insufficient to prevent me from toppling to the river below, yet I scarce took harm. 'Tis all a portent that the Lord hast afforded me His protection so that I might be of service. I have many plans that will benefit this town, measures that will indicate my gratitude for the Lord's good grace.

We are in sore need of almshouses for the elderly of good character but I digress. For now, I can do God's will and assist you in this terrible time of trial that has beset our town. Yes? Without doubt, I will be spared again."

Strange took a much-folded piece of parchment from his scrippe. As the mayor smoothed it out on his knee, Ravening recognised the opening of John's gospel, inscribed in faded ink.

"I have the talisman, as I see do you," said Strange, glancing at the amulet that was visible in the opening of Henry's shirt. It glistened as the sunlight caught it.

There was little Henry could say, after all, he too was convinced that he was protected from the sickness. Yet Strange's tales of his charmed life were of a different tone. Though he spoke of God's grace, there were those who, upon hearing the man's story, would be all too ready to whisper of witchcraft.

***

The stench of the sluggish summer river pervaded far beyond the quay. Rapacious gulls fed on floating carcasses that none dared examine too closely, lest they proved to be human. His conversation with Strange replaying through his mind, Henry made his way towards the top of the town. Yet another stricken family had sent word, begging him to call. It would probably be too late, he thought. Most times folk tarried until the disease was in its later stages, not that there was aught to be done if they sent for him when it first showed its evil hand. Henry was well used to the steepness of the street, yet the excessive heat gave him pause as he climbed the hill above the town. Reaching his destination, he knocked upon the door; there was no response. He lifted the latch and stepped tentatively across the threshold. The greasy straw was slippery underfoot and there was a rancid odour coming from the cooking pot. The ashes were cold in the hearth, a sure indicator that the goodwife had been taken from her duties, either by the sickness, or by the need to care for others.

"Chirgeon's here," called Henry into the silence.

There was a scuffling from the back room and Henry pushed aside a ragged curtain to find a woman kneeling by a mattress that lay in the corner. As Henry entered, she got to her feet and turned to face him. The strong features and bold demeanour of Goody Lloyd were instantly recognisable.

"She be gone chirgeon, there's naught to be done for this one but the laying-out."

Goody Lloyd was fast approaching her middling years and her clothes were filthy but there were still signs that she had been comely in her younger days. She held herself erect and the curl of dark hair that escaped from her coif as yet held no tinge of grey. Despite the rumour that, when she first came to the town, she was free with her favours when her husband was at sea, Goody Lloyd was childless. Folk muttered behind their hands that mayhap she'd cast a spell to stop her womb, to prevent any inconvenience. Yet God dictated that some women should be barren, thought Ravening. Of course, since the depths of time, there had been those who claimed to be able to prevent an unwanted quickening. Some innate instinct led women who found themselves in trouble to those who were none too scrupulous about what they did, or what remedies they offered. Despairing girls were prepared to part with coins they could ill afford and to risk their health too. The names of those who might come to their aid passed from one needy woman to another in a sinister wave. Occasionally, Henry was called upon when such measures had gone awry. More often than not though, the woman voided out her own life alongside that of her unborn child, or took an infection, if the remedy had been more invasive.

These wretched women were reluctant to tell where they had sought relief. Instead, they held last night's bad fish responsible for their stomach cramps, or they attributed their blood-loss to the heaviness of their monthly courses. In their delirium though, many would mutter and curse the woman who they had once believed to be their saviour. Thus, Henry was aware of those who preyed on the desperation of those in trouble. He knew that Goody Lloyd's name was one that was murmured when a girl's womb quickened afore she was wed. Ofttimes, those whose bodies were ravaged by the work of these goodwives, would let slip a name, as Henry tried to repair the damage. Yet never was the blame ascribed to Goody Lloyd. Mayhap her methods were more successful than most, thought Henry. The alternative, that she had stilled the girls' tongues by threat or by conjuration, was a thought that Henry dismissed from his mind.

Now Goody Lloyd stood before him, haughty, defiant, ready to defend her ways of dealing with the pestilence, against his reasoned argument. Fatigue prevented Henry from investigating how Goody Lloyd had sought to succour the poor soul who lay on the mattress, the rigor of death not yet upon her. He did not ask why he had not been called upon sooner. The woman was dead, it had all too probably been inevitable. Recriminations were futile. Mindful of Strange's words, Ravening addressed the woman who stood before him.

"I hear tell you've been tending to those who ail, Goody Lloyd."

The brief nod of confirmation held no hint of an apology.

"The mayor is seeking goodwives who have no fear of the sick. He is willing to pay those who are able to search the dead, to ascertain if 'twas the plague that has led to their demise."

At the mention of payment Goody Lloyd's eyes narrowed calculatingly.

"Is this a task that you'd be willing to undertake?" asked Ravening.

"Mayhap I would, chirgeon." There was a lilt to Goody Lloyd's voice that betrayed her. She was not from these parts. The years that she had spent in Byddeforde, since coming to the town with her seafaring husband, had not eroded all trace of her origins.

"'Tis not a task you'll find many willing to embark upon mind," she said, perhaps realising that her ready response might have lessened her chance of securing a high price for her services. "'Tis worth a goodly sum, to lay hands on corpses whilst the pestilence is still upon them."

"I know not what recompense the mayor has in mind," said Ravening, hastily. It was not his wish to become embroiled in negotiations. He had no doubt that Goody Lloyd would drive a hard bargain.

"Mayhap I'll see what he might offer," said Goody Lloyd, with a dismissive air. "Or mayhap I'll not. I have folk who have a need of me; I've herbs to gather afore sundown."

Despite her implication that she could not linger, Goody Lloyd made no attempt to pass Henry in order to reach the door. Instead, she faced him squarely, unmoving, staring, yet somehow mesmerising.

Henry tried to ignore his sense of unease. He was perturbed by Goody Lloyd's fixed gaze. Her eyes were a tawny colour, flecked with gold and Henry felt unable to look away. Surely no harm could come from a woman dispensing her strange remedies amongst the sick, he reasoned. Yet somewhere, deep inside himself, a primeval voice screamed its dissent.

Martha's Story
2020

Martha walked slowly into school, her head spinning with all that she had learned about the ever-widening religious divisions within the town in the mid-seventeenth century. She had never been particularly religious. Growing up with Hebe's pantheistic world view that blurred into paganism, mitigated against more conventional forms of worship. Yet Hebe's stance was as exclusive, as bigoted, in its own way, as the puritanical outlook of William Bartlett and his cronies, whom Martha had been studying. What part did faith have to play in setting people so vehemently against one another? she wondered. Why couldn't they just discuss their views calmly and agree to disagree? Mind you, she thought, we haven't learned from past experience, even though we are supposed to be more educated in the twenty first century. Intolerance. It surrounded her, as it did those she was researching. Religious fervour had appalling ramifications in the 1600s and you only had to watch the news to see that matters were not much better now.

Martha was so engrossed in her reflections that she cannoned into a group of boys loitering in the school entrance. She muttered an apology, hoping that they had other things on their minds, other students to torment. She recognised Jeremy, a thick-set boy with a perpetual sneer, who had been in her history class. The boys were in their PE kit, so presumably they were heading off for the inter-schools' athletics competition. Much to Martha's relief, after a few cutting jibes suggesting that she must fancy Jeremy in his shorts, the boys' attention was diverted by the arrival of the school mini-bus and they careered down the steps towards it.

As if she could possibly fancy anyone as inherently unpleasant as Jeremy. Who called their kid Jeremy nowadays anyway? Martha was vaguely aware of his parents, parents whose views he aped. His father was on the local council and had been an aggressively active Leave campaigner in the protracted debacle that was Brexit. Jeremy had turned up to school sporting large '#LeaveMeansLeave' and 'Immigrant Scroungers Out' buttons pinned to his lapel and had remonstrated when Mr Mortimer had asked him to remove them.

"That's censorship!" Jeremy had complained.

"It's not appropriate in school, Jeremy," Mr Mortimer had replied. "I agree that we live in a democracy and outside you are entitled to express any political opinions you may have. In my classroom, we are tolerant towards each other and politely listen to a range of views, without indoctrination or giving offence."

It was a pity that Jeremy had taken off his Trump-style "Make Bideford White Again" baseball cap before coming into class, thought Martha. She would have relished seeing Jeremy squirm when Mr Mortimer dealt with that one. The caps had been seen about the town off the back of last year's fuss about Bideford's longstanding nickname 'the little white town'; a strapline that appeared on the road signs as you approached Bideford. There had been a right hassle about that. Someone had complained to the council that the signs were racist. Sadly, thought Martha, there was a segment of Bideford's population who would be quite happy if the slogan was taken literally; those who were narrow-minded, fearful of the unknown, hostile towards difference.

Mr Mortimer had taken half a lesson, when they should have been studying the Spanish Armada, to explain the origins of the phrase. The Bideford cottages had been whitewashed in the mid-nineteenth century, in the belief that it would deter the spread of the cholera epidemic. As a result, Charles Kingsley had coined the 'little white town' epithet in his novel, *Westward Ho!* and the name had stuck. Martha supposed that, if you didn't know the history, the appellation might be regarded as offensive to people from ethnic minorities. North Devon tried, not altogether successfully, to make a living off the back of tourism, so it was not the best idea to alienate a significant proportion of potential visitors. The saga had rumbled on until it became yesterday's news, eclipsed by Brexit posturings and the snap general election that had dominated the run up to last Christmas.

Seeing Jeremy, Martha was reminded of the school's mock election that had been held at the end of the autumn term. Mr Mortimer, who taught A Level politics as well as history, had thought it would be a good idea to take the pupils through the process, from candidate selection and campaigning, to ballot box. Unfortunately, the aggressive smearing of the opposing candidates that was a feature of the real election, had been reflected in its school counterpart. Jeremy had, true to form, stood for the Brexit Party. Most of Jeremy's supporters were his so-called friends, many of whom had very little idea about the party's policies. What Jeremy stood for was irrelevant. He was their mate, he was popular, let's stick together and do what Jeremy says. Like their parents, they spouted the views of the right-wing press and without compunction, believed the more outrageous fake news claims about those of other races that they saw online. Fabricated propaganda it might be. No matter. If it serves the cause, why spoil a good story with the truth? The school had bubbled with barely concealed aggression. Fights took place between the adherents of rival candidates; graffiti was scrawled on lockers and abusive comments appeared on social media.

Martha was thankful that she had resisted Hebe's suggestion that she might put herself forward as the prospective Green Party candidate. The thought of competing for selection was daunting and she knew that she lacked the resilience to withstand the rigors of the leaders' debates. Poppy, a girl from year twelve, who had been chosen to represent the Greens, had been given a hard time by the climate change deniers and those who wanted to lift the hunting ban. Poppy had been narrowly pushed into last place by Jeremy, although there were rumours that his followers had somehow got hold of duplicate ballot papers and voted more than once.

Poppy was still nicknamed 'Greta', after the young climate change activist Greta Thunberg, someone whom Martha greatly admired but in Poppy's case, the nickname was not used as a compliment. Martha had overheard other year twelves deriding Poppy because, following the repercussions of the election, she had had most of the spring term off with stress. Martha regretted that she had done no more than put an X against

Poppy's name on polling day. Why had she not stood up for Poppy that time when she had seen Jeremy's bootlickers cornering her at the bus stop? Martha couldn't explain why she had walked away, self-preservation she supposed. She lacked the strength to expose herself to yet more taunts from her fellows. It was so difficult to put yourself out there, to dare to be different, to invite ridicule. So much easier to keep a low profile. Martha felt uncomfortable. Guiltily, she acknowledged that it was this very attitude that had contributed to the tragedies in seventeenth century Bideford. If you didn't speak out against the bullies, you were as bad as those who were doing the bullying. To be silent was to acquiesce.

Chapter 3
Arthur's Story
1649-1666

Iron nails were hastily hammered into the heavy beam that barred the rectory door. At the command of Reverend Arthur Gifford, men rushed to fasten the shutters of the downstairs windows. Underneath their calm exterior, panic was thinly veiled. That it should have come to this, thought Gifford. He had not made the decision lightly. Arthur was, both by nature and by calling, hospitable; his habit was to welcome any who reached his door. His role was to offer aid to the importunate but the men who were now making their way up the hill towards his home were not supplicants. Their purpose was not benign. Praise be that he had had sufficient warning of their approach. His attempts to secure the parsonage were, at best, a delaying tactic but Gifford was not a man to concede defeat lightly.

The five years of his incumbency had been beset with difficulties, he was haunted by those harrowing days when the pestilence menaced the town, plucking victim after terrified victim, extinguishing both life and hope. The image of the corpses stacked high in the churchyard, for want of a gravedigger, was forever scored in his memory. Some had turned to fervent prayer in their dread, others had reviled God. Stoically, Gifford had tried to dispense comfort to the fearful and succour to the grieving. Mayor Strange had been a wonderful strength in those times, until he too had succumbed. He'd left his legacy though and the newly constructed almshouses were a blessing. There were many in the town who were in sore need during the present troubles. Charities were overstretched. Just last month, he had been on hand when Mayor Andrew's dole had been distributed. It had been distressing to see that the queue to receive the loaves of coarse bread had been longer than ever this year. Where there was want there was always the fear of unrest and Byddeforde had seen overmuch strife of late.

The war of course, always the war. Fissures in the town had become gaping chasms, as those with opposing views were set one against another. Troops mustering in the fields beyond the town were already a common sight when Arthur first came to minister to Byddeforde, at young Sir John Grenville's behest. He barely recognised the man, his former self, who had first entered this very rectory, six years ago. Then he had been over-brimming with a young man's zeal, eager to spread God's word, to guide his flock in the one true way. He had little dreamed that he would see the day when the church was desecrated, its font turned into a horse trough. This late war had much to answer for. It was a relief that the organ, which had been purchased thanks to the public subscriptions of his parishioners, had been moved to the comparative safety of the vestry. The Grenvilles too had been brought low by the current regime. In the words of the ballad that was currently circulating, the world truly had turned upside down.

Arthur sank on to a nearby bench and put his head in his hands. He knew that he should pray but the words eluded him. He was barely in his forties, yet he felt as jaded as the ancients who begged alms at the church porch. Those who aided him were looking to him for guidance. He was a leader of men; he must act as such. Rallying, he ordered his allies to drag a heavy coffer in front of the door, the better to fortify it. There was a commotion outside. The time had come. This was his parish, his parsonage, his people. How could it be that he was being ordered to leave upon the whim of the Parliamentarian faction who now held sway in the town?

Arthur had always striven to be fair-minded, to overlook a man's political stance. His concern was with souls not affairs of state. Yet, somehow, the two had become inextricably entwined. He'd even made efforts to tolerate that renegade lecturer Bartlett, whom he had inherited from his predecessor. Dealing with Bartlett had plumbed the reserves of Gifford's Christian charity. If truth be told, tonight's incursion could probably be laid at Bartlett's door. Granted, the man had been in London these past months, ministering to the folk of Wapping but he had left behind a swirling foment of hatred and bigotry.

Gifford prided himself on his impartiality. It did not do to side too closely with one faction or another. He had never expected that he would fall foul of the Committee for Plundered Ministers, as his brother, John, had done. The Grenvilles, his kin as well as his benefactors, had long been ardent supporters of the Stuart line. It pained Arthur to think of King Charles climbing to the block in this winter's chill. He wished that he could have been amongst the hushed crowds outside Whitehall's Banqueting House. The news was but weeks old, few, on either side, had yet grasped the implications of this deed. When war first broke out, who had anticipated that regicide would be the outcome? Now that the king was dead there was little to restrain Cromwell and his supporters. Unlike his brother, Arthur had not followed the Grenvilles and taken up arms for the Royalist cause. John Gifford had distinguished himself at the Battle of Lansdown, had been present when Sir Bevil Grenville fell, whilst Arthur remained here in Byddeforde, tending to his parishioners. Where had Arthur's cloak of neutrality led him? He might just as well have cleaved to his inclinations and publicly declared for the king.

They were at his door. Arthur went to peer through an upstairs window. Mounted men, muskets glinting in the light of the burning torches that they bore. Hoof-prints marked the frosted grass. He watched as some disappeared from view, no doubt trying to gain entry from the rear. Gifford sighed. He was not going to leave without protest, why should he make matters easy for his captors, who were not even local men? No doubt the townsfolk wished to distance themselves from this heinous endeavour.

***

The shouting, the hustling, the jostling. He had tried but failure was inevitable. For the sake of those who had stood by him, Arthur had finally surrendered himself to the soldiers who sought him. It had not been fair to expect his men to continue to defend the rectory in the face of such hostile opposition. If it had been up to him, he would have upheld his right to remain with his last breath but in all conscience, Arthur could no longer stand fast against the incursion. He was jeopardising the safety of others and that he could not countenance. His shirt tore as he was pushed roughly into line between two burly soldiers. He shivered. The February night was chill and he had not been allowed to return for warmer attire. These were men from the Plymouth garrison, disinterested, uncaring. They had a task to do and they would carry it out with no thought for the man whose home, whose livelihood, whose very sense of purpose, was being ripped from him. No, these men did not know Arthur, felt no sense of loyalty or compassion towards him. Although those who were abusing him were strangers, Arthur could sense the hand of the town's Parliamentarians behind every move. His ministry was his vocation, it was being wrenched from him without thought or favour and with scant reason. Whilst he had not actively opposed them, he had refused to toady to Byddeforde's elite with sufficient zeal. That was the sum of it, his only crime. What lay ahead for him now?

The horses that surrounded Arthur grew restless. It was an effort to avoid the flailing hooves. On foot, his progress was too slow to satisfy those who were leading him towards the bridge, escorting him, as instructed, beyond the town. Several times he missed his footing, unable to discern the road's uneven surface in the darkness. He looked up in the direction of his beloved church but the deep night's blackness hid it from view. He could take no comfort there. The soldiers were reviling him now, uttering oaths that Arthur strove to ignore. A heavy clump of earth hit him in the chest, knocking the breath from him. A globule of phlegm scarred his cheek. Acts of derision these. He stumbled again. It was of small concern, naught mattered now. It was no less than his saviour had endured on the road to Calvary. Was that blasphemy, wondered Gifford, to compare himself to the Lord? Even his once sure and steadfast faith had become distorted by the events of the past few years. Nothing was certain.

Nine Years Later

Sheltering in the Torryngtowne home of Philip Harris these past months, Gifford was comfortable, yet not content. News reached him from Byddeforde from time to time. His greatest desire was to be allowed to return to his ministry there but at present, the prospect was bleak. He was as much an exile as the man whom he now regarded as his sovereign. Men were still at variance one with another; violent deeds were commonplace. He watched the flickering fire. The Harrises had been open-hearted, yet it irked him that this was not his own hearthside, not his own home. Mistress Mary bustled in.

She was a comfortable little body, sister to Philip and like Arthur, her status was ambivalent in this household. They lived here, yes, yet they were but inconvenient appendages. Dependants both, they had formed an unspoken alliance, taking pleasure in each other's company. Arthur had never before felt the desire to take a wife, he was untroubled by celibacy. Yet, under different circumstances, he might have entertained thoughts of spending his final years with Mary at his side. They were of an age to be beyond the needs of the flesh but companionship would be a blessing. Impossible of course. He had naught to offer. If matters were to right themselves, if he could once again be his own master, command respect, then perhaps.

"You have news from Byddeforde?" Mary remarked, observing the letter on his lap, its red seal broken.

Her rich Cornish lilt was like a balm to his troubled mind. It was in her nature to be solicitous.

"How fair matters there?"

"'Tis a poor prospect for those who do favour the king, I fear," said Arthur.

He lifted the second sheet of waxy parchment that the carrier had delivered just that morning.

"Grenville is ever faithful to the Royalist cause. The town has turned against him. In truth, I feared back along, when he put the manor to mortgage to raise funds, that we'd not see him reside in Byddeforde again. It seems it is his brother-in-law who dwells at the Barton now."

"Times have altered beyond our imagination. You and I, mayhap we've been too long in this world. We've seen too much. It sore grieves me to see our church is still not rebuilt."

"'Twas a sorry day that," Arthur agreed.

It was a dozen years since Torryngtowne's church had been destroyed and Fairfax's men had raised their standard in the town. Repairs were still not complete.

"Two score men were pressed last month," said Arthur, reading from his letter. "'Twill hit their families hard, with their menfolk taken."

"The gangs have been vigorous of late," agreed Mary. "Praise be, they rarely venture too far from the port and our young men here are safe."

"They send out gangs from Barnstaple to take them, knowing Barum men have no love for those in Byddeforde. Folk need to be wary. An over-indulgence in the ale-house and they lose caution, to the advantage of the press-gangs. It seems the odious gang-masters are lamenting that they did not take still more souls from their homes. As you know, I have little regard for our Lord Protector but he expects further trouble from the Dutch. We need men to defend our shores but it should not be like this. There are those who would go and willingly. These are sorry times when a Byddeforde man daresn't set foot abroad of a night-time, for fear of being pressed."

Glancing further down the page, Arthur grimaced at a mention of Bartlett. What new hurts could be laid at this man's door? It seemed that the preacher was amongst those who had put his mark to a paper, a covenant renouncing popery. Arthur had no time for papists himself, yet the relish with which they were denounced by the Independents, saddened him. There was vindictiveness in men's hearts.

Boldly, Mary patted the back of Arthur's hand. She could see that he was troubled. There was little she could do to console him.

"Is there nothing favourable to report?" she asked.

"It seems the school is flourishing. 'Tis as well they built out over the bakehouse last year, there was little enough room for the scholars to study afore I left. There's a surfeit of boys of rank who will study within its walls. At least 'tis a sign that the town is recovering from the losses during the pestilence."

Good news it might be but it evoked bitter memories. In a life that now seemed impossibly distant, Arthur had played his part in the education of the young men at Byddeforde's Grammar School. It was another aspect of his role that he missed. Schooling was a gift. It enabled men to think for themselves. His fond hope was that with learning would come discernment and the world would begin to realign. Upon his ejection from Byddeforde, Arthur had looked to keep a school in Westleigh, on the Torridge's eastern banks but Bartlett had lacked the compassion to accede to this request and Arthur's ambitions had been thwarted once again.

He read further. His brow furrowed. He felt the hairs on the back of his neck prickle. His throat constricted and his heart-beat quickened. Despite the good news of the school, all was not well in Byddeforde. Mary, attuned to his moods, sensed his unease.

"What be it? I see ee be distressed?"

Arthur's reply was little more than a whisper, "They've taken Mistress Ellyott for a witch."

Four Years Later

Byddeforde. It assailed his senses. Arthur had not appreciated how much he had missed the town during his exile. The shouts from the quay as a cargo of tobacco was hauled upon a ship bound for Amsterdam. The jingling of the bells on the leading pack horses as the train passed across the bridge. Folk hurrying lest they be squeezed against the parapet as the beasts swayed under the weight of their laden panniers. Even the biting smoke from the many kilns along Potters' Lane spoke to him of home. The comforting, deep sound of the church clock striking as he climbed the hill. Mid-day. The appointed time. Bartlett should be at the rectory to meet him.

Momentarily, Arthur wondered if Bartlett would have the temerity to stay away. That would make for further acrimony but no, there he was, by the rectory gateway, shoulders hunched and head bowed. He was stroking a heavy iron key that lay in his hands. Bartlett had aged since Arthur had last seen him. He was but a few years Arthur's senior, yet the times weighed heavily upon them all. Word was that Bartlett was passing some of his responsibilities on to his son and of course now he must relinquish still more to Arthur, whether that was his desire or not.

Arthur was within a pace of Bartlett now. They faced each other in silence. Bartlett placed the key into Gifford's open palms. Both knew that it was not just the object that was being proffered. That rectory key was a symbol of authority; one that Bartlett must now surrender. The order was once again a-changing. Bartlett lifted his head. The two men stared at each other in a rare moment of mutual understanding. There were tears in Bartlett's eyes and Arthur felt no triumph at the sight. For all their differences, they were strangely akin these men of God. Both were dedicated to the souls in their care. In another time, a gentler age, mayhap they could have been allies. Although they trod different paths, their shared love of the Lord and their concern for their fellow men might have brought them together.

Finally, Bartlett spoke, his voice, usually so firm, cracking with emotion, "I trust you are sensible of the weight of your charge."

With a flash of fellow-feeling, Arthur understood that it was a wrench for this man to abandon the congregation that had been his for more than a decade. Bartlett was now suffering as he, Arthur, had suffered in his turn.

"I shall do my best," replied Arthur, as he regarded Bartlett solemnly.

True, their relationship had lurched from veiled tolerance to outright opposition, yet they were both victims of the political machinations of the past few years. Years when the country had witnessed unimaginable deeds. Who could have predicted that a king would lose his head? Nor that, a few short years later, matters would come full circle and that that same king's son would regain his throne. A lesser man of course, Charles II, with his womanising and his merrymaking. The times were still unsettled. Fortunes waxed and waned at the whim of successive governments.

As Gifford regarded Bartlett, Christian compassion fought with antipathy. Not trusting himself to speak, Arthur turned away and walked to the parsonage, key in hand. Bartlett had chosen to live elsewhere, eschewing this accessory of the established church and the building had been sadly neglected during his tenure. Putting his shoulder to the oaken door, Reverend Gifford stepped inside to reclaim his domain. The air of neglect was overpowering. Arthur looked about him with dismay. Bartlett had let the parsonage to weavers during his absence and the remnants of their trade were evident. The furnishings that remained were dilapidated and dust-ridden but he was home, he was where he belonged, these were but minor irritations.

In the weeks that followed, Arthur sought to make-good the ravages of past years. It was not just the parsonage that had suffered. The back wall of the shippen had fallen away and the quarry that lay on glebe land was sadly depleted. Culm deposits had been reduced to naught. There were those who sought to curry favour by blaming Bartlett for the losses but Arthur knew that looters were quick to take advantage when a property was uncared for. He found it difficult to be patient with those who were swift to revile Bartlett. Arthur was no fool. He knew that a number of those who were now his most vociferous supporters were the self-same townsfolk as those who had been instrumental in his downfall. Just this week, after Evensong, he had finally lost patience, in a lamentable moment of irascibility. A worthy soul, renowned for her piety, had approached him.

"Reverend Sir, I's be that glad to have ee back. Narry the once have I set foot in this church during all the time of your absence."

Weary of the divisions in the town, Arthur had been exasperated by the woman's importuning. Prayers were required in these tumultuous times, regardless of who led them.

"The verier wretch thou," he had responded and immediately regretted his words.

Never before, in his dealings with his congregation, had he given in to flashes of temper. He needed a calming influence. Now he once again held office in the town, it was time to take Mary as his wife.

As Byddeforde struggled to adjust itself to the new regime, Arthur's religious duties took on a familiar rhythm. The circle of life and death continues, no matter whether there is a king upon the throne or not, thought Arthur, as he laid Richard Edwards in a pauper's grave. Young Richard had survived the dangerous earliest years, his parents might have entertained hopes that he would reach adulthood. There are no certainties, thought Arthur as he watched Davy Edwards lead his grieving wife away. Edwards' hollow cheeks and wracking cough told their own tale. Arthur feared that it would not be many months before Susanna Edwards and her children were without a man to support them.

Four Years Later

Bartlett and Gifford continued to lead their own brands of worship. Despite being ejected under the Act of Uniformity, Bartlett and his son held meetings in private homes and under the cover of darkness, on the outskirts of the town at Grange and in the woods behind Ford House. Bartlett led a charmed life, managing to elude the authorities. Arthur preached forbearance and encouraged those who climbed the hill to St Mary's each Sunday to care for their fellow man. News came of a devastating fire in London, one that had raged for five days and laid waste homes and churches alike. A further blow for the capital, which was already reeling under the ravages of yet another outbreak of the pestilence. Arthur was gratified that his parishioners had dug deep and added coins to the collection for those whose homes had been lost. Yet there were whispers of sabotage, those who laid the cause of the fire at the door of the French, or the Dutch. Fires were common enough, shrugged Arthur, more likely it was just an unhappy accident and the scale of the damage due to no more than the hot and airless weather. The country was jumpy, seeing enemies behind each door. On the surface, there was an uneasy calm in Byddeforde, yet all the dissention, the intolerances and the discord remained, thinly disguised, ready for some small incident to tip the town into turmoil once again.

Martha's Story
2020

Martha swung her laptop bag over her shoulder and waited for the school's automatic doors to open so that she could leave. Those heavy glass panels symbolised incarceration, oppression, unease. Passing through them to go into the building each morning required a supreme effort. Heart racing and palms clammy, Martha's anxiety levels would rapidly reach panic mode before classes had even begun. Would today be a day when she stayed out of trouble? Not trouble with the teachers, that was unheard of for Martha but could she avoid those who sought to taunt and belittle her? Could she find an excuse to stay in the classroom at break and over lunch, so that she could be alone, less vulnerable, hidden? Now though, the doors parted. A wave of warm air hit her as she left the air-conditioned atrium and stepped outside. Freedom. Escape. Safety awaited her.

That was the great thing about this school project. She could come in early and report on her progress to Mr Mortimer, then she was on her own, to research or write in some secluded place where she would be untroubled. She could seek out the sanctuary of the library or sit in her sunny bedroom and watch the birds in the garden, as words whirled and swirled in her head before marching to order on the screen in front of her.

Mr Mortimer had been very positive about her section on the religious upheavals.

"You have a very mature outlook, Martha," he'd said. "I can see why you want to do psychology next year. You have a real empathy for these people, a genuine understanding of what makes them tick. A lot more perceptive than many adults."

Pleased though Martha had been with his praise, she wished he hadn't made the remarks quite so loudly in a classroom full of people. Her delight flashed and was gone, as she heard sniggers behind her. She whirled round but could not be sure whose smug face masked the derision they had expressed. As if it mattered who it was, they all hated her, thought she was sucking up to Mr Mortimer; she was not one of them. She tried to tell herself that she didn't care but she was betrayed by the flush to her cheeks and the incipient tears.

"Ignore them," her mother advised, on the rare occasions when Martha shared her anguish. "Why take any notice of what a load of immature teenage girls think? They have no soul, no compassion. Just be true to your inner self and be proud of it. Difference is a gift; it should be praised and nurtured."

But it wasn't. Being different got you noticed and it was not the sort of attention that anyone would want. To be ignored was Martha's ambition. To be allowed to quietly get on with her life, unobserved, disregarded, invisible. She wasn't particularly bothered about having no real friends, she was quite content with her own company. If only they would just leave her alone.

Liberty brought reprieve; the rest of the day was her own and Martha resolved to return to the library. Monday was Joan's turn behind the family history help-desk and Martha was looking forward to sharing her latest discoveries and getting Joan's assistance with the characters who appeared in the next part of her story.

"I really want to concentrate on the witchcraft angle now," Martha said, as she settled herself beside Joan in the deserted library. It seemed that no one else sought the library's tranquillity when the sun shone and the beach beckoned. Martha opened her laptop and set it whirring, as she outlined her thoughts to Joan.

"At first, I did wonder if it might be more exciting if I left out the earlier stuff I've researched and just wrote about the three witches. Then I realised that the actions of the other people in Bideford, going back years before the witches, are vital to their story. Without the background, you can't begin to understand why they were accused. So I couldn't just start in the 1680s. It's been fascinating working on the civil war and religion and so on but I've decided that, this week, I need to actually look at the accusations themselves."

Joan smiled encouragingly and Martha continued, "I've been reading the book by Frank Gent that Mr Mortimer suggested and I've been on a few websites and it seems that the 1682 accusations weren't the first ones. Temperance Lloyd had been accused twice before and got off!"

"So are we going to look at those earlier accusations today then?" asked Joan, as she jiggled the mouse to stop the library computer hibernating. "I saw you had booked in a help-desk slot, so I opened up a few likely websites ready. Who do we need to find out about this time?"

"Well someone called Grace Elliott was accused in Bideford way back in 1658," said Martha. "We could try her but it is going to be a bit difficult to fit her into my timeline. I am already up to the 1660s with what I've written so far."

"You could always go back and add in a reference to her in the sections you've done," suggested Joan, "or you could have people remembering what had happened a few years before in the next bit, or both of course."

"That's a good idea," said Martha. "It could be a bit samey if I go into detail about every accusation. I do want see if we can find out anything about Grace though, just for completeness. Then perhaps I'll concentrate on the first time Temperance was accused."

"Who was involved in that?" asked Joan. "I'll make a list."

"Well, there's the Herbert family," replied Martha. "Mr Herbert claimed he'd been bewitched and Lydia Burman, she's going to be an interesting one. She was one of the main accusers in 1671. I'm thinking she might have been a bit old and embittered, you know?"

She looked up, wondering if Joan had been offended by her reference to being old, after all, Joan must be pushing sixty.

"Lydia Burman is a nice unusual name to work with," said Joan, who didn't seem the slightest bit upset by Martha's comment.

A few moments later, Joan had found Lydia in the baptisms' index.

"It doesn't look as if she was that old," she said. "This is probably her, baptised in 1632 just over the border in Cornwall. So it's likely she'd have been under forty in 1671. There are only a few Burmans in Bideford at this time. I'll just check the spelling variants as well."

Joan was busy opening up various entries, in order to see the images of the original records.

"Well, well. Look at this," said Joan, pointing at the screen.

The handwriting was reasonably clear in this part of the baptism register and Martha could make out, 'John the sonn of Liddia Borman baptised the 18th of June 1662'.

"Oh!" Martha exclaimed, "but there's no father mentioned, what does that mean?"

"It looks as if your Lydia, gave birth to an illegitimate son," replied Joan. "There's nothing to suggest that she was ever married. It would have been quite a disgrace at that time."

Martha was aware that there was no father's name on her own birth certificate. If Hebe referred to him at all, she called him 'the sperm donor'. She was thankful that, amongst her contemporaries, single-parenthood was commonplace. That at least was a stick that the bullies did not use to beat Martha with. In the 1600s though, Lydia must have had a hard time of it, living down the shame. Did that explain why she became so sanctimonious?

"So she wasn't quite as virtuous as she made out then," said Martha. "That's interesting."

"Everyone has their secrets," said Joan. "I think the scandals are what make family history so fascinating."

"I need to know what it would have meant to have had an illegitimate child back then," said Martha. "I know it would be very different to today when nobody cares if someone's parents are married or not."

"1662," said Joan. "It was after the Restoration but puritan views were still widespread. Lydia's main problem would be trying to support herself and her son. She wouldn't be able to work unless she could find someone to look after the baby. I wonder who the father was? It is unlikely that we'll ever find that out."

Already, Martha was imagining the sort of life that Lydia might have led. The hurts of the morning, when the girls had laughed at Mr Mortimer's praise for her work, receded and once again, Martha was transported back to the Bideford of the seventeenth century and its people. She needed to find out more about Lydia and how an unmarried mother became a self-righteous accuser.

Chapter 4
Lydia's Story
1670-1672

In the darkness of the February afternoon, old Maister Herbert was dying. Truth be told, he'd found matters arduous ever since the pox had taken his wife, some six years past. A lifetime of hard labour had left its mark on his once powerful frame. It had become an ever-increasing struggle to tend his livestock, or to till his fields to the south of the town. When it had first been suggested that he might be best served by sharing a home with his son, Will, he'd been reluctant. Pride and obstinacy had made him cling to his independence far longer than was prudent. Eventually though, he had bowed to his son's pleas and they'd rubbed along together quite satisfactorily these last few months. Now, in his sickness, Maister Herbert was in sore need and thankful for his family's aid.

His gnarled hand grabbed Will's arm, "I's bin overlooked boy," he hissed in an undertone. "Overlooked by that there Goody Lloyd. You be tellin' 'em boy. Tell 'em to seek the marks where she do prick me. She came to me begging for bread and I turned her away. I should ne'r have gainsaid her boy. She's done for me good and praiper now."

"Prick ee, faither?" asked his son sceptically. "When'd she be doin' that then?"

The old man became increasingly agitated.

"'Twas just afore Yule time," he said, his palsy becoming all the more evident in his anxiety. "There be fearful evil in this town boy. You 'member when the mercer's wife stood trial for sorcery. We heard tales o' that even out where I be."

"Mistress Ellyott?" queried his son. "Faither, that be a full dozen years since, you can't be thinkin' that aged dame Goody Lloyd had aught to do with Mistress Ellyott."

"Theys all be in it together, boy. Them cunning folks, wi' their devil's ways, ne'er work alone. You need to be a-sendin' for the minister boy. I's not long for this world. I need to put messen right with God afore I go."

"I thought you'd ne'er a good word for Reverend Eaton faither. You've been that lackadaisical 'bout church-goin' these past months."

"Needs must boy. I'll not go to me maker wi'out the fittin' words bein' said. I've matters I need to set straight. I need to see a man o' God and Maister Eaton be all we have, despite his strange ways."

The younger man hesitated before venturing, "I could send word to Master Bartlett faither. I know he be of the reformed faith but the corporation saw fit to engage him to serve as reader to Reverend Gifford back along. There be hundreds o' folk who do sit under his preachin' now."

"No boy. I've no truck wi' these newfangled ways. Look ee 'ow folk got fined last summer when the constables and churchwardens found John Bowden preachin' in Goody Dennis' house. You'll mind Bowden were minister down Exeter way afore ee took to siding with these 'ere Independents. They be nowt better than traitors; heretics even. If Maister Hill calls 'em fanatics, then that's what they be. Who knows better than our town clerk?"

Will well remembered the distressing incident of the previous year. It had set folk ever more firmly on one side or the other in the divisive debate about religion that raged in Byddeforde. Townsfolk shunned their neighbours. Insults were hurled and vitriolic speech had become the norm. Will was rare in his reluctance to publicly align with one group or the other. His father though was traditional in his thinking. The upsurge of religious hatred had served to harden the old man's stance; he had become fiercely opposed to the reformed way of thought. Will refocussed on his father's words.

"No boy. 'Tis not for the likes o' me to be havin' aught to do with such folk. I were brought up in the parish church and 'tis there I'll be laid to rest. 'Twill have ter be Eaton, for all they do say 'bout 'im."

Exhausted by the effort of such a long conversation, the old man lay back on his bed and rubbed his right arm that lay useless by his side.

"Faither, 'tis a mighty powerful thing ter be saying you be overlooked. 'Twill stir up a mort o' trouble in the town. I mind how 'twas when folk did speak out 'gainst Mistress Ellyott. Did set neighbour 'gainst neighbour and folk did clamour to point the finger at others, afore they be accused theirsen. 'Twas all for naught in the end anyroad. Master Ellyott stood surety and she were back in Byddeforde sellin' ribbons at market same as ever. It don't do to meddle in such matters."

"Ah but she weren't back fer long, boy. You recall, she be taken by the fallin' sickness not many years after. Though men did not dare to punish her, God saw fit to strike her down."

His son sighed; he was losing patience. He knew old folk were taken with strange notions but least said the better in his view. 'Twas as well not to go seeking trouble; who knew where it might end.

"Mayhap Mistress Ellyott was let go on account of there provin' to be naught against her, faither. Many a time there's folk that be taken with a fit and such. It can't all be the Almighty meting out punishment. If that were it, why did he not strike her down straight away? Not all misfortune be down to witchcraft neither."

"I be firm 'bout this boy. I'll lay my blood 'twas Goody Lloyd what has bewitched me. She has set her prints and marks upon me. You must see me avenged. You'd not deny a plea from a man in his final days? She's done for me boy, 'tis all there is to it. I be a-tellin' the reverend gentleman so. 'Tis said that, for all his faults, he be set firm 'gainst conjurations."

"I'll fetch the rector faither," said Will, reluctantly, "but just so as he might ease your passing, let's have no more talk o' bewitchment."

Will left hastily, before his father could say anything further. He climbed down the rickety stairs and went out into the small garden behind the smithy, where his wife, Margaret, was feeding the chickens, their two young boys playing at her feet. Green shoots were struggling through the soil. They'll suffer if we have another frost, thought Will, absently. Margaret put the empty basket in the outhouse and walked towards the back door.

"What's to do?" she asked; she could see that her husband was fretting.

"Faither be proper mazed," Will replied. "He be saying ee be witch-ridden."

"He be wandrin'. 'Tis 'is age. Can't be expectin' 'im ter be as sharp as ee were these years gone."

"I don't know," said Will, shaking his head. "He's sharp enough but he has these fancies. I tried to talk him out o' it o' course. Told 'im it were all a load o' old nonsense but there be some strange matters abroad in the town and his palsy did come upon him mighty sudden."

The gate creaked on its leather hinges and Mistress Lydia Burman entered the garden. The fussy little spinster was one of Margaret's gossips but Will found her sharp tones and continual harping about her neighbours distasteful. Margaret went to greet her friend.

"Oh Lydia, has Master Ackland no need of you this afternoon? I didn't not look to see you 'til tomorrow."

"I have left him dozing," replied Lydia. "He will sleep until dusk now. I am able to go about my own business as I please. I will need to be back afore he wakes though. I really do not know how he would manage, were I not there to tend him."

Mistress Burman was ever the one to exaggerate her own importance, thought Will, another reason why he disliked the woman. He could not comprehend why Margaret set such a store by Mistress Burman's friendship. Although Lydia's master, Humphrey Ackland, had once been prominent in the town, taking office as parish clerk, she was nonetheless just a servant, no more really than a maid-of-all-work, for all that she claimed to be indispensable. As he took his leave, Will could hear Lydia's shrill voice asking after his father. He was not under any illusion that her enquiry stemmed from genuine concern. Happen she wants to be the first with the news of his passing, Will thought.

***

Resentfully, Lydia turned to her task, stirring the hops to brew ale for the master. She did not want to be within doors when she could be wandering Byddeforde's lanes. Her thoughts turned to Margaret Herbert's revelation that old man Herbert believed himself to be overlooked and by Goody Lloyd no less. That would be a tasty morsel to spread abroad if she could just get to town before Margaret did. From the steamy brew-house, she had a good view of the lane. She could watch folk going about their business. Lydia was ever eager to know more of the doings of her neighbours. She called a greeting to the Misses Beale, who lived in Potters Lane. Young Dorcas Lidstone skipped past, her blond curls flying. She caught Lydia's gaze and embarrassed, slowed to a walk, mindful that she was nearing womanhood and should adopt a more decorous gait. Donkeys ambled down the hill, their laden panniers filled with produce to be sold.

There were shouts from afar. A great hog, its back ruddy from rolling in the earth, snorted and snarled as it made a bid for freedom, its once restraining rope trailed behind it in the rutted track. Those who had foolishly let the tether slacken called to others to step on the rope and halt the escape. Hearing the racket, Lydia abandoned the brew and rushed into the yard, just as the bewildered animal crashed into the rickety fence, sending staves a-flying. Lydia backed away hastily but the pig ignored her and careered on down the street.

She had been but a moment gone but the brew had caught and burned to the bottom of the cauldron, ruining both crock and ale. How had that happened in one brief moment? Lydia regretted her inattention. Master Ackland was rarely a harsh employer but iron pots were costly and inexplicably, this had near burnt dry. He would be displeased. Strange though, you could leave a pot like this an hour or more and it would take no hurt and she'd scarcely turned her back. Mayhap she could scour it clean, so that her negligence would not be discovered. She had looked to go to join her gossips when the brew was set, now she must start over and a cauldron to scrub as well. There would be no gadding about today. 'Twas all the fault of that red pig. It had had a look about it too, a wildness, an other-worldliness.

Yes, there was something to be feared in that pig, could it be that it was an imp taking on another guise? Was it mere happenstance that it had run into the fence just where she'd been standing?

***

The bell tolled and Will stepped forward at the sexton's bidding, in order to throw a handful of dark soil upon his father's coffin. Reverend Eaton intoned the words of the burial service. Although he had not been in the parish for long, Eaton had already fallen foul of a number of the town's elite. Nonetheless, thought Will, the rector's occasional visits had soothed his father somewhat in the past weeks, for that Will was grateful. Even so, until the very end, Maister Herbert had been adamant that his affliction was attributable to Goodwife Lloyd. Despite his initial scepticism, Will had begun to wonder if there might be some truth to the claims. Yes, his father was getting on in years but he had been struck down without warning and the old man's vehemence was convincing. Even so, Will would have been content to let things be, had Margaret not urged him to take action. It was Mistress Burman who had fired up Margaret's passions, putting thoughts into her head that were uncharacteristic of his normally placid wife.

Will stood by his father's graveside and wondered if he would regret his deeds. Recalling the events of the past few days, was disquieting. He was not altogether proud of his part in the proceedings. Should he have allowed himself to be swayed by others? He'd done as the old man wished. He'd placated his wife. He now needed to set things straight in his own mind. Will was not by nature a man of extremes but he knew that having begun taking this path, there could be no turning back. With reluctance, he had summoned the magistrates and laid an accusation at Goody Lloyd's door. He would have to stand by that, whatever the consequences.

Memories of the turbulent days since his father's death, crowded into Will's mind. He had scarcely had time to put the coins over his father's sightless eyes, before Margaret had accosted him.

"You should have paid more heed to what your faither was saying," she railed. "'Tis up to you now to do as he bid and see that Goody Lloyd be brought to justice. Her and her evil ways. You should harken to what Lydia has ter say 'bout her. 'Tis not just your faither who Goody Lloyd has cast her eye upon. Lydia soon showed me the sense to your faither's claims. I'll not let that spell-weaver go free for lack of those to speak against her. Mistress Ellyott may have escaped the noose but I lay my life I'll not let Goody Lloyd do the same. She'll not walk the streets of Byddeforde a free woman after this. You must go to the magistrates Will, afore she can take against other respectable folk. Lydia will speak out in our favour, add weight to our words, she's long been wary of Goody Lloyd."

Will had never seen Margaret in such a taking. It was, in part, the fact that her fervour was so out of the ordinary that persuaded Will to comply. He cast his mind back to Monday, only two days ago, yet it seemed like a lifetime. He had been to the magistrates with the tentative suggestion that his father's final illness had not been a natural one. He had uttered a name. Words once spoken could not be retracted. Will remembered the day when Margaret had plucked a chicken in the yard and then had found that the sack had a rent in it. A stiff wind had scattered those feathers abroad and they could no more retrieve them all than they could stem the tide. His speech was like those feathers. No matter that he now lamented his words, regretted being persuaded against his inclinations; what was done was done and there was no going back.

Matters had gathered momentum like a river in full spate. Other witnesses were sought. Lydia Burman had been the first to come forward, eager to align herself with the self-righteous, swift to condemn. The town was a-frenzy with gossip. All manner of folk claimed to have harboured their suspicions of the old lady who dwelt at the town's western edge. Little matter that those self-same indicters had, in more tranquil times, turned to Goody Lloyd if an animal sickened, a precious object was mislaid, or a wound was reluctant to heal.

"Goody Lloyd's been taken up for conjurations. Allus did say it wouldn't do to get backsides o' her."

"Bundled her off to gaol in Exeter they did, to await the Assizes. I seed her dragged from her cottage like she were no more'n a bundle o' rags."

"She deserves no better. Time was she tried to pass an apple to my little maid. Well I wuz havin' none o' that. Hustled the maid from Goody Lloyd's sight soon as ever I could and I told her, like I tells all o' my childer, don't you be goin' up that part of town maid, I said. There be no knowin' where 'twill end."

"And Goody Lloyd baint the only one by any means. There's others in the town who should be called to account."

"I hear tell 'twas young Maister Herbert what laid the charge. His faither were getting on in years but still he be struck down mighty unexpected like."

"Mistress Burman now. She be going 'bout the town like she was someone of consequence and all on account of her bein' called to speak out 'gainst Goody Lloyd to the justices."

"She be welcome to it. I'd not be journeying to Exeter if the devil himself were behind me."

"Husht. 'Tis best to guard your tongue and not speak of the evil one."

"I speaks as I finds. Happen there'll be no talking to Mistress Burman after this. She will be that full o' herssen."

"She baint half as respectable as she'd have you believe you know. Have you forgotten, back along ...."

***

The night-sounds of the Exeter inn could not distract Lydia from her thoughts. Sleep eluded her as she anticipated the excitements of the morrow. She could picture herself taking the stand, laying her hand upon the proffered Bible and reciting the oath in ringing tones. All would look upon her admiringly. It was she who would send Goody Lloyd to the gallows. She wished she'd been closer with the Herberts, perhaps helped to tend the old man in his last days, then she would have had more to say. The magistrates had asked for those to speak out against Goody Lloyd and Lydia relished the opportunity. She would make much of the incident with the pig. Of a certain 'twas no common pig that one. Yes, this would silence her naysayers. This would set her up as someone of standing within the town, someone who had been instrumental in upholding what was right. It had been worth every one of the forty saddle-sore miles on the back of a swaying beast. What a blessing that she had been able to persuade Margaret to harry her vacillating husband into action. Lydia settled back against the bolster and allowed herself to be lulled by the gentle snores of those who shared the room. Exeter was always crowded at the time of the Assizes, she had been fortunate not to have to share the bed.

Lydia dozed. The nightmare broke into her repose. She was gazing at the boy, the child she had borne in shame and in ignominy. His body had tinges of manhood, whilst his mind was yet that of an infant. She mourned for the loss of the man he would never be, for the grandchildren she would never hold. She could not shrug off her self-absorbed regrets for their lives lost. Her future was warped by this man-child's overwhelming anxiety, his incomprehension, his inexplicable anger. Women who brought forth babes who were misshapen in body, would ofttimes snuff out the flicker of life before it had scare begun but when it was your child's mind that was stunted, fractured, twisted, it was not apparent until they had grown into your heart. With each passing year, that which set her boy apart from his contemporaries became increasingly marked; his slowness of wit, ever more discernible.

Wretched, Lydia struggled with her grief. She reached towards the shadow man-child. Why could she not embrace him, this boy? Why was he always just out of reach?

She woke with a start. The room was chill yet sweat trickled between her shoulder-blades. It took her several moments to orientate herself, to realise that this was just another night-terror. Stupid, she thought. Her son, wherever he might now be, was but nine years old, not near full-grown. Why should her dream world imagine him to be feeble-minded? The sins of the fathers, so it was believed, would fall upon the child unto the seventh generation. Was her sin so great? If she could curtail the evil of the likes of Goody Lloyd, would this in some way atone?

As far as she knew, her boy, John she'd named him, was growing up whole and sound in the care of the family who had taken him. Childless they'd been, all too eager to pass coins her way in exchange for a mewling bundle, barely weaned. She did not have the luxury of more time with her son. Her meagre savings were exhausted. She must work. To give him up had been her only option. She had believed herself reconciled to his loss. It was rare now that he intruded upon her thoughts. In the years since his birth, she had established quite a position for herself, or so she fondly supposed. She had made herself indispensable to Master Ackland. She had gained the adulation of her gossips, simple women like Margaret Herbert, who esteemed her, valued her opinion, bolstered her sense of self-worth. Those who remembered that Lydia had once fallen from grace and given birth to a mis-begotten child, never mentioned it now, at least not in her hearing. Why had these memories risen up, unbidden, just as dawn was about to break on her day of triumph. It was unfair that the occasion should be tainted so, by the long-buried past.

***

Lydia revelled in the stir that her role in denouncing Goody Lloyd had caused. She needed to be abroad in the town whilst her part in the matter was still fresh in the minds of her fellow townsfolk. Granted, Lydia's sense of self-importance was somewhat tarnished because the foolish magistrates had, inexplicably, seen fit to acquit Goody Lloyd. After all she'd said too. Herbert's death could be regarded as the demise of an old man, whose time had come but it was galling that they had not recognised the gravity of her own bewitchment. They'd dismissed her story of the pig as being of no account. Nonetheless, the affair had made her gainsayers take notice; she would relish the attention whilst she could. Already, news of the trial was being eclipsed by other gossip, the latest raid on the non-conformists' meeting at Samuel Johns' house, for example. There was another instance of the guilty going unpunished, thought Lydia. True, Johns had paid his fine but the preacher had evaded capture.

It still rankled that somehow Goody Lloyd had gone free, free to roam the town and overlook those who had spoken against her at the Assizes. Lydia shivered. She knew she should rely on the power of prayer but what harm could it do to ward off evil in other ways, ancient ways, ways that might themselves smack of witchcraft.

Her gossips were eager to hear of her time in Exeter, anxious for her safety and for their own. Who knew who would be next to invoke the displeasure of one of the cunning women about the town? It was Mistress Gard who whispered a name, who told of a cottage where talismans were offered. Not that she had sought Mistress Gard's advice on the matter, quite the contrary. Mistress Gard spake with disparagement of the deeds of those who dabbled in the dark arts. Lydia had squirrelled away the knowledge. Reluctantly, under darkness' shade, Lydia had ventured forth to the cottage on the outskirts of the town. She'd tried to shield her face under her cape's heavy hood but she knew the woman could name her. A shiver of apprehension flickered and would not fully subside. A ridiculous sum the woman had asked for a small earthenware bottle, with intricate carvings on its flattened sides. The bottle rattled and liquid sloshed within but Lydia took care not to break the seal. All knew that a witch would enter a home through an opening. It was the door jamb, the chimney and the wind-eyes that allowed her ingress. Telling herself that she was merely protecting Master Ackland from harm, Lydia secreted the bellarmine upon a ledge in the far recesses of the chimney. She had had to let the fire burn away to ash to do so and even then the stones were hot enough to blister her fingers but she was comforted to think that no witch could pass that way. Then she turned and looked in dismay at the gently opening door.

Martha's Story
2020

Martha was sat beside Joan in front of the library computer once more. She had been looking forward to this visit. School had finished for the summer, so she could no longer get help from Mr Mortimer. Having spent the past week researching the Reverend Nathaniel Eaton, Martha was eager to show Joan how much she had unearthed online and to get advice about the contradictory accounts that she had found.

"So," said Joan, "who are we researching today?"

"The Reverend Eaton," replied Martha. "There's loads about him online. He was the rector of Bideford in the 1660s and1670s. I guess that means he would have had a lot of influence on his congregation; his opinion would have mattered. I thought he would make a good contrast to William Bartlett too. They seem to have hated each other."

Encouraged by Joan's smile, Martha went on, "Eaton's going to be an interesting character. He's not a bit like your typical vicar, very different from Arthur Gifford. It seems that he went from being a strict non-conformist to persecuting puritans. He was one of the early settlers in Massachusetts Bay Colony and was associated with what became Harvard University, although he left America in disgrace."

"He sounds like someone for you to really get your teeth into," said Joan, as she opened a search engine and brought up a website. "Let's try the Clergy of the Church of England Database and then the university alumni. If he was a vicar, he will have been to university."

"He doesn't seem to have been a very pleasant man," remarked Joan, looking up from reading Nathaniel's entry in the online Dictionary of National Biography. "Beating up his pupils and embezzling funds; not a great example to his parishioners!"

"But that is what makes him so fascinating," said Martha. "His influence might help to explain why such a lot of people in Bideford were so intolerant. He certainly seems to have been a bit of a fanatic."

"Hmm, Massachusetts, that could be significant," mused Joan. "It would have been after he left of course but the attitudes there resulted in the Salem witch trials in the 1690s. I wonder if the mindset that led to the persecutions there was similar to Eaton's and via him, contributed to the way of thought in Bideford too? This is all secondary information so far," Joan went on. "Let's see what original documents we can find to download."

She moved on to the National Archives' Discovery Catalogue and typed 'Nathaniel Eaton' into the search box.

"There's an inventory and some court documents," said Joan. "This is only the catalogue though; they haven't been digitised. You'd have to visit the National Archives if you wanted to see them. It seems from the index that your Reverend Eaton had some sort of financial dispute with a John Davie."

"Oh yes, John Davie was a merchant and the mayor at one point," said Martha. "I don't think I can go to London though, not unless there's a demonstration or something that my mother wants to go to."

"Not to worry," said Joan reassuringly. "Some of my genealogist friends live near to Kew and pop in and out regularly. I can ask them to get us copies but it will mean waiting a few days. Still, there seems to be plenty to be going on with."

Joan had moved on to search the documents available on the major subscription websites.

"Oooh look," she said eagerly, "a license to pass beyond the seas. That's a bit like a passport. I knew they existed but I've never used one before."

Martha was caught up in the excitement. This was great. So much better than getting sandy watching a load of stupid boys playing beach volleyball and pretending to be impressed when they scored a goal, or whatever they called it. Martha had succumbed to just a very quick peek at her social media accounts and she knew that this was where most of the girls in her class would be today. The prospect was chillingly unappealing to Martha, although, a few weeks ago, she'd cried in her room for hours when she'd been ignored and ridiculed at just such an event.

***

The following week saw Martha squinting at copies of the documents that Joan's friend had sent. Although she was getting a little more used to the old-fashioned handwriting, these proved too much for her and the lengthy account of a case in the chancery courts even defeated Joan.

"I can make out some of it," Joan said, "but I am afraid we may need to pay someone to transcribe that one for us."

Martha wasn't sure if the family budget would run to contributing to her school project but she didn't like to dampen Joan's infectious enthusiasm. Hebe had said something about being asked to run an 'alternative retreat' in a few weeks' time. Martha had only a hazy idea of what that might involve but perhaps it would mean that she could afford what was needed. Hebe's haphazard way of doling out money to Martha had its advantages as well as its disadvantages. Much as Martha would have liked a regular allowance, so that she knew what money she had to spend, Hebe's habit of flinging notes at Martha when she could afford it, interspersed by long periods when nothing was forthcoming, did mean that Hebe could be very generous when one or other of her many side-lines bore fruit.

Martha had enjoyed researching the Reverend Eaton. She could see what Mr Mortimer meant about psychology being relevant. What on earth had made Eaton behave in such a bizarre manner and to what extent might he have inflicted his views on others in Bideford? That might help to explain what happened later. The religious aspect of it all was harder for Martha to grasp. These people were all Christians for goodness sake and they were still tearing strips off each other, hardly very Christian. It seemed that religion was just as bad as politics. Being in Bideford, there weren't many different faiths represented at Martha's school, so the few Muslims and a Jewish family stood out. In fact, hardy any people she knew seemed to take religion very seriously. Martha knew that the two Muslim girls in her year were bullied for wearing the hijab, for being different. Then there was Lucie, whose parents ran the

Chinese take-away. When they'd been learning about China in geography, everyone had assumed that Lucie knew all about it but Martha remembered Lucie mentioning that her parents had been born in South London and that neither she, nor her parents, had ever been to China. Yet, as soon as the corona virus struck, there had been graffiti spray-painted across the shop window and Lucie had been shunned in school, as if her ethnicity made her somehow unclean.

It isn't just me, she thought, it is anyone who isn't exactly like everyone else. Is it because people are frightened, sort of a survival instinct maybe? Do people naturally feel intimidated by things they don't understand? Did this explain Eaton's behaviour? Does fear turn people into bullies, braving it out because they are scared; threatening others, ideally with the support of a gang, before they themselves are threatened? But why not just get to know them? Why not find out about them, then the bullies might realise that there was nothing to be frightened of, she thought. Shamefacedly, Martha realised that she was equally guilty, she rarely spoke to Lucie and she couldn't even remember the name of the Muslim girl in her maths class.

Painstakingly, Joan read out the inventory of Eaton's possessions. Martha was fascinated by the long list of kitchen items, candlesticks, cushions, a looking glass, bedsteads, curtain rods, a chicken pen and so much more. An image of Eaton's home emerged from the clouds of the intervening centuries and Martha could visualise just how it would have looked. She was itching to put into words the pictures that were forming in her mind.

Chapter 5
Nathaniel's Story
1672

In Byddeforde's substantial rectory, Nathaniel Eaton got up from his knees, his hand to the small of his aching back. Lengthy prayers were a burden on his aging body. Leaving the unadorned table-board, that did duty as an altar in his study, he reached for his Bible. It weighed heavily in his hands as he moved to the chair and lay the book upon the small table in front him. Nathaniel stroked the tooled leather binding, contemplating which passage he should study. He had found it difficult to concentrate on his devotions in recent times. Matters in the town were becoming troublesome. He needed to set an example to his flock, to stamp out the scourge of those who were mischief-makers and free-thinkers; free-thinkers as he himself had once been. Nathaniel had seen the error of his ways; any temptation to adopt puritan ideologies had long since been eroded. When he had first returned from Padua, armed with his Master of Divinity and his Doctorate, it had been expediency that had led Nathaniel back to the established church. The last few years though had seen him embrace its tenets with a zeal that bordered on fanaticism. The strength of his opposition to those who worshipped in the Independent Chapel was fuelled by a convert's fervour.

Of course, the reformed church had not been part of Nathaniel's early life. His father had been a clergyman of the Church of England. Brought up in the aftermath of the religious turmoil of the previous century, the Reverend Richard Eaton had stressed the need for conformity. His fear of anything that hinted of popery had been evident in every sermon, in every deed and in his dealings with his offspring. Briefly, Nathaniel wondered if his father's obdurate railing against Catholicism had played its part in leading Nathaniel and his brothers to a puritan way of thought. Richard Eaton's philosophy towards childrearing had been founded on the notion that regular chastisement was character-forming. As the sixth and penultimate son, Nathaniel had escaped the more rigorous beatings that had been meted out to his older brothers for the good of their souls. His eldest brother, Theophilus, had spoken of thrashings that left permanent scars. Fortunately for Nathaniel, by the time his turn came, apoplexy had weakened his father's arm.

The Bible remained unopened as Nathaniel became lost in his reverie. He wanted to consign the thoughts of his final encounter with his father to a deeply buried past but the memories rose up unbidden and consumed him. The nature of the misdemeanour that led to that last punishment could no longer be brought to mind but oh how Nathaniel remembered every stroke of that beating. He had been seven years old, the eldest boy remaining in the damp and creaking rectory of his birth. His older brothers had left to enjoy the independence of respectable employment in the mercantile trade, to study at university and at school. It had been cold, he knew that, cold as charity, with the tiny panes of the rectory windows encrusted with frost. Someone had thrown a green log on to the fire and it hissed and crackled as his father reached for the wooden stave that he kept by his writing table. The angry man stumbled as he walked towards Nathaniel and the table shook, as he grabbed it in order to steady himself. A newly made batch of ink spilled from its heavy glass bottle and marred the clean parchment that Richard Eaton had laid out, waiting for him to compose his sermon. This did nothing to assuage his ire and he grabbed Nathaniel by the ear and twisted viciously. Nathaniel could still feel the blows, still see his father's increasingly reddening face and bulging eyes as he belaboured the child in his grasp. Then the grip had loosened, his father had made a strange gobbling noise in his throat and crashed to the floor, overturning a stool in the process. Servants had come running, Nathaniel had been whisked away. Although his father had clung to life for a few days more, he never spoke again and Nathaniel forever held himself responsible for his father's demise.

Within weeks, Nathaniel had been sent, prematurely, to Westminster School, where his elder brother Francis had been for the past three years. In the shadow of Westminster Abbey, Nathaniel and his fellow pupils were fed a diet of rancid pottage, a classical curriculum and conformist Anglicanism. Nathaniel's abiding memory of his time at Westminster was the smell of beeswax that emanated from the long forms in the dusty school room. The senior boys had tried to scare the younger pupils with tales of hauntings by the monks who, it was said, once slept where they now learned Latin and Greek. Nathaniel revelled in his learning; he was soon challenging the masters, who struggled to keep up with the precocious young boy. Nathaniel's prodigious intellect did not endear him to his fellow pupils and in his unquenchable thirst for knowledge, he isolated himself, turning obsessively to his books.

In Byddeforde's rectory the candles in the battered iron candlesticks were guttering and outside dusk was gathering. Starlings swooped up from the glebe land out towards Cattshole and swirled towards the river, their harsh cries echoing between the twisted chimney stacks. A pile of thick parchment lay on the desk; documents that Nathaniel should be attending to. No, he could not bring himself to peruse, yet again, the false claims laid against him by John Davie. Assertions that he, Nathaniel, owed money and a substantial amount of it. Davie's country seat was Orleigh Court, some miles from Byddeforde but he spent much of his time at his town residence on the eastern side of the river. He had made a small fortune from the tobacco trade and from sending earthenware to Ireland and the colonies. Nathaniel was mindful of Davie's considerable influence in the town. It was not wise to fall foul of such a man.

Nathaniel's uneasy mind lurched between dwelling on his recent treatment by the Byddeforde elite and uncomfortable recollections of the past. His latest dispute with Davie and his sycophants had not been the only occasion upon which he had been unfairly treated. It seemed that money was ofttimes at the root of his difficulties, thought Nathaniel ruefully. How was it that these men could not see his true merits? He had only ever sought to do his work, to stamp out evil and above all to serve God. He shivered. The fire was dying down and the winter's chill added to his sombre mood. Evil lurked close by, aided by the acts of the ungodly. The devil had many guises. Whispers of witchcraft were surfacing again and not for the first time. A mere handful of years before Nathaniel had taken up his post, Mistress Ellyott had been fortunate to escape the hangman's noose. Then there was that business with the smith's father just last year. Old man Herbert had gone to his grave protesting that he'd been bewitched and bemoaning that he had not succoured Goody Lloyd in her need. It was never easy, ministering to someone in their last days, if they were troubled by sins of omission, thought Nathaniel.

Mistress Burman too, she'd played her part in bringing Goody Lloyd before the justices. He'd always admired Mistress Burman, when he had encountered her on his infrequent visits to Master Ackland. A well set-up woman, of middling years but sound in her opinions and some might even say comely, not soft and vapouring like others he could name. Nathaniel sighed, he'd buried Mistress Burman not so many months after Herbert and there had been those who'd wondered at the cause of her passing. Those who even then had muttered once more the name of Goody Lloyd. The pity of it was that Lloyd, with her wily ways, had somehow gone free when she faced trial over Herbert's death. They must be more mindful of the evil wrought by such women. Leniency, vacillation, indecisiveness, they had no place in trials of this sort. Firmness was what was needed, no matter that the evidence might be thin, an example should be set. The ways of the devil, of the worldly, must be set aside.

Nathaniel lamented those times in his youth when he had lost sight of God and had allowed himself to be tempted by the ways of the world. He had followed his father and brother Samuel to Cambridge University. He had arrived at that hallowed seat of learning in 1630, together with his younger brother, Jonathan. The two young men were bound for different colleges but it was reassuring to take on this new venture together. Jonathan was coming straight from the cloistered atmosphere of Westminster School. Nathaniel, who had spent three years nominally assisting his brother Theophilus with his mercantile business in London, felt himself very much the sophisticate, far superior to Jonathan who had seen nothing of the world. Theophilus was involved with the Eastland Company, who traded in the Baltic and Nathaniel had already made several trips beyond the seas on his brother's behalf. Nonetheless he found trade boring and he missed the rigours of academic life. When Jonathan was due to enter Cambridge, it had been decided that Nathaniel too would benefit from further study. Although he had no calling to serve in the church, Nathaniel knew that that was the intention, that he was being groomed for a life in the pulpit.

The brothers reached Cambridge on an unseasonably warm afternoon, at the start of the Michaelmas term. Their horses were sweating; it had been a hard ride from the tavern in Harlow, where they had spent the previous night. A potent miasma rose from the River Cam and drying ditches were filled with debris. Nathaniel had barely begun his studies when the ever-present friction between the scholars and the townsfolk reached a head, as the spectre of plague descended on the Cambridge. In the interests of self-preservation, the colleges had barred their doors. Provisions had been horded against such an eventuality; there were dried peas aplenty, sacks of flour and barrels of small beer. The masters, who were used to dining on salted ham and succulent beef, complained. For the scholars, whose diet was never very wholesome, the unrelieved pease pottage and ravelled bread, that was served each day whilst the college remained isolated, seemed little different to their usual fare.

In the town beyond the barricaded oaken doors, people perished in alarming numbers. Insidiously, plague stalked the cobbled high road and the narrow lanes. The occasional small boat plied the Cam. College servants, armed with stout staves, patrolled the Backs to ensure that those who might carry the seeds of this evil disease did not encroach upon college property. The desperate and starving townsfolk sent messages to the colleges, whose forethought in laying up food bred bitterness. Steadfastly, the university authorities refused to render assistance. Very few scholars succumbed but outside the university walls, the death toll soared. Once the dangers of the epidemic receded, the sight of a scholar's gown was an anathema to the surviving townsfolk.

Although he excelled at his studies, Nathaniel resented the strictures of university discipline; he found the petty regulations irksome after the freedom of his time working for Theophilus. He fell in with a group of fellow students who frequented taverns and occasionally, houses of ill-repute. Aware that his time at Cambridge was meant to fit him for a role in the established church, Nathaniel paid lip-service to religious observance. It was at Cambridge that Nathaniel was introduced to the reformed way of thinking. Those who wished to purify the church against anything that smacked of popery formed a strong and growing clique within the university. The country's fear of Catholicism, with its perceived link to social disorder, sparked the zeal of these young men. Theirs were the very beliefs that now endangered the people of Byddeforde. This evil perversion of God's will must be eradicated, thought Nathaniel. How could he ever have been drawn into such iniquitous puritan enclaves?

John Harvard had been of this Cambridge coterie of course, more a friend of his brother, Jonathan, than Nathaniel's own. Harvard and Jonathan had been at Emmanuel College together, whereas Nathaniel was a Trinity scholar. Harvard was treated with disdain by his fellow students, his origins as the son of a Southwark butcher a justification for their scorn. Nonetheless, Nathaniel had ignored all gainsayers and aligning himself with Harvard, he had become a passionate evangelist for the reformed church. Nathaniel shuddered at the memory. His association with Harvard had led to a period of his life when he had been dishonourably treated.

Having come down from Cambridge without taking his degree, Nathaniel had once again gone to live with Theophilus at Coleman Street and continued to travel on behalf of his brother, going to France and then Leyden. It was at Leyden that Nathaniel had first come under the influence of William Ames. Ames subscribed to Calvinistic thought and Nathaniel deeply regretted that he had been persuaded to adopt similar beliefs. Thankfully, he was beyond that now. He would be mortified if any of his parishioners in Byddeforde learned that there had been a time when he, Nathaniel, now a paragon of the established church, had been swayed by such ideas. That was why it was so important to counteract the growing number of Independents in the town. They must not be allowed to promulgate such mistaken doctrines. Still, Ames had a least shown Nathaniel that he was steeped in sin and urged him to abandon the heathenish debauchery of the lifestyle he had adopted since his time at Cambridge. Nathaniel reddened as he recalled the riotous celebrations that had characterised the students' Christmas season. He brushed his hands down his clerical garb. That too had been an abomination to Ames, who denounced such attire, believing that a man of God should be marked out by his piety and his deeds and not by a mode of dress. Ames' discourses against vestments were still circulated. Probably encouraged by the likes of Bartlett, thought Nathaniel.

At Ames' suggestion, Nathaniel had agreed to become one of his pupils. The time spent under Ames at Franeker University had turned Nathaniel into a fanatical Sabbatarian, insisting on the strictest regimen of Sabbath observance; a stance that he had taken with him to the New World. Nathaniel crossed himself, as if to ward off thoughts of his reformed self. The sign of the cross, with its tinges of popery, was something else that was abhorrent to Ames.

After his mentor died, just a year after the men had first met, Nathaniel had reluctantly returned to England, where he had secured a curacy in Wiltshire and taken up posts in two indifferent schools. Even then, Nathaniel had doubted that teaching was his vocation. Fresh from the influence of Ames' stringent way of life, Nathaniel had been shocked by the profanity and sinful conduct of both pupils and fellow masters. He had found it difficult to worship in the manner to which he had become accustomed in the Low Countries and Nathaniel had craved the company of fellow reformists. When the opportunity arose to join like-minded god-fearing folk in the emerging settlement across the Atlantic, it had seemed like an answer to his prayers.

Now, Nathaniel looked back on his time in the Massachusetts Bay Colony with distaste. He felt that he had been poorly served by the authorities there. It was a constant irritation to Nathaniel that those in positions of power failed to recognise his status or his merits. His worth had been underrated in the Colony and matters were no more favourable here in Byddeforde now. The expedition to the New World had started with such promise. He remembered the sense of expectation as he stood on the salt-tanged deck of *The Hector*, trying to quell his seasickness. His heart had been aflame with the prospect of freedom to worship in the new way and thoughts of what strengths he could bring to the emerging community. It had been Theophilus, newly remarried to Ann, together with John Davenport who had gathered the fellow puritans together. Nathaniel's brother, Samuel, had been of their number, not that he'd lasted long in the Colony, returning after only a few short years, to preach in a Congregational Church in Cheshire. Misguided of course and he'd died in his delusions, never returning to the one true way. Nathaniel sent up a fervent prayer, thankful that, unlike Samuel, he had seen the dangers of the dogmas of the reformed church.

The brothers had persuaded their elderly mother to accompany them across the seas but she'd deserted him, thought Nathaniel, petulantly. Mistress Eaton had left for New Haven with Theophilus when Governor Winthrop's regime became unpalatable. Theophilus had done well for himself as Governor of New Haven; he was dead too, these ten years or more. Would matters have been different if he had followed Theophilus to New Haven? Nathaniel had chosen to remain in Newtowne, revelling in Winthrop's firm hand and harsher outlook. He had misjudged Winthrop, thinking they were in accord but Winthrop too had turned against him. The injustice of what had happed in Newtowne still rankled. Even now, Nathaniel could not bring himself to refer to the settlement by its new name of Cambridge. He had merely been doing his duty, yet he was the one who had been unfairly maligned.

Once in Massachusetts Bay Colony, Nathaniel had presumed upon his acquaintance with John Harvard. Thus, he had secured the position of master at the college that had been set up as a result of grants by Harvard and others. Nathaniel still blamed Harvard for dying prematurely. Had he lived, he might have supported Nathaniel in his adversity. The scheme to found a seat of learning was poorly conceived and without Harvard's guidance, did not prosper as it should. The sums of money set aside for the running of the new establishment were paltry and Nathaniel was offended by the meagre plot of land that he had been granted for the college building. He was a teacher not a builder. Little wonder that he had taken himself off to Charlestown, whilst those more used to menial labour set about erecting the accommodation and teaching rooms in Cowyard Row. Such a prestigious institution as the Colony's first college deserved to be sited somewhere that did not reek of manure but Nathaniel's protests had gone unheeded. True, he had later been allocated an additional two acres from the former pasture where the plough oxen had grazed but he had been ill-used from the outset, thought Nathaniel, peevishly.

Now, with the passage of more than thirty years, the faces of his first scholars were beyond recall. The young men were universally intractable, slovenly and in need of frequent correction in order to instil the essential qualities of obedience and prayerfulness. The settlement's leaders insisted upon regular beatings, a duty that Nathaniel had carried out with relish. All knew that sparing the rod spoiled the child and the puritans, in particular, advocated the habitual chastisement of their children and servants. Although their features eluded him, Nathaniel could still bring to mind the names of some of those assigned to his tutelage, Henry Saltonstall, Sam Hough, George Downing, Samuel Bellingham, William Hubbard, Tobias Barnard, their names tripped from his tongue like a roll-call but to Nathaniel, they were an amorphous mass, any individual facets of their personalities had blurred into a corpus of obstinate young manhood. Then there was all that fuss over the lad Rowe, who had been foisted upon him with the intention that Nathaniel should demean himself by teaching the boy Latin. Rowe he could visualise; he had been a particularly unpleasant specimen, overweight, lazy and plagued with a pustule-ridden skin. Nathaniel was not going to stoop to bothering with the likes of Rowe. If the youth needed tuition, that was the job of the ushers. Nathaniel blanched again. The unstoppable tide of memories was crushing.

Nathaniel was adamant that he had done everything a God-fearing man should have done. He had acquired a wife, Ellen, a sure protection against the sins of the flesh. He had dutifully sired children upon her. Thoughts of his first wife, were consigned to that compartment in his mind that Nathaniel rarely visited. Considering his time with Ellen provoked recollections that were inextricably linked to the nadir of his career.

It had been an impossible job to run the College on the derisory funds that he had been allowed. True, despite being a gifted mathematician, the reckoning of accounts was another duty that Nathaniel had resented and therefore ignored. What if he had run up a few debts? It was not his fault. Naturally, Ellen, charged with providing meals for the scholars, had been frugal. Young men would not appreciate good meat. An excess of rich food only heighted the blood and made men lustful. Give youths too many vittals and they become slothful and inattentive. Hunger pains sharpen the mind, Nathaniel knew that from his own time of study. So, Ellen had routinely served porridge and pudding. Granted there had been a few unfortunate incidents. He should have rebuked Ellen, prevented her from being so free with her tongue when they were summoned before the Governor. What had possessed her to admit to providing dishes of un-filleted mackerel or hasty pudding mixed with goat's dung? She should have stood her ground and denied all the allegations that were laid at her door. Naturally, Nathaniel had beaten the scholars for recalcitrance and stupidity, yet, unfairly, that had been another reason for complaints against him. Nor was it his fault that the blackamoor, who was meant to be emptying the chamber-pots and taking out the slops, decided to lie in Sam Hough's bed. Yet he had been censured for that too.

The greatest injustice was the incident with Briscoe, whom Nathaniel had appointed as an usher. After only three days in post, there had been an altercation and Nathaniel had been compelled to upbraid the man for insubordination. He had taken a stout walnut stave, after all the man was taller, younger and a fair few pounds heavier than Nathaniel. As he had castigated the fellow, laying about him with the cudgel, Briscoe had drawn the knife that he carried in order to cut his meat. When questioned, Briscoe had had the temerity to claim that he feared for his life and had wielded the weapon in self-defence. The knave had uttered blasphemies that obliged Nathaniel to prolong the beating. Briscoe had twisted that too, saying he had merely been calling upon God to save him. How foolish, when God, with Nathaniel as his instrument, was clearly on the side of righteousness and the man deserved to be punished. Then others had intervened, attempting to prevent Nathaniel from meting out the warranted beating. Small wonder that Nathaniel had gone to the General Court, laying a complaint against Briscoe for attempting to draw blood.

He had expected support from the elders who presided over the Court. Far from denouncing Briscoe, they had turned the accusations upon Nathaniel himself. The sheer hypocrisy of the elders, Mather and his ilk, beggared belief. Students came forward, emboldened by the support of their peers and claimed that he, Nathaniel, had beaten them excessively. Excessively! He'd merely been ensuring that they confessed their faults. In the end, Nathaniel had debased himself before the Court, acknowledged what they perceived to be his fault and begged their pardon, much as it pained him so to do. At the time, he had been confident that this would be sufficient to allow him to keep his post. The fines were punishing. A hundred marks to the Court and then they expected him to pay that buffoon Briscoe forty-five marks. Remonstrating was pointless, they would brook no argument.

Realising the futility of attempting to state his case, in the face of the censorious Court, Nathaniel had turned on his heel with the parting shot, "If sentence be passed, then it is no end to speak."

The General Court had been hostile enough. Nathaniel could not contemplate facing the rigours of the ensuing Church Court. He was not going to stand in front of those same men, albeit in a different role and be humiliated and vilified unjustly a second time. Before matters could become even more unspeakable, Nathaniel had absented himself from Newtowne and naturally, he had taken the money that was due to him. Nathaniel allowed himself a small moment of self-congratulation as he recalled how he had got the better of those dolts of constables, who Governor Winthrop had sent to apprehend him at Piscataqua. Nathaniel had agreed to pay an exorbitant sum to Captain Neale, who was about to set sail for Virginia. He'd duped the constables by feigning compliance and had begged to be allowed on board the ship to reclaim his baggage. The constables had been chosen for their physique and not for the sharpness of their wits. Nathaniel almost raised a smile as he replayed the scene in his mind. Two of the constables remained on the quay, leaving the youngest of their number to accompany Nathaniel. It had been comparatively simple to give the unwary fellow a hearty shove. Captain Neale, mindful of the gold that Nathaniel had passed into his hands and observing the dilemma that his passenger was in, had hauled the final anchor and sailed out of the harbour. The hapless constable was left floundering in the wash, with his colleagues raging impotently on the shore.

Having abandoned Newtowne, Nathaniel had been fortunate that he had been able to settle in Accomack

County and that the congregation in Hungar had been in need of an assistant minister. Not that it paid more than a pittance and debts were inevitable. A man had to live according to his rank if he was to gain the respect of his flock. He'd done the right thing, sent for Ellen and the children but they'd set sail and not a stave of the ship had ever been found; likely the vessel had fallen victim to the autumn gales. He'd heard that Ellen had left their eldest, Benoni, behind in Newtowne but Nathaniel had been wary of drawing attention to himself by making too many enquiries. A man, particularly a man of God, needed a wife and the widow Ann Graves had seemed eminently suitable, biddable and not ill-favoured. In the privacy of their home however she'd proved to be a shrew and reluctant to perform her marital duties. Small wonder that he had left alone for Merry Point, when his creditors became importunate. Briefly, Nathaniel wondered if Ann was still alive. Best not to dwell on the matter, he thought. If Ann still lived there might be those who'd cast doubts on the validity of his marriage to his current wife, Mary.

Eventually, it had seemed prudent to quit the New World entirely. Given the political turmoil of the years whilst he'd been overseas, pragmatism dictated that, on his return to England, Nathaniel should present himself as an ardent adherent of the established church. It had gained him a living, at first in Bishop's Castle and subsequently here in Byddeforde. No sooner had he arrived, some three years ago, than he was regaled with tales of evil deeds. Had he realised that he was stepping into a maelstrom of non-conformity, he would have been less enthusiastic about taking up the position. That arrogant Bartlett was ardent in his whipping up of disorderly factions with Independent leanings.

Nathaniel had not long been in post when Bishop Sparrow remonstrated with him about the crowded state of the churchyard. Well, Nathaniel could hardly be held to account for the growth of the town. It seemed that every week more folk moved in from the country around. Nor was it Nathaniel's fault that so many of the inhabitants died and required burying. Sparrow had complained that the dead should be treated with more reverence. At least now they had additional land, granted by the Earl of Bath, upon which to extend Byddeforde's burial ground. That was one less irritation for Nathaniel to contend with.

The town was in disarray and not just spiritually. There was filth cast in the hedgerows and swine were running amok in the streets. It was yet another symptom of moral decline. Cleanliness was indeed next to godliness and so many of the newcomers to the town had scant regard for either. That Hugh Langdon for instance, he had had the audacity to let his pigs wander into the churchyard. What would the Bishop have to say about that? Nathaniel wondered. The fellow had not even looked contrite when the warden had had strong words with him about the matter. There were dung heaps everywhere, if they did not take care there would be another visitation of the plague. After Cambridge, Nathaniel did not feel that he could contend with that, not at his time of life. That rogue Joynt was paid to clear the waste but he was found to be in dereliction of his duty. Thankfully, the aldermen had required the coopers to put barrels in the street to collect the refuse, mayhap that would help matters.

Nathaniel was aware that, whilst his thoughts had been wandering, most of the candles had burned out and he was now sitting in near darkness. Pushing his unread Bible to one side, he got up to summon the maidservant to replenish the candles. As he did so, there was a vociferous banging on the rectory door. He pushed aside the thick hangings and peered through the blemished glass to the street below. Three burly men were outside. One raised a staff to hammer yet again on the oaken door, the brass tip of the rod glinted in the light of the lantern held aloft by one of his fellows. A bright arc fell on the faces of the men, as the maidservant opened the door. Nathaniel shrunk back behind the curtain, not wishing to be observed should one of the men glance upward. Their chilling words reached him.

"Master Davie sent us. Is Reverend Eaton within? We've a warrant for his apprehension on a charge of debt."

Martha's Story
2020

Martha poured the remains of a box of sugar-free muesli into her bowl. She was eager to get on with the next stage of her research and she had earmarked the next few days for investigating the 1679 witchcraft accusations.

"You need a day off that laptop, today," remarked Hebe as she squeezed a fresh orange into a jug.

This was out of character. Hebe rarely paid much attention to what Martha was up to.

"No. The weather is glorious, you need to get some vitamin D; you've been looking positively anaemic of late. Go and commune with nature, remember your mindfulness. It is all vital for your wellbeing."

Martha sighed. Perhaps discussions at Hebe's recent alternative retreat had reminded her that she had a daughter. There must be a reason why she was attempting to exert some parental authority for a change.

"Go for a walk along the beach," suggested Hebe. "I am going to an Extinction Rebellion meeting, I can give you a lift. Let the rhythm of the waves heal your soul."

As much as Martha would rather continue submerging herself in stories of seventeenth century Bideford, she did acknowledge that she'd done nothing else since school broke up. Hebe obviously had some hidden agenda of her own that necessitated having an offspring that wandered alone along the shoreline.

"Take Calliope for a run."

Ah, so that was it. What Hebe actually wanted was for Martha to take their rough-haired mongrel for a walk. Calliope was Martha's saviour when things got really bad at school. Martha could sit on her bed and bury her face in the coarse fur, pouring out her hurts. Guiltily, Martha acknowledged that she hadn't taken Calliope on one of the rambles that they both loved since she'd been caught up in her project.

"I can't take her on the beach. There's a dog ban for the summer," Martha reminded her mother. Hebe was always oblivious to the practicalities. "Can you drop us off at the park instead?"

"Victoria Park is hardly the wilds of the great outdoors," said Hebe. "But if you will allow yourself to be trammelled by petty bureaucracies, the park it is."

***

It was blisteringly hot. Calliope sat panting in the dappled shade on the slope by the swings, hoping to be given the tail end of Martha's ice cream cone. Martha was pretty sure that there was something in Hocking's ice creams that did not conform to Hebe's exacting dietary restrictions but she didn't much care; they were delicious. It seemed that the wariness about crowded places, that accompanied fears of COVID-19, was forgotten. The screams of small children rose up from the paddling pool. Adults lay face down on towels, their scarlet flesh squeezing from swimming costumes that they had persuaded themselves were still a good fit. Rapidly reddening shoulders suggested that some people would later regret their sun-worship. Martha wiped her sticky fingers on the dry grass and wandered towards the area beyond the skate park, which was usually quieter.

There was nothing peaceful about this part of the park today. A large group of boys from Martha's school had abandoned their skate-boards, mountain bikes and cans of energy drink to watch a fight that was taking place. On the periphery were the girls; a few cast derisory glances in Martha's direction. Her jeans and tee-shirt did not fit their uniform of bikini tops and tiny shorts. Today though there was fresh bait. Normally, Martha would have turned and walked away as quickly as possible but emboldened by Calliope's presence, she looked at the two boys whose fight was the focus of attention. She recognised Hunter, a tall, wiry boy with streaked hair and a floppy fringe. Martha knew him as one of the sporty crowd; he'd been praised in assembly for gaining the county high-jump record. Martha remembered that he was one of the few who had spoken up for Poppy during the mock election.

Hunter was currently dodging the blows of a heavier boy, whom Martha couldn't name, although she'd seen him hanging around with Jeremy.

She began to distinguish the crowd's taunts from the general blur of noise.

"Bloody Fag."

"Homo"

"Paedo. No way is my little brother going to athletics training, if he's taking it."

Martha's phone bleeped with a notification. She stood on the edge of the crowd and scrolled down. Within moments it became clear why there had been fewer posts directed at her lately. Her social media feeds were pulsating with the latest gossip. Hunter had come out as gay, making Martha's geekiness pale into insignificance. Actually, it transpired that poor Hunter hadn't intended to broadcast his sexuality to the world at all. He'd told one other person and for some unfathomable reason, he had chosen Jeremy. Maybe it was because they were both on the athletics squad. How could Hunter not see that he had picked the absolute worst person to tell? thought Martha. The invective swept across the internet with the virulence of wildfire. The abusive comments, taken up by Jeremy's crowd and the likes of Tyrone, were embellished with every succeeding post. Martha felt for Hunter, yet underlying her empathy was the secret relief that she was now old news. The shouts were growing louder. Slowly, Martha began to pace backwards away from the throng, a whimpering Calliope at her side.

Chapter 6
Dorcas' Story
1674-1679

John Davie struggled to conceal his unease. The man who stood before him had been shown into his study by an apologetic servant. The interloper was a low sort of a fellow, scarcely one who would normally be granted an audience but the servant had been swayed by the man's persistence. It was fortunate that he had. The intelligence Davie had received was of vital worth in the crusade against insurgency. Davie sighed. It seemed that much of his term of mayoral office had been taken up by dealing with troublesome dissenters. Old man Bartlett was a perpetual thorn in his side. Dismissing the informant with a wave of his hand and a proffered coin, Davie summoned his manservant. This was a task for the constables; they needed to act swiftly and with a show of strength that would be a deterrent to these malcontents.

***

Six burly constables gathered outside a house in Potter's Lane. They were accompanied by two Serjeants at Mace bearing their staffs of office and a single, reluctant churchwarden, his colleague having feigned sickness when the nature of the undertaking became plain. It was not the first time that the constables had been called to this pottery of late. It was only a few weeks since the owners, brothers Thomas and Gabriel Beale, had been fined for stacking furze against their front wall. Jeopardising the safety of their neighbours in this way was prohibited and for good reason. Potters needed to fire their kilns of course but a sudden spark might easily ignite the thatch. Nonetheless, for ease of working, several potters preferred to keep their firewood close to hand; disregarding the regulations that said they must store no more than 300 bundles of lightings at a time and that these must be a full eighty yards from a dwelling. All along Potter's Lane, roughly tied faggots of twigs lay in haphazard piles, openly flouting the directive. Yet it was the Beales who had been made an example of and here they were, in trouble once again.

A low murmuring could be heard coming from the shippen attached to the rear of the potters' home. The nine men slipped round the side of the house and squeezed into the back of the crowded out-building.

"There's nigh on four hundred folk here," whispered one of the constables, "It must be a quarter of the town!"

"'Tis more than we were led to believe," said his companion, looking warily about him. "I thought these meetings had ceased; we've not had word of such a gathering for many a month."

"We have the mayor's authority," said another, beginning to force his way through the press of people, belabouring those nearest to him with his stave.

Their presence had been noticed now and a wave of alarm flickered through the throng. At the front, on a raised platform, William Bartlett was addressing the crowd. His resounding tones belied his advancing years. The mayor's men forged their way forward. Exclamations, from those who realised what was occurring, grew ever louder. The old man never faltered in his speech; he merely exhorted his listeners to call upon God to deliver them from gainsayers. Devout most of the crowd might be but the incursion was not conducive to pious thought. The minds of many were now on self-preservation.

Near the back of the congregation, stood young Dorcas Lidstone, a somewhat reluctant participant in the proceedings. Dorcas was not a dissenter by nature, it was a combination of expediency and curiosity that had brought her to the meeting. That and if truth be told, the fact that the Colemans were amongst the worshippers. Dorcas was ruthless in her pursuit of a husband and a well set-up man such as Jack Coleman, like to be master of his own ship afore long, was an ideal candidate. She had been a little bored by the lengthy service. It had been a relief when Master Bartlett the younger had sat down after giving a tedious address but there was to be no respite, as his father had immediately taken his place. For Dorcas, the disturbance had been a welcome interruption.

The fracas had reached the front of the crowd. Dorcas contemplated making a timely exit but she was hemmed in by those around her. Despite their disquiet, very few seemed to be attempting to leave. Dorcas had stationed herself a discreet two ranks behind the Colemans, so that she could admire the object of her affections from an appropriate distance. Jack Coleman and his family remained steadfastly focussed upon preacher Bartlett's words. Nervously, Dorcas glanced across the assembled congregation. At the front, the two Misses Beale were looking anxiously at their husbands. These stout women, mainstays of Byddeforde's puritanical faction, were very alike in appearance, being sisters; Dorcas never could distinguish one from the other. Over there were the Thomas family, Grace and Eliza, with their elderly father. Dorcas' mind was momentarily diverted from the commotion playing out before her. Grace was standing dangerously close to Jack. The woman must be nigh on forty; surely she could not have designs on Jack, though Dorcas proprietorially.

The crowd hushed as the Sergeant rapped upon the plain deal table upon which the preacher's Bible was laid. Finally, William Bartlett halted his oration.

"By what authority do you meet in this house?" the Sergeant roared.

Quietly but firmly, Bartlett responded, "I preach here by the same authority that constituted the mayor to hold office in this town."

There were murmurs of agreement in the crowd. Surely, Bartlett and his son were licensed to preach. Ignoring the officials, Bartlett resumed his sermon but the Sergeant was determined to impose his authority.

"This meeting is an infringement against the late Act made against Conventicles. All here present will hereby be fined five shillings. For many for whom this is a second offence, the fine will be doubled," bellowed the Sergeant.

Some of those closest to Dorcas looked doubtful; five shillings, could not easily be found. There was a shuffling of feet, yet most remained where they were, whilst Bartlett finished his address. Dorcas could see Jack Coleman steadfastly standing his ground, making no attempt to avoid the constables, who were struggling to note the names of those they recognised. The incident had done far more to convince Dorcas of the attraction of the Independents' cause than any of the preachers' words. She could be a part of this group of worthy people, she too could be brave in the face of the men sent by the mayor. She would call out against those who did not follow the true way and the mayor and his constables could do as they pleased. The more stringent requirements that might accompany adherence to Bartlett's followers now seemed a minor deterrent. She could eschew frivolity, give up her gewgaws and furbelows for more modest dress. She would persevere with her reading, as industrious women of the reformed faith should. No longer so she could read the salacious broad sheets but in order to study the Bible. She too could frown upon the tipplers and merry-makers, who danced to viol and flute. She could belong.

***

Dorcas shifted the weighty basket into her other hand, its handle had left bright indentations across her fingers. Why should she have to undertake such tasks? she thought, resentfully, as she walked away from the bustle that surrounded the market stalls at the bottom of the High Street. Essential errands were an irritation. No matter that the preachers promoted diligent toil as an indication of a commitment to a godly path. Actions that might ease her way to heaven, they may be, yet she was but sixteen summers. Time enough to pay more heed to the afterlife when the distractions of youth had lost their appeal. Despite her now regular attendance at prayer meetings, Dorcas could not subdue her self-absorption, as she knew she should if she were to take her place amongst the elect. She would far rather be strolling in the late summer sunshine, tattling with her gossips and hoping to catch a glimpse of the likes of Jack Coleman.

Dorcas stored away secrets with relish and the more sensational the better. Sanctimoniously, she told herself that it was solely for the benefit of others. After all, awareness of their failings allowed her to pray for those who fell short; thus might sinners be given the opportunity to reform. She had learned that patient listening was often the way to encourage the confidences of her friends and neighbours. Only today, on her way to market, she had stood quietly on the periphery of a conversation about the newly appointed rector.

"Well you'd scarce think he'd be worse than Reverend Eaton but seems we've another who will send folk flocking to the likes of Master Bartlett and Master Beale."

"I am sure I heard him uttering a profanity just the other day, mind 'tis hard to make out his northern speech."

"They say he hails from Scotland way, how can he be knowin' aught 'bout the likes o' us? Not that I could ever take to Reverend Eaton messen but this new man….."

Being a follower of the Independent way of thought, at least nominally, Dorcas had not yet encountered the man who had recently arrived to replace Reverend Eaton. Nonetheless, every little morsel of gossip could be tucked away, stored and used to her advantage at some undefined point in the future.

"I know one should not speak ill o' a man o' God but they do say he is oft in strong drink. I heard it from one who should know, her sister's husband's aunt be servant up at the rectory."

Dorcas obediently joined in with the horrified intakes of breath.

"Chaplain to the king some be sayin'. Well, I be tellin' you, we don't want all those fancy ways down 'ere. He can go back to Lunnon soon as."

The conversation moved on, "D'you hear tell about Reverend Eaton? They say he's died up in that Lunnon prison."

"Hard to think on, our vicar in gaol. Like as not he were under close guard."

"Well he broke his bail that one time did he not? Passed a coin or two in the right places they do say. Though where he got money from to ease his time, there's no tellin'."

"No, indeed, being as 'twas debt what put him under lock and key in the first place."

"'Twas no more than he deserved."

Dorcas had heard enough. Eaton was old news. She slipped away, she could linger no longer; she was anxious to deposit her load and seek her companions. It was too warm for hefting baskets weighted down with the market's offerings. There was talk that the flourishing market should be re-sited at the top of the town, where there might be more space for traders to display their wares. Dorcas sighed. She did not relish the prospect of the steep climb up and down the hill if that were to happen.

Eager for her errand to be over, Dorcas quickened her step. She overtook an older woman, whose progress along the street was more leisurely. As she passed by, Dorcas recognised her neighbour, Jane Dallyn and she turned in acknowledgement as Jane uttered a greeting. Dorcas was shocked to see that Jane's eye was an angry red, with swollen lids that were beginning to close. Glad of the opportunity to rest her heavy basket on the ground, Dorcas paused to exchange brief banalities about the warmth of the weather. Jane eased a laden pannier from her shoulders and rubbed the back of her hand across her eye. Dorcas was prompted to enquire as to the nature of the hurt.

"Do you have a speck in your eye Mistress Dallyn?" she asked. "Or mayhap it be a bite or sting. 'Tis greatly inflamed and I believe you are in some discomfort?"

"I know not what 'tis," replied Jane. "My sight has dimmed with advancing years. I can scarce make out the words in my Bible now, for all they are so familiar. Yet this irritation has come upon me sudden like. 'Tis of but a few days duration and I know not the cause."

Dorcas rarely concerned herself with the plight of others but she was keen to put on an outward show of sympathy, lest any be watching. Furthermore, the Dallyns were close with the Coleman family, happen she might hear something of Jack if she engaged Mistress Dallyn in conversation.

"Should you be abroad, mistress?" asked Dorcas.

"In truth the sunlight pains me," Jane acknowledged, pulling her hood forward to shade her injured eye. "Yet I am in need of provisions. I have collected as much as I can carry but there is more that I require, so 'twill be back to the market again for me in an hour or two. Despite my discomfort, I cannot stay within doors."

Dorcas had no inclination to dally. Offering to fetch the goods on Mistress Dallyn's behalf would be too great an inconvenience. Advice though took little time and it did no harm to give folk cause to be grateful. Dorcas picked up her basket and continued her homeward path. She would slacken her stride so that Mistress Dallyn might keep pace with her but she had no time to loiter. The two women walked on together.

"Have you no ointment to ease it mistress?" asked Dorcas, more to break the silence than out of genuine compassion.

Mistress Dallyn looked embarrassed. "I've none to hand. Just afore I was took bad, Goody Lloyd did come around offering her potions and the like but I sent her away. No tellin' if there might have been something that she had to offer that might have aided me but anyroad, I'll have naught of her concoctions."

Dorcas wrinkled her nose in distaste. Standing firm with her new acquaintances of the reformed faith, she sought to avoid those such as Goody Lloyd, whose incursions into the lives of the respectable townsfolk were at best akin begging. It didn't do to dwell on the more sinister undertones that were said to be an accompaniment to Goody Lloyd's ministrations. The ancient dame, with her bedraggled appearance, sour odour and constant importuning, had a particularly dubious reputation. It was but a few years since Master Herbert had condemned her as a witch. Had Mistress Dallyn been wise to refuse aid from one who might do her harm? In the case of Herbert, the decrepit old woman had walked free of course but it didn't do to cross cunning folk such as Goody Lloyd. If it had been me, I'd have taken her offering and thrown it in the midden when she was beyond sight, thought Dorcas but she did not communicate her unease to the woman beside her.

Instead, Dorcas remarked, "You should send word to the new apothecary, Master Ball. Though he is but young, he is highly regarded. Mayhap he will have a remedy that will ease you."

"Indeed but 'tis not yet the season for loosestrife. There's none better for darkening sight."

Mistress Dallyn was right, it would be a full month before the pink spikes of the loosestrife showed themselves on the marshy ground by the river.

"Is there nought else that can aid you?"

Dorcas did not set great store by housewifely skills and had been inattentive on the numerous occasions when her exasperated mother had encouraged her to learn what herbs might succour the ailing.

"A concoction of eye-bright, is usually efficacious at these times," said Jane. "I'll mayhap call upon Master Ball when my marketing is done. I did not reckon on the brightness of the day inflaming it further."

Dorcas' capacity for exuding sympathy was diminishing. Mistress Dallyn had not once mentioned the Coleman family, as Dorcas had hoped that she might. She had scant interest in Jane herself, whom Dorcas regarded as being of little account. True, the Dallyns were respectable folk, Dorcas would scarce have passed the time of day were it not so. Jane's husband, Symon, was master of the *George*, and plied the channel to Bristol with cargoes of pipe clay and earthenware but Dorcas set her sights higher. She longed to be someone of importance in the town, someone whom folk would hold in high esteem. How this was to be achieved Dorcas could not yet determine but one day, she resolved, one day soon, she would be a person of note, one who was looked upon with deference and envy.

Three Years Later

The summer had been a dry one, the fields were parched and tempers were short. The water dredged from wells and conduits was brackish and foul-smelling. Women argued with their neighbours. Any who had the temerity to walk from the well with more than one bucket of syrupy brown liquid were rebuked for their greed. Food too was scarce; crops had failed and many were reduced to eating poor quality produce that would, in more bountiful times, have been fed to the pigs. Livestock grew lean and was slaughtered untimely. It made for poor eating but there was little left to feed animals when families were starving. 'Twas better to put them in the pot, rather than watch them waste away.

Even though the season was turning and the harvest, such as it was, was in, it was uncomfortably warm. Where possible, the townsfolk avoided going abroad in the heat of the day. The fiery sun striped the water with orange and gold, as it lay low over the river. Dorcas slipped her arm through that of Ann Fellow. Ann was a recent connection, cultivated because her father was an Officer of Excise, a man of some rank in the Byddeforde. Ann was just the sort of girl Dorcas sought in a friend. Pretty, in an insipid sort of a way, with watery blue eyes and flaxen hair. Of course, Ann's hair was poker-straight, Dorcas flicked her own abundant gold curls. No, Ann was just right, it didn't do to be seen with anyone dowdy, yet she did not want to associate with one whose looks might overshadow her own. Eager to flaunt her new friendship, Dorcas was hopeful of encountering other acquaintances. It was growing dark as the two young women strolled through the butt garden. No one practiced archery here after Sunday service nowadays but the old name lingered. A noisy crowd was gathering ahead of them. Ann drew back, anxious to avoid trouble. Fearful of missing some titbit of news, Dorcas urged her on. The thickening throng circled two brawling men. Dorcas pushed her way to where she had a better view, dragging a reluctant Ann behind her. In the dim light it was difficult to make out the identity of those who were fighting but Dorcas' keen ears picked out fragments of conversation in the crowd.

"Surely that be Master John Collacott, you recall, him out Alwington way, 'tis rare you see a gentleman scrapping in the street."

Dorcas didn't not recognise the fellow who was at this moment trying to wrestle another to the ground but his fine clothes certainly suggested that he was a man of status.

"Just this day he were fined for swearing at the mayor, no less, for all he calls hisself a gentleman."

"'Tis the drink that be in them. In truth we've that many ale houses in Byddeforde, 'tis little wonder we've become a town full of tipplers."

"I don't hold with strong drink messen. Even the alehouse keepers be insensible in the street."

"They say Bagilhole be worse than the rest, him what used to take in tailoring afore he took to sellin' spirits."

"Drinkin' the stock more'n like."

Impatiently, Dorcas shifted her position. If this was indeed a gentleman who was being attacked, she needed to ascertain the name of his assailant. In truth, it was not clear who had cast the first blow. The fighting increased in ferocity. Dorcas was near the front now, with Ann cowering behind her, entreating her to come away. Dorcas was torn between appeasing her friend and finding out more. How gratifying it would be to be the first amongst her associates with this tasty piece of gossip. A hefty man pushed his sweaty body against Dorcas as he swayed in the press of the crowd. Dorcas looked at him with distain. She knew him as Richard Allen, a bricklayer who had recently come to Byddeforde to work on some of the fine new houses that were springing up as the town prospered. The privations of the poor harvest did not extend to the wealthy tradesmen, who aspired to have homes that flaunted their affluence. Dorcas attempted to move out of Allen's orbit. She might be able to name him but she wanted naught to do with such a base fellow, one who was frowned up by Bartlett and his followers. Allen was notorious about the town, forever before the authorities for uttering profanities. In alarm, Dorcas realised that he was carrying a stout stave. This he passed to the man who was, at that moment, cowering under Collacott's blows. The fight was moving to a very different level, yet Dorcas was reluctant to leave. She needed to identify the man who was now wielding Allen's stick with effect. Allen and his drunken cronies were shouting encouragement. Dorcas did not have to wait long before one of the women in the crowd told her more.

"I know who 'tis. 'Tis him that works up at Clovelly Court for George Carey. I mis-remember his name but he's ofttimes in town on some such errand or another."

"'Tis not a fair fight, him armed with a stick 'gainst a man wi' just his fists. Has someone sent for the constable? One will take serious hurt else."

"There never used to be so much trouble in our younger days."

"A body can scarce walk down the street now without fear o' being attacked. These ne're-do-wells are no respecters of rank."

"'Tis terrible that we've sunk so low. 'Tis not so long since the Reverend Ogilvy went to the mayor afeared of his life."

"I ne'er heard tell o' that. Who'd dare to put a bloodwick upon a man of God?"

"Master and Mistress Cole, that's who the Reverend spoke out 'gainst."

"I's not be knowin' o' they. Baint from hereabouts then; though there's Coles over to Buckland, be it them?"

"There be too many strangers in town o' late. 'Tis the cause of much of this arguifing."

The fight was intensifying. Others were weighing in on one side or another. Dorcas stepped back in alarm and yelped as a man fell at her feet. The woman behind her remonstrated as Dorcas had landed heavily on her toe. It was time to go, she had learned much that was edifying.

Two Years Later

Dorcas knocked politely on the Fellows' door. Despite her close acquaintanceship with the family, she did not presume to enter unbidden. It was an imposing house, conveniently sited beyond the end of the recently extended quay, where Master Fellow could keep an eye out for those landing untaxed goods. Dorcas hoped that they would not answer her summons too speedily, she wanted others to see that she was calling at a home such as this. Over the past couple of years, Dorcas had taken

to attending the prayer meetings that were held at the
Fellows' home. These were small, intimate gatherings of
no more than a dozen and gave Dorcas an opportunity
to flaunt her religious fervour in appropriate circles.
Dorcas wore her piety like a mask. She found the ways
of the Independents ever more restrictive, yet she still
felt that, through them, she might somehow achieve the
adulation that she so craved.

So, demurely feigning compliance, Dorcas joined
them in their worship, aped their actions and parroted
their words. Their opinions became her own. They
reviled people, Dorcas did likewise; this was the way to
acceptance. Her plan was working, albeit rather more
slowly than Dorcas would have wished. She was now
regarded as part of the coterie that surrounded Mistress
Fellow. Most were older women, Mistress Coleman,
Jack's mother, was one and Dorcas had striven to gain
her approval. Mistress Bremmicombe, kin to Mistress
Coleman, was another matron of import. Her husband
was one of the town's wealthy tobacco merchants, with
ships on the run to Maryland. Sometimes Mistress Davie
came and she was gentry. Then there was Mistress Ball,
a little nearer in age to Dorcas and Ann, not long since
married to the apothecary. Thoughts of marriage
brought Jack Coleman to mind. He was finally taking
notice. Urged on by his mother, he ofttimes exchanged
a few polite words with Dorcas after Sunday meetings
and on several occasions, she had caught him casting
admiring glances her way. Dorcas smiled to herself,
gratified with the way matters were advancing. She
knocked again; a flustered Mistress Fellow came to the
door.

"Oh, Dorcas, 'tis you. There be no prayer meeting today. Ann's took to her bed."

"What ails her?" Dorcas' concern was sincere, she had become genuinely fond of Ann.

"You'd best come within," said Mistress Fellow, ushering Dorcas inside.

"May I see her?" asked Dorcas. "When was she struck down?"

"Just yesterday," replied Mistress Fellow. "Her humours are greatly disordered," she dropped her voice to a whisper, despite the fact that there was no one within earshot. "'Tis a mite strange, she says she's being bitten or pricked, yet there be no mark upon her."

Dorcas shuddered. Icy fingers caressed her spine. This smacked of the dark arts. It was symptoms of this nature that folk mentioned when they muttered behind their hands of malfeasance, of spell casting, of ill-wishing.

"'Twill be some insect or another, of a certain," said Dorcas, with more conviction than she felt. "There's many a creature abroad now the days be a-warming and the miasmas be coming up from the river."

"Master Ball called earlier," Mistress Fellow said, as she led Dorcas up to Ann's chamber. "He left a purge but he was at a loss to know the cause of her distress."

Ann was lying on her bed, a finely-woven blanket drawn up over her. The strident cries of the gulls could be heard through the shuttered windows. Dorcas rushed to clasp her friend's hands; they were deathly cold, despite the warmth of the day.

"Why do you sit in darkness Ann?" queried Dorcas. "Shall I throw back the shutters? 'Tis a fine day outside."

"As you wish," replied Ann, listlessly, "'tis of no matter now."

"Oh, Ann. What's this to do? Of a truth it matters to me, I wish to see you well. What ills are these? Your mother spoke of bites."

"'Tis the pricking I can't abide. Pricking in the palms of my hands and the soles of my feet. There's one who has wrought evil upon me."

"But Ann, you are so good and sweet, who would wish you ill?"

"Dear Dorcas, you are too kind. Do you not harken to Master Bartlett, we all be sinners. 'Tis a punishment for my lack of charity."

"Punishment? For lack of charity? You are far more free with alms than I," said Dorcas truthfully. "If God saw fit to punish for mean-handedness, 'twould be me that suffered not you."

Ann smiled sadly, "'Tis not God you see Dorcas, this affliction is from the evil one himself."

Incredulity and panic fought in Dorcas' consciousness. Underlying these feelings, buried deep was an unacknowledged resentment. It was not every day that someone claimed to have been overlooked. Why should it be Ann who had been singled out? Now it would be Ann whose name would be on every tongue; timid little Ann, Ann whose place was in Dorcas' shadow. Dorcas shuddered. She didn't want to fall foul of those who might wish her ill, of course she didn't. Did she?

"They've entreated me to give a name," said Ann, "but I daresn't, not to my mother or my father, not to Master Ball, nor any of them. But you are different. I don't need to tell you. You know." Ann ignored Dorcas' puzzled expression and went on. "It was last week at market. You recall Dorcas, you were there when Goody Lloyd came upon us a-begging for a crust."

Dorcas barely remembered the incident. There were always poor folk importuning their betters and Goody Lloyd was just one amongst many. It was time that the corporation took action, one could scarce walk down the street unmolested these days. Only today, on her way to see Ann, she'd been plagued by daft Mary craving a coin. Everyone knew daft Mary. Normally, Dorcas would cross the street if she saw her approach. She lived in a tumble-down cottage on the edge of the town and had struggled to make ends meet since the deaths of her parents, Trugeon and Honour Trembles, a few years since. Best that the simple-minded were overlaid at birth, thought Dorcas. She turned her attention back to Ann.

"The good book says what we do for one of his children we do for Him," said Ann. "'Twould have cost me little to give her a morsel but I was too taken up with my own affairs. God in his grace has forgiven me but Goody Lloyd, she knows I need to be punished."

"Surely not Ann," Dorcas was placatory now, the sooner Ann was up and about, the sooner folk would stop fussing over her. "You'll be out in the spring sunshine afore long."

Nought that Dorcas could say lessened Ann's conviction that she was witch-ridden. As Dorcas went to take her leave, with promises to return on the morrow, she saw that, despite the cancellation of the prayer meeting, several worthy dames were congregated in Mistress Fellow's parlour.

"Oh, Dorcas," said Mistress Coleman, "how did you find Ann?"

"Yes, we are greatly concerned," added Mistresses Bremmicombe. "Greatly concerned," she turned to Mistress Ball beside her. "When your good Master cannot find the cause for her ills, well then 'tis grave indeed."

"Mopish," Dorcas was monosyllabic.

Ann this, Ann that, poor Ann, it was all about Ann, thought Dorcas. Despite her affection for her friend, bitterness was now to the fore. This was not how matters were meant to be. The conversation flowed on. Dorcas was pushed to the periphery. Scarce a word was addressed to her. The talk turned to darker matters.

"There be something not natural 'bout my Ann's sickness," said Mistress Fellow. "Pricking, biting, being watched, she says she is. And sometimes 'tis as if her limbs be not her own."

"There's evil abroad in this town, that's the truth of it," said Mistress Bremmicombe. "Ladies we should pray upon the matter, seek deliverance for the poor child who lies so afflicted."

"There's those of you that mightn't recall but there's been things that baint natural in Byddeforde these years past," said Mistress Coleman. "Take Master Herbert and afore him Mistress Ellyott."

"Yes," agreed Mistress Ball. "There's been several ills of late that my good Master has not had the bettering of. Ailments that do not seem natural like. I remember when we was first married, nigh on five years since,

Mistress Dallyn succumbed to an infection in her eye, died o' it in the end she did and there was something not quite right about that."

Dorcas was poised to contribute her knowledge of Mistress Dallyn but Mistress Ball had begun to recite a catalogue of untimely demises and Dorcas had missed her chance.

Mistress Bremmicombe cut across the younger woman's diatribe, "If 'tis witchcraft then the spell must be lifted. The wrongdoer must be tested, made to confess her fault, punished."

"She'll come for us all else," agreed Mistress Ball, "who's to say who will be next?" The young wife looked anxiously at the sleeping baby in her arms.

Mistress Fellow sighed, "She'll not tell who 'twas, narry a word has my Ann uttered 'bout who be the cause o' it all. We've need of a name to take to the justices."

"Goody Lloyd," blurted Dorcas and then again, more loudly, "'twas Goody Lloyd what cursed us in the marketplace. Why, I am fortunate not to have been struck down myself."

Suddenly, all attention was upon her. The women bustled round, expressing shock, concern, gratitude, praise. The constables must be summoned. Dorcas must give her account. How providential that Dorcas had borne witness to the incident. Was Dorcas that certain that she was in good health? Dorcas basked in the adulation. This was better. Momentarily, she had considered claiming to have been overlooked herself. Not that she wanted to be spell-ridden, of course not but it might have diverted the interest from Ann. No, this was infinitely preferable. A witch would be brought down thanks to her, Dorcas Lidstone; all would applaud her, speak her name. Of the consequences for the old woman she had denunciated, Dorcas thought not at all.

***

Dim shadows played across the floor of the upstairs room. Temperance Lloyd perched awkwardly on a stool in the corner. Her knees were drawn up to her chin, her feet rested on the stool's rim. Blackened toes with thick, yellowing nails poked out from under her worn petticoat. Ropes binding her wrists to her ankles rendered a more natural pose impossible. Yet this was preferable to the walking. Hour upon hour she had been forced to put one aching leg in front of the other, round and round. Ten paces one way, twelve the next, turn the corner again, ten paces more, her feet shuffling and stumbling on the dusty floor. On and on, times without number, with the others watching, waiting, ensuring that there was no rest, no respite, no time to gather her scattered thoughts together. Night had come and gone whilst she had been incarcerated, yet she had not been allowed to sleep.

She looked at her tormentors, respectable women these, women who knew no hunger nor want. You could not set any raggle-draggle to this task, unpleasant though it might be. No, these women needed to be upright, honourable, highly regarded. Temperance sniffed in derision. She knew better, they banded together these goodwives, eager to maintain their position in the rank of the accepted, to do anything, to say anything, in order to fit in. Not one of them was free from the burden of convention. Yet they all harboured their secrets. She recognised Sisily Galsworthie. Yes, there be tales that Temperance could tell 'bout her. Mistress Galsworthie was ofttimes called upon by the church to examine a corpse as it lay in its coffin, to swear that the winding sheet was of wool, as the regulations demanded. Of course, there were the gentry who might seek a silken shroud and be willing to pay the five pound fine for the privilege. There'll be no silken shroud for the likes o' I, thought Temperance. More like the parish coffin and a pauper's grave.

When her elderly body could stagger no further, her tormentors had grudgingly allowed her the use of this rough wooden stool. In fear, they had bound her. Rest was still impossible, trussed as she was like pheasant ready for the pot. She'd complained of a full bladder, Mistress Galsworthie had loosened the bonds with an exasperated hiss and gestured towards a pot in the corner. The fastidious watchers summoned a servant to clear it away immediately afterwards. Her bodily fluids offended them. Not her body though. These women knew it intimately, they had stripped her naked and had poked and prodded every crevice and cavity, searching, exclaiming, despairing. They rarely spoke to her of course. The actions they required of her were communicated by rough shoves and jabs.

Once again, they untied the fraying ropes that confined her and tore off her ragged clothing. Despite the prying fingers, the violation, the humiliation, the sharp air playing across her papery skin, Temperance could not but be gleeful at her tormentors' vexation. She had the measure of these women, for all their pretentions. They might plague her now but she would be the victor.

"There be nought! Not a teat, not a mark!"

"There must be. How else would she suckle her familiar?"

"You baint be lookin' aright, hold that candle closer, lift her arm, lift her paps, part her legs once more."

"The men could not extract a confession with their hard questioning. Master Fellow won't be best pleased if there is nothing with which to condemn her. 'Tis up to us to find a mark, or other indicators of her guilt."

"All night she's been up and one or more of us has been on watch. Did none of you spot her entering into converse with a rat, or bird, or fly? Happen you was dozing, you'll have missed the chance."

Sisily Galsworthie was indignant, "Happen I was not! She be too cunning, that's all there is to it. Hoodwinked us all, she has."

"There's folk of rank eager to condemn her. She cast her spell on those who spoke against her when Master Herbert was took, I vow she'll not cheat justice this time."

Temperance looked sideways at the four women as they huddled in the corner. They might mutter and mumble but she knew what they were saying, could sense their desperation, their hostility, their frustration and their fear as they failed to find aught with which to denounce her.

As the women resumed their fruitless searching with increased fervour, Temperance's thoughts turned to her accusers. Mistress Fellow thought herself so high and mighty that one did. Temperance had marked her out back last autumn, when Mistress Fellow had railed at her in the street, shrieked at her she had and all for giving a windfall to a little maid. Where was the harm in it? That wasn't the only time she'd had an unpleasant encounter with Mistress Fellow neither and she'd overheard what the woman had to say 'bout her an all. She was not sorry that the harpy was suffering, her and her daughter, the one who now cried witch. 'Twas all bluster, they could point their fingers but it did no more good than pissin' in the wind. They sought to accuse her with vagaries and unsubstantial tittle-tattle for their own ends; puffed-up meddlers every one. Take Mistress Davie, well o' course, it was ofttimes folk of rank who were free with their allegations but as for Mistress Davie, she'd no more to say than the rest o' them. Oliver Ball the apothecary. He had allus bin a naysayer, infuriated because her simples were more effective than his costly offerings. More than once he'd raged 'gainst her for taking custom from his door.

Young Dorcas Lidstone, simpering little maid, forever tossing her curls and looking up under her lashes, for all she claimed to be a puritan. No doubt Dorcas had seen an opportunity to ingratiate herself with the Fellows. The young uns were the worst. Maids of her breed 'ud tell any tale to turn heads. Of a certain, that Dorcas 'ud say aught to gain favour from the likes o' Mistress Coleman and Mistress Coleman was amongst those who sought to condemn her. Temperance felt bile rise in her throat; she resisted the temptation to spit. Best not give rise to the thought that the devil was leaving her.

She'd lead them a merry dance, that was her power. Temperance shut out the bustle and the chatter around her. Mayhap the voices would come to her and she would do their bidding. She'd sit silent, that'd enrage them and she would best them that she would, as she had afore. If she closed her eyes, her one-roomed cottage was as clear as if she were stood in front of the fire. Yes, there it was. The embers' scarlet glow, the darkening shadows in the unlit corners, the battered cooking pot, the drying herbs and there, right there, on the roughened table-board, rusting pins and a straw poppet with flaxen hair.

Martha's Story
2020

"I want to concentrate on the witches themselves. I think I'd like to do something on Mary Trembles," said Martha, responding to Joan's enquiry as to what they were going to research that day. "We've neglected her a bit. From what I've found out so far, it seems she was easily led and sort of got mixed up in the witchcraft stuff almost by accident. What I want to know is why these women went out begging from people in the first place. I suppose it's a bit like our rough sleepers but wouldn't they be on benefits or something?"

"Well, sort of," replied Joan. "There was parish relief by this time, under the provisions of the Elizabethan Poor Law."

"Oh, of course. I should've known that," said Martha. "We did Elizabethan England for our exams. Poverty was one of the topics but I suppose I hadn't really thought about it in connection with my people in Bideford nearly a century later."

"They almost certainly wouldn't have been given money," Joan went on, "but they could go to the church and ask for food, or fuel, or clothes, in times of need."

"They don't seem to have done that though do they," said Martha, "or they wouldn't have needed to go out begging. Why didn't they just go to the church and ask for help?"

"Pride, maybe," said Joan. "It was a real stigma to ask the overseers for poor relief. Fear perhaps. You see, each parish had to look after their own poor and the Settlement Laws set out the rules, so you knew which parish was responsible for you in times of trouble. Often it was wherever you were born, unless you had done something to change your settlement, like rent an expensive house, or work for year and a day for someone who belonged to that parish, or served as a parish official, things like that."

With thoughts of her twenty first century life fading, Martha started to take notes. Joan was so interesting and she knew masses about life in the 1600s. This sort of background information was just what Martha needed if she was to really appreciate what her characters went through and what motivated them. She was getting closer to understanding how layers of intolerance, that had built up in Bideford over decades, might have led to three elderly women being put to death.

"Of course," Joan continued, "married women always took the settlement of their husband. We know Susanna was local but maybe her husband wasn't and the other two were probably born away from Bideford and didn't want to ask for help because they'd be sent back to wherever. Or it could be that they were just suspicious of authority."

"Can you just go over that again, please?" asked Martha eagerly. "Did you say they were called Settlement Rules?"

***

The music's incessant thud and the stench of stale smoke and spilt beer assaulted Martha's senses and made her wonder, yet again, why she had thought that coming to this party would be a good idea. She had never enjoyed parties before, why on earth had she expected that this one would be any different. The message had gone out on social media, "Oldies away guys, get yourselves over here, the more booze the better. It will be THE place to be tonight." Martha was not usually the recipient of such entreaties. It turned out that this was not the only party planned for the evening and this particular host was keen to outdo his rival by boosting the numbers at all costs, without regard for the social acceptability of his guests. Martha was skulking in the kitchen amongst the discarded cans of cider and bowls of stale crisps. Someone had already thrown up in the sink and failed to wash away all traces of their excess. The reckless host would need to do an awful lot of cleaning up before his parents got back, thought Martha.

She was still feeling bad about the Hunter incident, regretting her inaction, her impotence. Normally Hunter would be here, he'd been close friends with the boy giving the party. His absence was chilling. Rumours online said he'd been to A & E with three broken ribs but who knew if that was true? The loud music made conversation difficult but she had overheard the scathing comments, as those who were still in ignorance of the latest scandal were brought up-to date. The animosity directed towards Hunter was universal. Cliques formed in corners and the news eddied and flowed round the gathering, becoming more sensational with each retelling. No one addressed Martha directly. That suited her.

Periodically, a lurching party-goer or two would stumble into the kitchen and slosh vodka into a plastic cup, or crack open a bottle of beer, before heading back to the living room. Much to Martha's relief, they rarely gave her a second glance. She knew she was dressed all wrong, her make-up, which she rarely wore, was too unobtrusive and worst of all, she was drinking coke, enough to make her a total pariah. Aside from the fact that she didn't really like the taste of alcohol, the advantage of coke was that you drank it out of the bottle. Ever since that time last year when someone spiked her lemonade, Martha took care to choose bottled drinks and made sure that she didn't put the half-empty bottle down. The tempo of the music changed and Martha knew that people would be pairing off. There had already been couples writhing on cushions in the corner when she'd abandoned the party room.

The door flew open over-exuberantly and crashed backwards into the fridge.

"Ooops," said the taller of the two giggling girls, who stumbled towards the bottles and cans that were littering the sticky worktop.

"It's a glass door, Kayleigh," warned her friend, stating the obvious.

"Well, people shouldn't have glass doors if they don't want them broken. I'm sure it must be against some health and safety thingy, having a door that's glass. People could hurt themselves."

Only if you hurtle through the door when you are off your face, thought Martha, mentally crossing her fingers, hoping they'd be too preoccupied with selecting their drinks to notice her. Kayleigh, with her cutting remarks and sarcastic social media posts, was one of those girls that Martha strove to avoid. Martha's luck was out.

"Oooh look Skye, it's the freak," shrieked Kayleigh. "No wonder she's in here, no one would want to get with her looking like that. Look at that hair! Those glasses! Why doesn't she get contact lenses or something?"

Much as she tried to supress it, Martha felt a blush wash over her cheeks. I won't let them make me cry, she thought. I won't.

"Well she likes the more mature type, doesn't she," giggled Skye, digging Kayleigh in the ribs with her elbow. "Maybe that's the sort of look someone old, like in their thirties maybe, would appreciate."

"Oooh yes, of course, she's got a thing for Mr Mortimer. 'Oh Mr Mortimer, can you pleeese just go over my homework with me,'" Kayleigh minced, batting her eyelashes in a melodramatic fashion.

Ever the sycophantic acolyte, Skye collapsed into giggles and looked appreciatively at Kayleigh.

"I bet she isn't that mature though, is she Kayleigh, know what I mean?" Skye patted the pocket of her skinny jeans.

"No way," replied Kayleigh. "She looks like she's barely out of primary school, even my little sister wouldn't dress like that and she's eight."

"Not even out of nursery," said Skye, easing a small piece of folded paper from her pocket and shoving it into Kayleigh's hand. "Go on, she'll never do it."

Kayleigh walked up to Martha and waved the paper in her face. Martha felt tears pricking the backs of her eyes. She hated people invading her personal space at the best of times and Kayleigh was antagonistic, threatening and way too close.

"Gonna be a big girl and take one of these then?"

Kayleigh unfolded the paper to reveal a few white tablets.

"Go on, show us you're not such a freak after all," urged Skye from the side-lines.

The room began to sway. There was no escape. Please let someone come in, thought Martha; please let something happen to get me out of this.

"Why won't she talk do you think Kayleigh? Does she think she's too good for us or something?"

"She's stunned into silence because we look so hot," sniggered Kayleigh.

"Or maybe she is scared. No way would she have the guts to do anything really grown-up."

"What like you and what's his name were in the hall you mean?" responded Kayleigh. "Looked like you were really getting it on out there."

"Nah," replied Skye dismissively. "No idea what his name is but he's a right bore anyway."

Whilst the attention was momentarily diverted from her, Martha tried to compose herself but the respite was short-lived.

"Come on then," said Kayleigh, holding out the pills once more. "Get one of these down you, they'll liven you up a bit. They get rid of your in-he-bish-ons, don't they Skye?"

Skye nodded, knowing that her role was to hang on to Kayleigh's every word. That way she would keep her place as Kayleigh's best friend.

"She never will Kayls, she's not the sort. Too much of a nerd, aren't you freak?" the last comment was addressed to Martha.

Martha remained unmoving and silent. She made no attempt to take one of the pills. This was now a battle.

Kayleigh was frightened that she would lose face with Skye if she couldn't get Martha to take the tablet. "Tell you what freak," she said, "seeing as it's bound to be your first time, we won't even charge you."

"Hang on Kayls, I paid loads for them, they're supposed to be extra special, know what I mean."

"Shut up Skye," said Kayleigh sharply. "What's one tab between err friends?"

She advanced towards Martha again. "Come on freak, Mr Mortimer's going to love you after you've had one of these. He might even give you extra tuition." She winked, exaggeratedly.

Suddenly, there were shrieks from the other room, a flustered girl rushed into the kitchen.

"You still got stuff on you Skye? It's a raid, some scabby neighbour must have complained. Out the back door, quick. It's too late to lock yourself in the loo and flush them away."

The girls dashed out into the garden. Martha followed more slowly. Her tormentors were letting themselves out of the back gate. A rotating blue light pieced the night-dark sky. Martha took off her glasses and polished them vigorously on the bottom of her tee-shirt. Tears were stinging her eyes and she could not stop shaking. She only lived around the corner, it was one of the reasons she'd thought she might as well come to the party, make yet another attempt to do what was expected of her. She knew that these houses backed on to the woods, the girls might be lucky and avoid the police. Martha struggled with her feelings. Did she really hope that they would get away undetected? Should she try to sneak out through the woods too and risk being caught? Should she go back into the house? Now that the music had been turned off, the ringing in Martha's ears made her realise just how loud it had been. She looked at her phone, 11.30pm. Maybe she'd just slip off home.

Chapter 7
Mary's Story
1679-1680

"Come Mistress, you've seen a mite too many summers ter be particular. There be rent owin' an if you've no coin fer me, then there's other ways ee can pay."

The burly man filled the doorframe of the ramshackle cottage. His stained clothing reeked of tobacco and his few remaining blackened teeth were loose in his gums. Mary tried to close the door but he put his foot across the threshold.

"I've naught left ter sell sir. Naught but the shift I stand in. Even me cauldron be gone now and I be beggin' fer me bread."

The man looked her up and down. "I weren't so much thinkin' o' you selling a few old pots," he leered. "I'm sure it would not be the first time you've had your back 'gainst the wall."

"Oh! Please sir, not that," Mary begged. "Time was you was aboard ship wi' me faither. He'd not want to think you'd use me ill."

"'Tain't my concern if Trugeon Trembles saw fit to die wi' out making proper provision fer his daughter," replied the man, although mention of his former crewmate had given him cause to hesitate.

"Ma and me, we done the best we could since he be gone," babbled Mary, her words tumbling from her. "'Twas easier afore ma were took, she knew best how to earn a coin or two. We'd walk to the farms out Littleham way and help with plantin' and harvestin' and such but I's der get muddled and ofttimes lose me way. I know not 'ow ter find those who might need an extra hand."

The man sighed. He knew that Trugeon's daughter was a mite addled in her wits. He thought better of his intention to take advantage. After all, she was well past being a young woman and had not been easy on the eye, even in her youth.

"If ee don't have the coin then I'll have to put you out of doors dreckley," he said. "You can't be stayin' here. If I go back and say there be no rent money, then 'twill not go well for me, unless I says you be gone."

He kicked at the rotten doorframe. "Mark you, 'twill not be easy to find those who'll take the place on in this state. 'Tis all but a ruin."

"'Tis me 'ome," Mary sobbed. "We've allus lived 'ere. Ever since we came up from Cornwall backalong. You'd not put me out on the street sir? Have a care for a poor woman in sore need."

The man hardened his resolve. He had a job to do after all. This was no time for sentiment.

"Well, baint your home no longer," he said. "If you've no chattels ter gather up, you can be gone now and I'll board the door 'til it can be let out to those who can pay."

Mary looked despairingly round the hovel's single room. There was nothing for her to take with her. The rats had left little of the straw-filled sack upon which she slept. Not a pot nor a crock remained. The man stood over her, arms folded, determined now, his moment of weakness gone. Sighing, Mary gathered up her empty basket and her moth-eaten shawl and walked slowly out on to the street.

***

Rain slaked the fields. The roadways were an impassable mire and the farmers feared for the harvest. When food was short, little was handed to those who might beg a crust. The inhospitable hedgerows were poor shelter for the homeless and the destitute. Pickings were scarce. Mary's feet were cut from walking. Always walking. Traversing the same streets again and again, not daring to knock upon doors where the occupants had already turned her away. At first, she hovered within the environs of the town, reluctant to rove far from the byways that she knew. Soon though, her hunger drove her further and further from the familiar lanes, to the farmland beyond. She searched for berries at the field's edge but they were few in number. She lacked the skill to trap a rabbit or fetch a fish from the stream.

Mary pulled her shawl more tightly about her but the wet wool could not keep out the freshening breeze.

From across the sodden field, an elderly woman approached. Perhaps she could be prevailed upon to part with a morsel or two, thought Mary. The woman's aged limbs moved slowly, it was some minutes before she was within hailing distance. Mary sighed, she had hoped a farmer's wife might be passing, perhaps with produce for sale at market. The woman who stood before her looked as if she was as much in need of charity as Mary herself. Still, the poor looked after their own and it was often those who had the least who were readiest to give.

Mary held out her hands, "Have ee a crust or aught you can spare for a poor famished soul?" she whined.

The old woman tipped her basket to show it was empty, "I've naught to give mistress, 'tis lean times and no mistake. Best we hasten for shelter, the weather be comin' in ag'in."

The women faced each other, unspeaking. The rain stung their faces and dripped from the edges of their shawls but neither made an effort to seek the protection of the trees nearby. Mary swayed, she felt dizzy from lack of food and she was soaked to her shift.

The older woman broke the silence, "Have you no place to go then? No lodgin', nor kin in these parts?"

"I was turned from my door. I've nothin'," Mary replied. "There was only ever just me an' faither an' mother. I never had no brother, nor sister. First faither did sicken, then, not long after, mother be taken. The past few years I's been alone."

"And have you ne'er had a man ter sustain ee?"

"No mistress, not a husband, nor a lover, nor a babe to suckle," said Mary wistfully; there were times when she'd longed for a child.

"Kin be no good to ee anyroad," a globule of spittle hurled from the old woman's mouth, to emphasise her disgust. "You'd not think I had childer about these parts would ee. Every three years, sure as, another babe. None could say my Davy weren't regular in his attentions. Six times I were brought to bed, afore age stopped my womb. Me eldest," the woman sniffed derisorily, "lovely little maid she were but she went to the bad. No tellin' where she be to now. Kathryn too, she's no better than she ought to be, just this year she be brought to bed of a babe. She'd not name the father, nor have me to help at the birthin'. Happen she wouldn't have laid her boy in the ground if she'd let me tend to him. No, she'll have naught to do wi' me and mayhap 'tis best thus. Then there's my Bess, ofttimes I'll see her about the town with her little lads but she looks the other way. I be naught but a shame to her see, now she be wed above her station."

A daughter who would not cleave to her mother in times of need, or indeed times of plenty, was beyond Mary's comprehension. Her own mother had been everything to her.

Mary's thoughts turned to her own plight, "There be no one. There's naught to be done. I've not had bread these past days. All that's left to me is to seek aid from the parish."

The old woman started to walk back towards the town and Mary followed; she had nothing else to do.

It was some minutes before the old woman spoke again, "Well dinna ee be a-thinkin' the overseers be settin' ee up right praiper in them there new almshouses up Meddon Street. They baint fer the likes o' us. You baint from these parts be ee?"

"What mean ee, not from these parts?"

"Well ee baint Byddeforde bred be ee?"

"Nay," Mary answered. "I did come up from Kilkhampton, when I be nobbut a maid but mother and faither, they be laid to rest in the churchyard here, don't that count for zummat?"

"Where you been these past years? Have you not heard tell how the church won't have no truck wi' those who be not native born? They'll ship ee out soon as. Constable'll see ee past the parish boundary stone and you'll be on your way, back to where ee belongs, afore ee can blink twice. There be no relief fer those from afar now."

"They'd send me back to Kilkhampton? But my family's long gone from those parts and faither and mother, they left on bad terms. There's none back there who'd know me now, nor care."

The two women had reached a cottage on the outskirts of the town. The elder paused, her hand on the latch.

"That be no concern o' the overseers. They be charged wi' keepin' the poor rate down fer the rich folk. There be no relief fer the like o' us I tell ee. I been born in this very cottage but they'd not look twice at me on account o' me husband being from Wales see. Soon as I be wed 'twas his home parish they'd be a-sending me off to. I've no notion where it be, some powerful long name that I ne'er could get me tongue round but that's where they'd send me, no matter that I've scarce been more'n a few miles from Byddeforde in all me days." The woman paused, lost in the depths of memory. "Aside from the war o' course, then I didst go about but ne'er did I set foot on Welsh soil."

"What's to do?" whispered Mary. "I've no place I can seek aid."

There was a pause, "I'll see ee right," replied the other. "Ne'er let it be said that Susanna Edwards let a poor woman, whose been as ill-used as she, be in need. You bide what I say to ee and you'll not want for aught and I'll see ee dressed praiper. There be ways of coming by a coin or two that I can teach ee. You'll earn your keep mind. I baint as nimble as I once were. If ee can turn a hand to gathering herbs for me simples, 'twill be most welcome. 'Tis the stooping see, me back do pain me ofttimes, when there be dampness in the air."

Such was her relief that Mary would have agreed to anything that Susanna demanded.

"I'll mind what ee say mistress," she said, eagerly. "I'd be that grateful for a morsel or two and shelter fer the night. I'd do aught fer that. I be afeared o' crossing all that way back to Cornwall 'mongst strangers see. 'Tis Byddeforde I knows and here I'll bide if I can. I'll not be goin' to no overseers. I be that relieved ee did caution me 'gainst doin' so."

"Mind ee don't. 'Tis best we keep from meddlin' eyes see. We don't want they pryin' in ter what we be about."

***

Sunlight streamed in through the cottage window; no covering kept out the elements. Mary blinked and rubbed her eyes. Susanna had long since risen from the pile of bracken in the opposite corner. Now the old woman was muttering to herself as she stirred the steaming pot in front of her. In the few weeks that Mary had been at the cottage, she had become accustomed to Susanna's ways. She helped her to gather the herbs when the time was fitting, be it at dawn, at dusk, or by moonlight, as the receipt dictated. Many a time folk came to Susanna's door seeking a cure for an ailment, or help to secure a lover. Occasionally there might be a whispered request for something less benign. Mary was not party to these transactions and was hustled outside whilst the negotiations took place. Dried herbs were strung across the beams, poultices and concoctions were set in earthenware jars on the single shelf in the corner. Susanna never hesitated when seeking out the ingredients she needed. Mary could recognise the more common herbs but Susanna's remedies called for many a plant that Mary's mother had never shown her.

"Ah. I's a-wonderin' 'ow long ee'd be abed," said Susanna. "There's work ter be done and iffen ee do get along well, mayhap I'll let ee try some o' this. 'Tis mighty, err strengthening, I think you'd say."

Susanna cast another handful of herbs into the pot and a pungent aroma was released into the room as she stirred carefully, three times clockwise, three times widdershins. Mary had learned that Susanna set great store over the stirring.

"There," Susanna eased her back into as upright a position as her advancing years would allow. "We'll leave it to steep and by nightfall 'twill be ready for ee. 'Twill be a praiper treat for ee. You'll never have known the like."

Mary tried to look grateful but the overpowering stench of the murky-coloured, thick liquid was anything but appealing. Susanna noticed her hesitation.

"Ee baint goin' ter drink it you daft body. 'Tis more of err, more of an ointment see. You be gettin' on in years baint ee, we all do need summat ter keep us lively."

Mary looked dubious. Susanna was ever complaining of her own lack of vitality. Why did she not use the potion on herself if it was so powerful?

"How many summers have you seen?" asked Susanna. "Five and thirty? Forty? It can't be much more as you still get your monthly visitation."

"'Bout that mistress,' replied Mary. We never did take much account o' how old we be. Happen there be some writing someplace, which some clerk did pen at me baptism but I know not where that be. Cornwall I reckon, though 'twas said me ma were from Ireland and that's where faither did find her and back they came, wed already, did cause some stir so they say. I've not heard tell if I were born across the sea or no. Faither's family did take 'gainst mother, on account of he wouldn't put her aside when she could bear no more childer, for all that he needed strong sons to work the boat. It all got too much for ee and when I was nobbut a maid we came to Byddeforde. During the wars that was. I recall the soldiers hereabouts and faither used to say how as her got work labouring ter build the fort, afore he went back to sea."

"Happen you be nigh on forty then," calculated Susanna. "My maister, he fought in the wars," her eyes glazed at the memory. "Followed the flag I did, messen, with a babe in arms and one on the way. The years be catchin' you now Trembles' daughter. They be creepin' up on ee. You be too old ter catch a man's eye these several years gone but there be ways, see. Yes, happen there be ways."

Susanna never addressed Mary by her given name, always it was Trembles' daughter, as if Mary had no identity in her own right.

The harvest, such as it was, was gathered in. Even the rich folk had bellies that rumbled and there were few gleanings for the poor. Susanna dragged Mary beyond the town to gather herbs and berries and to beg for bread. Susanna would not return to the cottage before dusk and Mary trailed after her, longing for autumn, when the days would shorten. On this Thursday though, Susanna seemed unusually excitable. She chivvied the reluctant Mary along, with promises of the remedy that awaited her on her return.

"'Twill have thickened nicely mind, time we get back," Susanna said, reassuringly. "Happen you'll not have known aught like it."

Indeed, by the time they returned, the glutinous mass in the pot had reduced to a still-odorous slime. Not yet satisfied, Susanna set to straining the mixture through some tattered linen to remove the remnants of the liquid, whilst Mary squatted obediently on the earthen floor, soiled straw around her feet. There was no food to prepare, so Mary waited and Susanna muttered.

Finally content that the ointment was ready, Susanna turned to Mary. "There ee be Trembles' daughter, rub that on ee."

Gingerly, Mary put her finger in the pot and rubbed a little of mixture on to the back of her hand.

"'Twill take ee fer ever if ee do do it like that!" exclaimed Susanna. "You need plenty and all over ee. Happen you'll need to remove yer shift ter do it praiper."

Hesitantly, Mary loosened her bodice and petticoat. She clung to her shift, loath to stand naked before the other woman.

"Get on with ee woman," urged Susanna, "do ee not recall that ee did say you'd do as I bid?"

Slowly, Mary lifted her shabby shift over her head and shivered as the cool night air from the wind-eye stroked her body.

"All over mistress, all over," shrieked Susanna gleefully, gesturing towards the ointment. "On yer belly, on yer breast, on yer privities. No part must be neglected."

Seeing no option, Mary did as she was commanded, whilst Susanna stood appraising her, uttering the occasional word of encouragement, entreating her to apply more of the evil-smelling concoction. As Mary anointed herself with the last of the mixture, Susanna turned and proffered a horn cup.

"Drink this down Trembles' daughter, you'll sleep sound this night," Susanna's cracked laughter resounded from the walls.

Mary took the cup and sipped hesitantly, the taste was sweet, pleasant, with a faint hint of valerian. A warm feeling spread over her. Eagerly she drained the final drops. Suddenly aware of her nakedness, Mary turned to look for her shift. She was finding it difficult to focus and the tattered garment was nowhere to be seen.

Susanna followed her gaze. "You'll not be needing a shift ter keep ee warm this night Trembles' daughter. Lie upon the straw and see what comes to ee."

Mary stumbled across the room and lay flat on her back on the straw, her arms crossed to hide her breasts. Susanna reached over and put Mary's arms to her sides. Mary flinched, it was the first time that the woman had manhandled her and it was not a gentle touch; nonetheless, again she submitted. Mary's eyelids felt heavy. Despite her sense of foreboding, despite the feeling that she needed to be wary, the lure of slumber was overpowering.

Mary looked down upon herself stretched out on the straw. She was flying from a great height, yet there she was, lying as Susanna had left her. There was no sign of the other woman. Whispered words came from outside the cottage. Mary struggled to make sense of what she could hear but it was as if they were uttering a foreign tongue. A creature entered the room, hirsute and howling. It reminded Mary of the crudely-painted lions that she had seen on swinging ale-house signs. It approached the Mary below as the Mary above looked on in horror, in fear and then in wonderment. Shaking back its mane, the creature towered over the makeshift bed. Slowly it knelt before the Mary who lay prone, beyond the reach of the other-worldly Mary. The room twisted, shifted and swirled, the mist came down and dimmed the eyes of the Mary who floated, who flew, who dreamed she was invincible. An anguished, pain-ridden cry came from the Mary on the floor below her.

The ground was cold and iron-hard. Dew seeped into her skin. Drowsily, Mary realised that she was prostrate on the muddy patch outside the cottage. Fuddled, as if she had partaken of too much strong March beer, Mary lay inert, as she tried to marshal her thoughts. Stupor gave way to wakefulness. Every pore felt enlivened. Her acute awareness of her skin, her muscles, her very bones, was a sensation that was alien to her, yet deeply satisfying. Never had Mary felt more conscious of her own body, of her oneness with nature. The night-scents of the earth, of the cow-parsley and the musky mallow, could not deaden the stench of the ointment that was still smeared across her body, accompanied by another rank smell that she could not identify. Her body ached, her breasts were sore and there was blood upon her thighs.

Mary struggled to raise herself up onto her knees. In the glimmerings of the early dawn light she could see Susanna at the door of the cottage, talking to a heavily bearded man. He was powerfully built, with light hair flowing past his shoulders. He looked like one of the seamen who plied the ships from the Baltic, which ofttimes brought timber to the quay. They were of a type, these blond giants and they set the maids' hearts a-fluttering, to the disgruntlement of the local men. Mary shrunk into the shadows; she would have to wait until he took his leave. She hugged her knees in an attempt to warm herself, the sun had not yet broken through but the birds were already heralding dawn's imminent arrival. How had she come to be naked on the grass?

Why was she so cold? Mary saw the man hand Susanna a coin. Her only thought was gratitude that there would be food for them both that day.

***

The harvest moon rose iridescent and blood-red above the oaks. Soundlessly, the hunting owl swooped across the rough ground beyond the rectory. Eerie night-shadows stretched over Parsonage Close, giving cover to the man who watched, who waited. In his dark cloak, with his hat pulled low over his brow, he blended into the shadows, invisible, except to the keen sight of the hunting owl. The silent killer ignored the man; it was intent upon smaller prey. The man rubbed his leg and shifted to ease the ache that was a legacy from his time serving under Black Tom, many years past. He'd been scarce more than a boy when he'd left his ship and taken up arms for Parliament, lured by the thrill, by the chance to show he was a man full-grown. Ill-prepared though he'd been for the blood-shed, the tumult, the fear and the sheer tedium of the life of a soldier.

In four short years, that felt like a lifetime, he'd learned to kill. Kill or be killed; 'twas ever thus in times of conflict. This war, his war, had been different though. Somewhere 'mongst Hopton's men had been his brother, his father; adversaries, yet those he held most dear. Each volley that was fired, each ball that left his musket, might find its mark, might leave him fatherless, brotherless. Such thoughts had warped his mind. That and the blow that he'd taken at Stratton. His carelessly fastened helmet had been dislodged in the confusion that followed the initial push of pike. The enemy foot-soldiers, pikes abandoned, had reached the first rank of musketeers, where he stood waiting for the call to fire. A lad as young as he had flourished a sword. He'd thought he was done for but the enemy he faced seemed reluctant to deliver the fatal blow. His foe was too raw a recruit, too much of a coward, those were his last thoughts before the sword was brought down across the side of his head. He'd been left for dead on the battlefield. Out cold a full two days afore he'd come round, bootless and minus his breastplate. It seemed none had thought his breeches worth the effort.

Nigh on forty years ago that was and the black moods still came and they went, mostly they came and he knew that, when it was one of his bad times, he'd lash out without good cause. His sweetheart left him, married another, saying she'd not be doing with the shouting, the swearing and when he was at the depths of despair, the violence. He'd never married, never found a woman who would put up with his irascibility. When he needed release, he sought a woman from the back streets, who would take his coin and be grateful, even if there were times she'd be left with blackened eyes or bruises round her throat. Word spread fast; the whores were a close-knit group. It was harder now to find one who would lift her petticoat for him. He was left with the old, the desperate and the diseased.

When the war was done, he'd worked the Newfoundland run 'til his strength failed. Women in every port, taken, used, forgotten. No doubt he was carrying the French pox, a legacy of too many encounters with dirty whores. 'Twas ever the fate of a seaman. Some sailors he'd known had taken the mercury cure. He'd not have mercury injected up his man's yard for no-one, more painful than the bloody pox that'd be. So he'd ignored the rash and the lesions and they'd gone. There were folk that said the pox could lie hidden, coming back after years to claim a man. All the more reason to indulge in a bit of princum prankum whilst he still could. The man scratched his groin and shook his head like a beast trying to rid itself of pestering flies.

It wasn't the head wound that was paining him as he hid in the copse at the edge of Parsonage Close. His leg was numb beyond feeling. He'd taken a musket ball to the calf in the skirmish on the common land outside Torryngtowne. Fruitless bloody exercise that had been. The King's men had been wily that time, leaving lighted matches in the hedgerows and scarpering off. Whilst the bloody Royalists were supping in the Black Horse, he and his comrades had been expending precious shot firing at the flickering lights across the aching expanse, aiming for what they'd believed to be the match-light of the Royalist musketeers. It had been Royalist match-light alright but not a king's man tarried in range. The musket ball that shattered his leg had been loosed in frustration by an inexperienced musketeer in the rear file. The ignominy of being shot by one of his own men still rankled; frustration and anger heaped on top of the physical discomfort.

A slight noise and the man stiffened. A woman, clad only in her shift, crossed the field, her bare feet heedless of stone or thorn. She wore no coif; her straggly locks fell across her face. Even at this distance, the man could tell by her gait and her bent back that she was no youngster. Mayhap she'd being willing to take his coin, he thought. She looked like she'd not be finickity, might even be grateful for a dalliance. Not that he was up to much now, his age had sapped him of his virility but she looked to be a woman who might have a trick or two to satisfy him. There were some advantages to the older crones, whose experience could ofttimes compensate for their lost youth.

Time to see how she'd respond to his proposition. As he approached, he could see the woman was even more aged than he'd first thought. He got this far and he was hot for a woman however old she might be; he was not going to draw back now. Someone of her advanced years had likely been starved of a man's attention for many a month. He might not even need to offer her payment in return for a fondle of her sagging breast. That would save him a coin or two. He stepped from the shadows; the woman looked up with a start but her eyes failed to focus. It was as if she saw a distant spectre and not the man in front of her. Uneasily, the man cleared his throat.

"Be ee poor mistresses?" he asked, jangling the few coins he held in the pocket that sagged from his worn leather belt.

Her vacant gaze gave no indication that she was aware of his presence, yet she'd heard his question. Hands clasped in front of her she lowered her eyes and sketched a bob. "Aye, I be in sore need."

Despite her mask of deference, the man could not help but feel the ancient dame was mocking him. Nonetheless, he resolved to take advantage of her seeming acquiescence. He leered and bent over her, pulling a coin from his pocket as he did so.

"If you will meet this one request, thou shalt not want for meat, nor drink," he plucked at the woman's soiled shift, "nor clothes."

She did not recoil from his touch but still would not meet his gaze. Once again, her eyes, filmed with the milk of old-age, were staring at the trees beyond. A silence stretched between them. From the depths of the undergrowth, a fox's shrill scream. Someone was getting it tonight thought the man, the old dog-fox knew what he was about. The woman remained in front of him, motionless, unseeing. He rested a heavy hand on her unresisting shoulder. He ran it down to cup the pendulous breast and squeezed her roughly through the coarse linen. The man was breathing heavily now and fumbling with his breeches.

The woman made no attempt to pull away but spoke in a harsh whisper.

"In the name of God, what is it that I shall have?"

***

Mary had scarcely fallen asleep after a long day roaming the fields, when Susanna shook her roughly on the shoulder.

"'Tis time to waken, Trembles' daughter. 'Tis no time to be a loiter-sack, we've herbs to gather whilst the moon is full. Goody Lloyd be here to aid us. There's matters that do need her powers see."

Mary was shaken. 'Twas one thing to mix the odd potion or two with Susanna but she had not thought to be within doors with such as Goody Lloyd. Yes, best to be wary of the likes of Goody Lloyd, who had twice been condemned as a witch but had twice, inexplicably, escaped the noose. The devil had looked after his own, folk whispered. Fearfully, Mary rose from the straw and pulled on her petticoat although Susanna stood in just her shift. Temperance Lloyd, older even than Susanna, yet sprightly still, watched Mary appraisingly.

"Will she do Goody Edwards?" asked Temperance. "You know we do need someone who be close-mouthed 'bout these affairs."

"Trembles' daughter mayn't be as sharp as you or I but she knows what she's about," replied Susanna.

Mary went to fetch the cauldron from its place beside the fire. Susanna snatched it from her hand.

"I be carryin' that this night Trembles' daughter. You take the bucket, for we've need of water. It all has to be just so. We've a remedy to mix for such a customer as you'd not believe." Susanna's laughter echoed round the room. "It seems that for all their high-falutin' words an' speechifyin' there's those who still have a need o' the like o' us."

"Have a care that your words do not give aught away," cautioned Temperance, jerking her head in Mary's direction.

"Well folk've not a good word to say for the man. A man of status he may be but he be quarrelsome and his coarse words would put the foulest seaman ter shame. Ofttimes he be in strong liquor; 'tis no wonder ee be wandoughty, 'tis ever the complaint of those in drink. We was best off with that there....," hastily, Susanna stopped herself from uttering a name. "That there, errr, other fellow, for all he were in debt."

"Hush," urged Temperance. "Even those with addled wits can tell of whom you speak. The man paid good coin and if he be struck down with the frailties of his age, well, we do know how to restore his vigour do we not mistress?"

Ushering the other women out of the door in front of her, Temperance set off towards Parsonage Close.

Mary was glad that she had stopped to gather her shawl, for the night air was chill. Susanna set the cauldron on the uneven ground and Temperance cast herbs from her basket within it.

"The water, Trembles' daughter," urged Susanna, "'tis time to add the water."

Mary did as she was bid. It seemed that the feral cats were making the most of the full moon's light, hunting mice across the Close and mating in the hedgerow's shade. Their yowling and shrieking rent the air.

"Must we tarry longer?" asked Susanna as the cats screeched again. "Thrice the brindled cat hath mewed. Mayhap 'tis a portent that we might squeeze payment from our man three times over."

"He'll not be long now," said Temperance, glancing towards the rectory beyond. "We'll need to wait, for we need something from him to ensure the potency of the remedy."

"Ensure the potency," shrieked Susanna, "'tis his potency we need to ensure!"

"Hush woman, you'll waken folk in the town with all your clattering," cautioned Temperance. "He's nigh, look you."

Mary looked in the direction of Temperance's pointing finger. A man skirted the walls of the rectory and crossed the rough ground towards them. Shrouded by his dark cloak, his face was hidden by his hat's deep brim. Although he was close enough for Mary to smell the alcohol on his breath, she could not distinguish his features.

"Do ee have what we need sir?" asked Temperance.

"Nail parings," the man replied gruffly, "will that suffice?"

"Indeed, good sir," said Temperance, "aught from your body, nail parings, hairs and such, all will aid the efficacy of the remedy. Do cast them into the pot good sir."

The man obeyed and Temperance added more ingredients from her basket.

"Beat the water, Trembles daughter," said Susanna.

Mary stepped forward and grabbed the stick that Susanna had cast on the ground. She stirred slowly. After a few moments, Temperance put her hand on Mary's arm. "'Tis enough," she said.

Temperance ladled the mixture into an earthenware pot and held it out towards the man.

"You've coin?" she asked.

The moonlight gleamed on the money that the man pulled from under his cloak. Solemnly, he handed a coin to each woman. Mary looked wonderingly at her dirty hand, with the bright object glistening on her flattened palm.

"I'll be takin' that," said Susanna, snatching the coin. "You be owin' me fer bread and board and anyroad, you've not the sense to be havin' coin about you. There's folk as might take advantage."

The man's retreating figure merged into the darkness of the stone walls of the rectory. The moon disappeared behind an errant cloud and the night was still.

An Hour Earlier

The man walked up from his home in Honestone Lane. He'd spent the hot summer's day on the quay, quaffing ale and yarning with other old sailors but now he felt in need of a whore. When he'd been young and vital, he'd derided the halt and the aged, such as he'd now become. Scarce had he dreamed, when he had his first woman, that he might be capable of lustful thought, four decades on. Here he was, he'd seen nigh on sixty summers, yet still there were times when the urge was upon him. He'd try his luck up Parsonage Close again, he thought. Mayhap he'd encounter the old hag he'd met last time. Not that she'd given much satisfaction but needs must and he could ill-afford to be particular.

He reached the rectory, a fine building it was, recently renovated, as befitted one of Reverend Ogilvy's rank. He peered across the garden, newly laid-out in the French style. Not a candle-glimmer shone from the windows; happen the inhabitants were abed. That meant he could lurk unseen in the shelter of its stone walls. He crept round to the far side of the building and looked out across Parsonage Close, peering through the darkness. The distant church clock boomed the midnight hour. Three shapes hove into view. Three of them, that'd be a novelty, he thought, it might even spark his jaded interest. He hesitated, watchful. An iron crock squeaked as it swung from the hand of one of the women. She placed it carefully on the ground. As she turned, the man recognised her from his previous encounter. Again, she was clad only in her shift, lacking petticoat, coif or shawl, yet she seemed unaware of the coolness of the summer's night.

The three women circled around the pot. The man blinked and shook his beer-befuddled head. They cast things into the crock in turn. The shortest of the three grabbed a fallen stick and began to stir. Across the silent night air, the voice of one of the women came to him.

"Thrice the brindled cat hath mewed."

Her companions' harsh laughter set roosting birds a-flight.

"Beat the water, Trembles' daughter, till the tempest gather over us; til the thunder strike with wonder and the lightening flash before us! Beat the water, Trembles' daughter, ruin seize our foes and slaughter."

The cracked voice reached his ears more clearly this time. She'd uttered but a few words when they had met before; now her tones were mesmerising, he could not turn away. An icy sweat dripped between his shoulder blades. He was transfixed. What was this that he was witnessing? As the incantation dried on the woman's lips, a shrouded figure emerged from the rectory behind him, a dark hound at its heels. The animal sniffed the air and lowered its muzzle as if to follow a scent. The man shrank back in the shadows. Despite his limp, he'd had lost none of the stealth he'd acquired during his time as a soldier. 'Twould not do to be discovered now but there was little to be done 'gainst a hunting dog. He squeezed his eyes shut, as if that would render him invisible, undetectable.

His heartbeat was as loud as a striking clock. Surely he could not remain hidden. The silence was broken only by his own thudding heart and ragged breathing. He could no longer hear the slavering hound. He opened his eyes and peered through the gloom. He had naught to fear, the hound had gone, dissolved into the darkness, as if it had never been. The newcomer crossed the grass towards the three woman and wordlessly, handed each a coin that gleamed in the moonlight. Then, drawing his long cloak tightly round him, the shadowy spectre melted back from whence it had come. All desire dropped from the watching man in an instant, the heartening effects of the ale he'd consumed were gone. He was left alone, raw, vulnerable, aching. Slowly, he retraced his steps toward Honestone Lane, thankful that he had not been seen.

After a restless night, during which the incident replayed in his mind with ever-increasing horror, dawn broke. Within the safe embrace the of day's light, the man tried to rationalise what he had beheld and to calm his sense of unease. He felt compelled to share what he'd witnessed, trusting that relating the scene would serve to assuage his disquiet and help the memories to fade. At least it would make a tale to tell back down on the quay and he'd see to it that it'd lose naught in the telling. The distinction between what he had observed and what had merely been part of his terror-ridden dreams, was blurring. He was convinced that hound had been a spectre. Surely, there had been cloven hooves masked by that long grass and of a certain, that was a spiked tail he'd glimpsed under the long cloak as the figure swept back towards the rectory.

Martha's Story
2020

Martha pulled the duvet over her head. She'd spent a night of tortured dreams and fitful rest. What with the Hunter thing and then the awfulness of the party, her brain was a whirling, churning mess. She could hear Hebe calling her but the thought of facing the day was overwhelming. The glimpse of a new-found confidence, that starting her project had given her, was gone. It had been an illusion, tempting her with the idea that she could be different, stronger, happy. Now, frozen by reality's harsh hand, she knew that it was impossible. That brief period of contentment accentuated just how far away from okay she felt this morning. It made the return of all the old feelings harder to bear. How could she possibly have imagined that anything would ever get better? Stupid. Stupid. Of course, nothing had changed, everything was just depressingly the same as it had always been. She would always feel like this. She didn't deserve to be happy. She was so useless. Why should anything good happen to someone who was so pathetic?

It wasn't even a school day. In term time, every morning was an effort but the holidays weren't usually this bad. Her head told her that she should get up but her body betrayed her. It would be so much easier just to stay here, like forever, maybe. The incident at the party haunted her, twisted her mind and hacked into her every thought. Yesterday's enjoyment, researching with Joan, was forgotten. All she could focus on was the sick feeling in her stomach. However hard she tried, Martha could not help replaying the scene with Kayleigh and

Skye over and over in her mind. They were right. She was a loser. No one her age had fun working on a school project. Who enjoyed spending time in a library with a middle-aged woman? Maybe she wouldn't bother to finish her research. It was not like it was compulsory or anything. No. It was all too difficult. She wouldn't get up, why should she?

Hebe's calls grew more insistent but Martha curled herself tightly under the duvet and gnawed at her finger nails.

"Suit yourself," Hebe was saying. "I am off now. I've got to go and sort your Gran out. She's got herself in a state again. She shouldn't be living on her own any more really. I'm going to have to miss my poetry workshop. If you don't want a lift you'll have to get the bus, you've only got an hour. Don't forget you said you'd drop that stuff off at the food bank on your way to the library."

The front door banged. Loud. Final. Martha struggled not to cry but it was a losing battle. Why did they have to live in this stupid village? Why did she have to go to that awful school? Why did no one like her? Why had she thought that a history project might solve everything when life was just crap anyway? Any remnants of self-esteem were buried under the fog of past taunts. It was so much easier just to stay in bed and do nothing. She was still hollow, still alone but the alternative, encountering the real world, was beyond contemplation.

It felt as if she'd lain there for hours. She'd not had breakfast but Martha wasn't hungry. The monsters that she confronted robbed her of her appetite. There was a sudden weight on Martha's legs. With a scuffle and a companionable wuff, Calliope settled on the bed. The little dog was not her usual exuberant self, it was as if she sensed her young owner's anguish. Reluctantly, Martha reached out and ruffled the fur between the mongrel's ears. A rough tongue scraped across Martha's face. The dog whined and cocked her head on one side.

"Oh Calliope, I suppose you want to go in the garden for a wee," said Martha.

She'd spoken aloud. The broken sound of her own voice shocked her. Calliope was already bounding down the steep stairs and scratching at the back door. Martha hauled herself out of bed. The last thing she needed was a load of dog wee to clean up, or worse. She caught sight of herself in the landing mirror. Pale face, puffy, black rimmed eyes, unruly hair and it looked as if she had a spot coming. Urgh. How could anyone bear to look at her.

Martha hovered in the kitchen, whilst Calliope sniffed round the garden. It was sunny again but still early enough for the air to be fresh, inviting even. Martha poured herself a glass of water. Three bulging jute bags slumped against the larder. Hebe was thoughtful with her food bank donations; the bags contained not just tins of beans and peaches but toiletries and ethically sourced chocolate bars. Martha was reminded of the hardship of her seventeenth century characters. No food banks for them, just begging, or the insurmountable stigma of poor relief. Maybe there were people going to Bideford food bank today who would need that stuff. Maybe she should have gone into town and taken it; Joan was expecting her too. Pity it was too late to catch the bus. Or was it?

Martha glanced at the clock. Maybe she could get ready in time. She could grab a panini in town, so no need for breakfast, her laptop and notes were ready, if she had a quick shower she might just make it.

"Come on dog," she called, "I need to go out."

***

Martha went into the food bank and stood in the queue behind an elderly lady who was being offered a drink whilst the volunteers made up her food parcel.

"Oh, I don't know as I should stay for a cup of tea after all," the woman was saying. "You've other folk to see to. It's not as though I usually come here. It is just this once because I've had a bit of bad luck. I shall be back on my feet once I get my pension. I don't need charity you know."

"It's not charity at all," said the volunteer behind the counter. "All sorts of people need a bit of a helping hand now and again. You've got your voucher; you are entitled to what we can offer."

The woman still looked uncomfortable. She kept glancing behind her, as if Martha's presence was adding to her embarrassment. Martha wasn't sure what to do. The lady was probably a few years older than her gran. They were of a generation who fended for themselves and looked down on those 'on the social'. It must have been really difficult for this woman to come and ask for help. The volunteer began to pack various items into the woman's wheeled shopping bag.

"I've not queued for food since I was a small child during the war," the woman said. "Rationing didn't end until the 1950s you know. Dried egg we had and us children didn't know what sweets were unless we managed to get some from the Yanks. They were here training for D-day at Croyde and Woolcombe. They opened a club for the G.I.s over East-the-Water and we kids used to hang about outside hoping they'd give us gum. Of course, the older girls were after nylons and some of them got more than they bargained for."

Spurred on by her memories, the old woman had gone from reticent monosyllables to garrulous reminiscences in a matter of moments. Martha was fascinated; there was so much about Bideford she didn't know. She had no idea that Americans had been stationed here in the war. It was one thing researching life in the town three hundred and fifty years ago but this was within living memory. People should know about it. With a start, Martha realised that she hadn't really ever asked her Gran about her past and now Gran's memory had started to wander. Would it still be possible? Although Gran got confused with the present day, she did still seem to remember what happened years ago with piercing clarity. Someone should write this old lady's stories down as well, before it was too late. Maybe she'd ask Joan about it. The second volunteer arrived with a cup of tea and a biscuit and sat at a table with the woman, who continued to chat about her past. Martha heaved her bags onto the counter and reluctantly took her leave.

***

Martha's head was aching. Even though she'd not been drinking alcohol at the party last night, she still felt like she'd got a hangover. The fact that she'd scarcely slept didn't help. She was beginning to wish that she had stayed in bed after all.

Joan looked at her quizzically. "You seem a bit quiet today," she said. "Are you sure you're ok to do some work?"

Martha nodded, swallowing hard. She mustn't start crying again. Her eyelids were already swollen.

"Who are we looking for this time then?"

Martha struggled to put all thoughts of her disastrous, non-existent social life from her mind. She'd really much rather be here researching with Joan than hanging out with a load of idiots who condemned someone for being gay; or those who thought groping with some dim boy in a hallway, or getting off their head on drink and drugs, was the only way to enjoy yourself.

"Yes. I'm fine," said Martha. The parroted response, the conventional reply of both the fine and those who were far from fine. People asked if you were ok but did they actually want you to say, "No I'm feeling crap, I've got no friends, my life is a mess"? Of course they didn't. They just wanted you to join in the ritual, say you were fine and get on with the next part of the conversation. Why had she even come out today? She didn't have to take that stuff to the food bank, her mother could have done it tomorrow. Joan was looking at her with a mixture of concern and expectancy. Martha wondered if she should tell Joan just how close she'd been to staying at home. If it hadn't been for Calliope wanting to go out, she'd still be in bed. Better not mention it, she decided.

Joan might be cross, especially as today wasn't her regular day on the help-desk; she'd come in especially to work with Martha.

Dredging some emotional strength from who knew where, Martha said, "I can't help thinking how hard things were for Susanna and Mary and others like them. It must have been so difficult with no proper income and no help from anyone. I know there was poor relief but like you said, they probably didn't want to ask the church. There must have been so many who were struggling to feed themselves and their families."

"There were several bad harvests around then too," said Joan. "It was difficult for them to bring in food from other parts of the country when transport was so poor. There were private charities of course. In fact, I've some news for you about that. I've been doing some digging and I had a word with Peter Christie. He's the author of a number of books about Bideford and he writes in the *Journal* too. There was a mayor in Bideford called John Andrew and he left money for loaves of bread to be given to the poor on New Year's Day. There's records of who was given it and in 1681 there were names you'll know!"

"Oooh, who was it?" asked Martha with a flash of interest.

"Temperance Lloyd and Widow Edwards!" said Joan, triumphantly.

"Wow, so they were desperate enough to seek help in the end," said Martha.

"Maybe," replied Joan, "or maybe they were just chosen by whoever was in charge of giving out the dole."

"I can't imagine not knowing where the next meal is coming from," said Martha. "I know there were shortages with everyone panic buying because of corona virus but we never thought we were going to starve. I was up at the food bank today, giving in some stuff mum had collected and there was an lady there, she must have been in her eighties, in a way she reminded me a bit of Susanna Edwards. She really didn't want to be there and was so embarrassed when I turned up. Next thing though she was chatting away to one of the volunteers about all the Americans who were stationed here in the war. Someone really ought to write it all down."

"She needs to be part of an oral history project," said Joan. "There's a group called Way of the Wharves working on the history of East-the-Water. Maybe they could put a poster up in the food bank and hope she spots it, or ask the volunteers to speak to the lady when she next goes in."

"I've been thinking that I ought to ask my Gran stuff too," said Martha. "Trouble is she's got dementia. She's not too bad yet. She still lives on her own, though she probably shouldn't. Mum's up there now because something's happened. She does still talk about when she was a girl and when she was married to Grandad and the 'swinging sixties'. She spent time on a commune, it's where my mum was born. It is everyday things like remembering to eat her breakfast that confuse her."

"You should ask her questions while you still can," said Joan. "The Family History Society has got a recorder I could lend you."

"She does get a bit angry sometimes," said Martha, "but I think she'd be okay with it on a good day, especially if I stretched the truth a bit and said it was for school. When she stopped being a hippy, she used to be a teacher. I'd love to borrow the recorder, if you're sure it will be alright."

"No problem," replied Joan. "I could bring it in and show you how it works. Maybe you'll start to research your own ancestors, not just the families of the residents of seventeenth century Bideford."

Martha was aware that any family history she could do would be distinctly one-sided but the idea did appeal. She needed to get this project finished first though. Her early morning mood, the anguish she had felt, the memories of the party, were momentarily pushed aside.

"How can people not be interested in history?" she asked. "Everyone thinks it's irrelevant and boring but the present is just a reflection of the past. People don't change, studying history helps us to understand how people behave now. I love all that; it's why I decided to do psychology as well as history. At one point I thought I might not be able to do A Level history at all, as there were so few of us wanting to do it but thankfully, the school have said it can go ahead."

"Who's under the psychologist's microscope next?" asked Joan.

"I think I'd like to look at another accusation," said Martha. "I know we've done the Herberts and Dorcas and Ann Fellow but this is an older woman, Grace Thomas. I wonder if there was something about these people that made them blame witchcraft rather than just thinking, oh I'm ill, that's bad luck."

Chapter 8
Grace's Story
1680-1682

Grace Thomas pushed open the wooden shutters of the upstairs room in a fruitless attempt to cool her flaming skin. The flush washed over her, leaving her sweat-drenched and discomforted. It was a few years since her menses ceased, yet still these signs of the change of life plagued her. It was a source of resentment that her sister, Eliza, did not seem to suffer in the same way. Although they kept up an outward show of sisterly affection, their bond had loosened since Eliza's marriage. There was no denying that Eliza had done well for herself. It had seemed that the Thomas sisters were destined for a companionable spinsterhood, as they cared for their ailing father. Yet somehow, despite being beyond child-bearing, Eliza had caught the eye of prosperous shop-keeper and merchant, Tom

Eastchurch. After the quiet wedding ceremony two years ago, Eliza had established herself in a comfortable position as one of Byddeforde's respectable non-conformist matrons. Although she had been invited to live with the newly-married couple, Grace had felt side-lined, shunned, of no account. Her health began to suffer and gradually she had assumed the role of the ailing, dependent relative, an inconvenience who was tolerated for form's sake. She was on display to all-comers as tangible evidence of the Eastchurchs' Christian charity, that was her destiny.

A commotion in the street below heralded the delivery of another consignment from Tom's ship the *Delight*. Much of the cargo would be sold on but the choicest produce would be proudly offered to the Eastchurchs' most select patrons. Grace withdrew from the open window; it offered her no relief in the summer's heat. Following her sister's lead, Grace would not contemplate demeaning herself by serving even the most prestigious of customers. Yet, secretly, she took pleasure from time spent in the spacious shop. She rejoiced in the scents of the spices and the cloying, sickly smell of the soft brown sugar. She was fascinated by the exotic fruits, the coffee, the chocolate, newly-popular items that only the wealthiest could afford. She sighed as she sank back on the stiffly-padded, brocade-covered chair; it too an indicator of the affluence of her brother-in-law. The humidity of the afternoon was enervating. Grace wore her invalidism as a badge of office. She had long since ceased her regular jaunts in the town; the effort was beyond her and gadding about did not sit well with her claims of ill-health. She found her self-imposed confinement tedious, yet she revelled in Eliza's concerned glances and the solicitude of the neighbours.

A tread on the stair and a discrete knock on the door signalled the arrival of Annie Wakely, who was the source of much gossip. Grace missed the tittle-tattle of town life and looked to Annie to keep her informed of the latest goings-on.

"Good day to thee Grace and how be ee this day?"

"Much the same I fear, Annie. I find this weather most fatiguing." Grace fanned her face with her hand. "I hoped that you might call with news that could enliven me. How is poor Master Bartlett? I have prayed that the Lord would strengthen him in his distress."

"Indeed. It goes hard with a parent when their child dies afore them. Master Bartlett conducted his son's burial with dignity, as you would expect of such a man. We are so fortunate to have him to guide our worship."

Grace leaned forward eagerly, "And what news of the odious Reverend Ogilvy? 'Tis little wonder that folk be turning to Master Bartlett when such a man holds sway at the rectory. I am so thankful that we hold fast to Master Bartlett and have long since eschewed the parish church."

"Oh Grace, there's been such a to-do. As you know, I've little time for our town clerk Master Hill."

Grace nodded enthusiastically; John Hill's aggressive persecution of Bartlett's flock meant that the clerk had few friends in non-conformist circles. Neither the Wakelys nor the Eastchurch household had any time for men, such as Hill, who made life difficult for those with Independent leanings.

"But," Annie continued, "I have it on good authority that there was a confrontation after church on Sunday and Master Hill received the brunt of the rector's anger. Reverend Ogilvy's speech was most unchristian and he held out his staff and threatened Master Hill. Then he spoke ill of the Bishop's surrogate!"

Grace gasped, this was scandal indeed, yet perhaps unsurprising, given the nature of the men involved.

"What prompted this? What did he say?" she asked.

Annie lowered her voice, conspiratorially, "Well, the bishop's man was pressing Reverend Ogilvy to take his recommendation as a curate and Ogilvy was having none of it. Would you believe that he said he could find it in his heart to kill Crymes, that's the bishop's surrogate you know."

"Kill him! 'Tis strong talk from any man but a man of God….."

"And Master Hill remonstrated with him, told him that to speak in such a way was a grievous offence and that the rector should be of a mind to take the curate, as Crymes advised."

"It seems that Reverend Ogilvy is forever in dispute with one fellow or another," said Grace.

Annie was warming to her theme; it was gratifying to have the older woman hanging on her every utterance. "Indeed, he has vilified many of those of standing in this town, calling the magistrates knaves and such like. Of course, Reverend Ogilvy is an immoderate lover of strong drink; his profanities are highly unbecoming in a clergyman. But you've not heard the worst of it. He has allowed Master Hann, you know, he whom Ogilvy reckons as his curate, to administer communion and

Hann's son too, yet both have been ejected from the church. The congregation have denounced the rector for it, yet he will brook criticism from no man."

Grace was shocked by these revelations, so much so that she had to remind herself to strike a suitably frail pose.

"Oh, Annie," she whispered, "your news is enough to bring on one of my turns, you know that Doctor Beare has cautioned against over-excitement."

Much to Grace's gratification, Annie immediately looked contrite.

"Oh Grace, I did not wish to discommode you," said Annie. "Should I take my leave?"

Grace smiled weakly and put a restraining hand on her friend's arm.

"No, no. It alleviates the tedium to hear of such matters."

Annie settled herself back in the chair and resumed her diatribe.

"It isn't even as though Ogilvy is a suitable rector when he's sober. I hear that one of his flock confronted him after divine service and complained about the nature of the sermon."

"And how did the Reverend gentleman respond?" asked Grace, thankful that Annie had gossips who were stout Anglicans and who could report first-hand on the machinations of the maverick rector.

"He said that he wished all his parishioners were of a similar mind, then he would have little to do!"

Grace tutted and shook her head but Annie had moved on to other matters. "Did I tell you that Richard

Sleeper had been obliged to take down his sign at the Blacksmith's Arms?" she said.

"No! Why is that? Does it mean that he will no longer be a victualler?"

"Happen he will still keep his locksmithing business but no doubt the mayor will see to it that he can no longer purvey ale. Sleeper has brought this upon himself with his disrespectful words and unseemly language."

"It seems that many of Byddeforde's men are short of temper these days," said Grace.

"In truth 'tis a feature of our times. Folk have scant patience one with another. The mayor had little choice but to act when Sleeper addressed the chief magistrate in a most contemptuous manner, in front of the borough council too. Sleeper spent time in the lock-up for his pains. Bagilhole, odious man, he's another alehouse-keeper who has been condemned for his rough speech."

Grace had little interest in the town's inn-keepers; for her, strong drink was an anathema.

"What news of others of Master Bartlett's persuasion? Do you hear much of Mistress Bremmicombe or Mistress Fellow?"

"Oh my dear, such sad news, Ann Fellow was taken from us just this week. She has been ailing these many months past as you know. She was resigned to her fate and died in the sure knowledge of her salvation but it is distressing to see one so young fall into a decline as she did. Mistress Fellow is quite beside herself and young Dorcas Coleman, you know, Dorcas Lidstone that was, she that married but a few weeks since, it has cast a shadow upon her happiness. She and Ann had a firm attachment."

One Year Later

Grace took a deep breath. It was refreshing to feel the autumn sun on her face after being within doors for so many weeks. The crisp edges of the browning leaves and the mist on the river foreshadowed the shortening of the days but for now, there was pleasure in being outside; it revived her spirits. Grace felt in better health than she had done for many a month. She was thankful that she had decided to venture out today. She climbed the High Street. As Grace neared the rectory, she was plagued with a stitch in her side and she paused, hoping that it would ease. She rested her basket on the ground and looked about her. A man passed by, clad in black, in mourning mayhap, mused Grace. So short of stature was he, that at first Grace had thought him to be but a child, yet a straggly beard gave the lie to this. There were those whose growth was stunted by some quirk of nature of course. The man was a stranger to Grace, a traveller, it seemed. He walked on towards Higher Gunstone, without acknowledging her presence. Approaching from the opposite direction was an elderly lady. The man stopped and the couple exchanged a few words before continuing on their way. It seemed that the man was known to some in the town after all. Of course, many new folk had settled in Byddeforde in recent times and she had not been about these past months to acquaint herself with newcomers. Perhaps the diminutive man had but lately moved to Byddeforde. Yet surely, if he was known within the town, Annie would have commented on one whose appearance was so remarkable.

The old lady drew nearer. Grace's eyesight was no longer sharp but she recognised Goody Lloyd. All knew of the ancient dame, with her lilting speech, her cantankerous ways and her unprepossessing appearance. Her grey hair straggled from under a grubby coif and her petticoat was soiled. Grace wondered if she could hold her tuzzy-muzzy to her nose without appearing rude. The woman stank of rotting cabbage and a sickly odour that Grace could not identify. It would be a relief to inhale the smell of sweet herbs. Despite Goody Lloyd's unsavoury aspect, some spake highly of her remedies. Yet Grace had not thought to consult her in her sickness, preferring to rely on the expertise of Doctor Beare.

Goody Lloyd was muttering to herself and clutching a loaf of coarse ravelled bread under her arm. On spying Grace, she fell to her knees, discarding the loaf on the hardened earth. Goody Lloyd's hands, with their knotted knuckles and grime-rimmed nails were clasped on her lap, in a parody of prayer.

"Mistress Thomas, I be glad to see ee so strong ag'in," whined Goody Lloyd.

Grace, embarrassed by the show of emotion from a woman that she would scarcely call an acquaintance, let alone a friend, was unsure how to respond.

"Why dost thou weep for me?" she asked.

"I weep with joy to see ee so well ag'in," Goody Lloyd responded.

Grace had no notion that Goody Lloyd was aware that she had been indisposed but it was charitable of her to express her gratitude, even if the reaction did seem somewhat overstated. A breeze sprung up and the sun slid behind a cloud. Grace shivered. Muttering her thanks, Grace set off for home, casting anxious glances over her shoulder at the retreating figure of Goody Lloyd. The encounter with Goody Lloyd was disquieting, unsettling and somehow sinister, despite the old woman's expressions of gratification at Grace's improved health. Her new-found vitality ebbed away and Grace realised how much the excursion had fatigued her. Perhaps she should not have undertaken such a long walk for her first outing for many weeks.

Eight Months Later

"Oh Annie, I am that glad you have come, the pains be worse than ever now."

"Hush Grace, said Annie, chafing at Grace's arms in an attempt to restore colour to her friend's pallid flesh. I have told Eliza that I will stay here as long as is needed. She has to be about her own concerns and you should have someone in attendance to nurse you through this malady. Eliza is not always on hand to enquire if you have need of anything."

"I be that grateful Annie but I do not wish to inconvenience you. What about young Willie, who will tend to him if you are with me?"

"He's rising six years old now," said Annie, "my Alice can keep an eye on the lad; they can fend for thessen a bit. 'Tis no inconvenience, so's you're not to fret."

Gripped in another wave of agony, Grace's face contorted. She could scarcely focus on Annie's words.

"Oh my dear, it distresses me to see you in such pain. Eliza has sent for the good doctor. Hark! I believe I hear him downstairs now. I'll go home for a space whilst he tends to you. We must hope that he will have a draught that will ease your hurts."

Eliza ushered the doctor into the room; Annie exchanged a brief greeting before taking her leave. Grace flinched as Doctor Beare opened the shutters and light flooded the room. She groaned and turned her head to the wall.

"'Tis my head, doctor, I've such pains in my head, there be no tellin'. 'Tis as if pins and awls are being thrust within my body from the crown of my head to the soles of my feet, as if I be laid upon the rack. Night-times be the worst, then 'tis beyond all bearing. It has been bad these months past, ever since I walked out to take the air in autumn time, I can endure it no longer."

The doctor looked grim as he examined Grace. For form's sake, her sister hovered in the doorway. It would not be seemly for the doctor to be alone with a female patient. Doctor Beare's appraisal was brief. He uttered meaningless platitudes and left Grace to her thoughts. The pain was intense. She was sure that Eliza thought she was exaggerating, as, in truth, she had in the past but this, this was something new. How was she to survive it? Was she to die here in this sunlit room? The outside world taunted her. Grace regretted that she had remained in her chamber on occasions when she might have enjoyed going to market or attending Sunday service. Now she could scarcely stand, let alone walk the town. Was this agony to be her punishment for feigning illness? Doctor Beare had pulled the door to behind him but it was not firmly closed. It was difficult to hear Eliza's softer speech but Grace could make out the doctor's booming tones.

"I regret that your sister is so afflicted Mistress Eastchurch. I admit, the cause is one that is difficult for me to ascertain. It is of grave concern to me and she is not the only good dame whom I have seen in such straights. I encountered something similar last year when Master Bremmicombe summoned me to Mistress Coleman's side. She was taken with pricking in her arms, her stomach and her heart, not unlike your sister's complaint. There was little I could do to alleviate her suffering. She too found that she was unable to leave her chair, despite assistance from her husband and from Master Bremmicombe, sturdy men both. She could scarce move nor see. Mistress Barnes too has been struck down, 'tis most perplexing."

Grace did not catch Eliza's response but the doctor's next words struck a chill to her heart.

"The laws of science cannot explain what ails your sister. It is with regret that I must conclude that this is the devil's work. Has anyone uttered evil words against her, or might she be subject to some conjuration?"

***

Annie's eyes turned to the far corner of the room, where the candlelight failed to alleviate the gloom. A bragget cat paced silently from the flickering shadows. Annie wondered when Eliza had acquired another animal. This was not the familiar tabby who grew fat keeping the mice from the shop's precious goods. Grace was whimpering piteously but was no longer thrashing her limbs, as she had been earlier. Annie made to straighten the bedclothes. There, on the bottom of the bed was a little maid's poppet. Surely Grace did not still cherish such a trinket from her childhood? Folk became fanciful when they were sick 'tis true but 'twas rare that they clung to a remnant of their past in this way. Annie picked up the crudely carved wood. The face was indistinct but it was wrapped in a scrap of cloth, cloth that was similar to that of Grace's new petticoat. Strange enough that such a toy should be kept by a woman of Grace's mature years, thought Annie; stranger still that she should dress it in new cloth. Annie laid the poppet to one side.

Then Annie noticed a piece of leather on the floor. Where had that come from? The maid-servant had been summoned to clean the room just that evening. There had been no sign of any leather when she left. A maggoty-pie, with iridescent wing, had alighted on the sill. Before Annie could rise from the chair to shoo it away and fasten the shutters, it had fluttered to the floor with a flurry of feathers. When birds are trapped they are fearful but this one cocked its head and fastened a staring eye upon the room's occupants. After a full minute, it took flight and flapped from wall to wall before claiming freedom in the skies beyond. Annie had closed the shutters firmly. She was not a believer of cold air in a sickroom in any case but Grace had insisted that she craved sight of the sky. The bird had left evidence of its visit, so the girl had come up with the besom and cleaned the boards. Grace had ordered that the whole room be swept, including every corner and crevice, under the bed and behind the dresser. It was a strange notion but it was as well to humour the sick and Grace had been insistent, despite complaining that the dust aggravated her throat. Annie was sure the leather had not been there then. No one had entered the room since. Odd, most odd but 'twas of no account. Annie smoothed the leather under her fingers. It was of poor quality and had been pricked several times with an awl, it was good for naught. Annie discarded it on the dresser with the poppet. She would dispose of it later.

***

Grace woke suddenly, a cold sweat prickling between her shoulder-blades. The candle still guttered in the brass candlestick; it could not be long since she had settled for the night. All that pother with the bird had unsettled her. Grace shook her head; the pain addled her mind. The bird had been there, of a certain, that was not a fancy. Grace dug her nails into her palms and tried to order her thoughts. The bird, yes, she remembered the bird and how adamant she had been that all traces of its presence be swept away. There was something about that bird, something disconcerting, terrifying even. She glanced at Annie who snored gently in the chair by the window. Surely, surely it was not Annie who had tended her none too gently. It had not been Annie who had squeezed her belly and her breast, that had been Goody Lloyd. Why had she been sent for? Grace couldn't comprehend it. Annie and Eliza would never countenance such a thing. Like Grace herself, they deplored the ways of the cunning women of the town, who preyed upon the fears and the desperation of the needy. So how had Goody Lloyd gained admittance? Had Annie been here when the old woman was at

Grace's bedside tormenting her? If help were needed, why had Doctor Beare not been summoned? What exactly had the Goody Lloyd done? Grace remembered the pain as those blackened fingers gripped and prodded her flesh. She knew that she had cried out when Goody Lloyd's ministrations had become too rough. What had happened then? Why could she not remember?

As Grace struggled to clear her mind, the pain shackled her with its intensity. She was bound in chains. Her shoulders, her arms, her hands, her thighs; it was as if her flesh was being torn from her. She beat her fist helplessly upon the bolster.

"I shall die. I shall die," she cried.

Annie, awoken by Grace's shouts, rushed to the bedside. She tried to restrain the stricken woman who was writhing on the mattress, the coverlet wound between her legs. Horrified, Annie saw that Grace's belly was distended, as if she were with child and the birth was but days away. What new trouble was this?

Martha's Story
2020

Guiltily, Martha pocketed her phone, as Joan came back into the library. Everything had been fine whilst they'd been working together, finding out about Grace Thomas. Then Joan had popped out to get a sandwich for lunch, leaving Martha alone with her thoughts. She had been looking at her social media accounts to see if there was any news about Hunter. Her feeds were still full of the party. Posturing girls, drinks in hand. Boys with their arms draped round one or another of her scantily-clad classmates. Given that the night had ended in a police raid, Martha wondered how wise it was to publicly advertise that you'd been there but clearly this was the furthest thing from the posters' minds. They'd had internet awareness days at school. Surely they knew that potential employers and those considering your applications to uni' sometimes looked at your online profile. Apparently, few people in her year cared about that; providing they were seen to be associating with the socially acceptable, nothing else mattered. It was no co-incidence that Martha appeared in none of the photos, who would want to be seen with her? For once, it was a relief that she'd not been part of the frenzy to upload the image of the night. One that would gain the most likes and meet with the approval of those that counted. Alongside the poorly-lit pictures though, were the messages, messages that horrified Martha, leaving her with a churning stomach and racing heart. She struggled to concentrate on what Joan was saying.

"Been checking your phone?" she said, smiling at Martha. "That reminds me, before we start, I must just check the ancestry hour tweets. There's been a lot of discussion about the latest DNA updates."

"Ancestry hour?" queried Martha. "What, on Twitter? I never thought about family history being something that people tweeted about."

"Oh yes," said Joan, there's hundreds of genealogy Twitter accounts you can follow. Archives, family history societies, leading genealogists across the world and people who just have fun tracing their family history. Every Tuesday at 7pm is Ancestry Hour when people ask questions and tweet the latest news but sometimes there are discussions in between. If you've got Twitter, I can suggest some good people to follow. Or you could search for the ancestry hour hashtag and see what people have been tweeting."

Martha thought about the people she followed on Twitter. A list that was dictated by those whom her classmates deemed acceptable. Each other of course, though few followed Martha back. Pop singers, TV stars, the latest cohort of reality show contestants, celebrities who were famous for nothing much but being famous. Martha had even felt embarrassed about following Greta Thunberg and a few other environmental campaigners. They were not the sort of people you were meant to follow. She had no idea that her newly discovered world of research could overlap with things like Twitter. This was a shock. Looking through social media might be something she could anticipate with interest and excitement, rather than dread.

Martha's mind was drawn back to what she had been reading when Joan arrived. The photos of the early hours of the previous day's party were followed by general speculation about who had told the police. The neighbours were soon exonerated, apparently they were on holiday. If not the neighbours, then who? Swiftly, the consensus was reached. It must be one of them. Who had they not invited? Who might have a reason to shop them? As Martha scrolled through the posts in chronological order, names were mentioned, names that flicked in and out of the early posts and were dismissed. Martha was glad that hers was not one of them. Perhaps it was a good job she had turned up at the party after all.

Reaching the more recent messages, one name stood out. It was repeated again and again, tossed into the social media maelstrom never to be retracted. Hunter. Martha had felt bad enough when she'd been the topic of everyone's posts. These attacks on Hunter were far far worse. So much for the social media providers acting responsibly and cutting down on online abuse. The things people were posting, were suggesting, were truly appalling. How must Hunter be feeling? First there was the coming-out thing, that had been thrown idly from account to account, gaining in momentum, ever since the fight. To have your sexuality paraded for all to see must be hell, especially when you hadn't really been ready for the world to know. He probably wasn't intending to tell his parents just yet and now he had to face his family. Hebe would be fine about something like that but Martha knew that it wasn't the same for all her friends' parents and what about grandparents? Gran, in the old days before dementia claimed her, wouldn't have worried if her descendants announced they were gay but you only had to listen to people tutting on the bus to know that not everyone would be so accepting. Now, on top of all that and worse maybe, somehow people were convinced that it was Hunter, excluded from the party, who was the informer.

Martha was shocked by the intensity of the reaction. Amongst the posters, alongside the usual suspects, Jeremy, Tyrone, Kayleigh, Skye and their hangers-on, were people she knew. Not friends exactly, well, she didn't have any of those but people she thought were relatively sane. How had they suddenly got swept up in all this hate and venom? She could just about understand that the people at the party were angry. Even though the ones with the drugs were in the wrong, she could see why they might be annoyed at being raided. This was way beyond being annoyed. Waiting for Joan to come back, Martha had scrolled through threat after threat. Warnings of ostracisation were nothing new, Martha had experienced a good few of those herself. This, this was so much more, here were promises to do physical harm. Someone had set up a 'Lynch Hunter' WhatsApp group. They'd even invited her to be part of it. That smacked of desperation, no one ever invited her to join WhatsApp groups. Martha had swiftly removed herself from the group but the words of the posts were branded on her mind. She stared at her phone as if it was contaminated. How had she got dragged into all this?

Joan had moved on from Twitter and was chatting about who she followed on Facebook and Martha tried to tear her thoughts away from what she had seen.

"Anyway," Joan was saying, "that's enough about Facebook, you can look at that later. If you've finished researching Grace Thomas, have you got someone else in mind to work on this afternoon?"

Hastily, Martha thumbed through her notebook. With all that had been going on, she wasn't really prepared for this session.

"I've been trying to work out exactly what happened in the weeks before the final trial," she said. "It is very difficult to sort out the contradictory accounts and get the story straight. Everyone seemed keen to get in on the act and fling accusations about."

***

As soon she left the library, Martha reached for her phone. She quickly discovered that, during the afternoon, the messages that were directed against Hunter had spiralled even further out of control. Martha was relieved that she was not part of the frenetic scramble to post the most outrageous, the most hateful comment. She could remain detached. Or could she? Here she was, reading the posts every bit as avidly as those who were joining in. Her emotions were engaged. Okay, so she was horrified rather than thrilled by what she saw but she could not deny that she was involved. Not as a perpetrator maybe but certainly as an onlooker. She'd ignored Poppy when Jeremy's lot were laying into her. She hadn't made any effort to stick up for Lucie or to get to know the anonymous and isolated Muslim girl in maths. She'd backed away from the fight in Victoria Park. How long could she keep this up? If you acknowledged that something was wrong, evil even and remained a bystander, if you didn't speak out, you were part of the problem. Right now, Martha acknowledged, she was indeed part of the problem.

Chapter 9
John's Story
Summer 1682

After more than twenty years as Byddeforde's town clerk, John Hill was weary. Weary of the unending battle against the growing number of non-conformists in the town. Weary of the continual friction between himself and Reverend Ogilvy and now this altercation after morning prayer on Sunday. Ogilvy had preached yet another unsatisfactory sermon; that alone was sufficient to rouse the ire of the congregation. Still worse, it was plain that the rector was once again in drink. As his parishioners filed out after the service, some of the men took exception to the way Ogilvy bade farewell to their womenfolk. He'd grasped Mistress Jones' hand overlong, as she recoiled from his wine-laden breath. Hill was one of the last to leave the church, so he did not witness precisely what had occurred to prompt

Bennet Dunscombe to take hold of Ogilvy's arm so roughly. As Hill well knew, the rector was quick to anger and could seldom be made to see reason. With voices raised, the argument became personal.

"I'll wager a guinea that cask of Madeira I had from you was watered," Ogilvy blustered. "I'd look to the master of your ship, if I were you."

"I'll not have a word said 'gainst Master Dennis," Dunscombe replied. "He's captained the *Speedwell* for many a year. You might as well accuse Abbott here of adulterating his cargo."

Christopher Prust stepped forward and attempted to pull Dunscombe away.

"You'll not win an argument 'gainst the rector, Bennet, best leave it be."

Dunscombe shook himself from Prust's grasp.

"He may be a man of the cloth but there's no call for him to speak thus. I'll have him afore the justices for slander, as God be my witness. He'll not walk away from this."

Hill had no intention of becoming embroiled in yet another confrontation with Reverend Ogilvy, so he side-stepped the angry men and made his way home.

***

There was an unease about the town. An uncertainty. Folk looked to their rector to set them right, to temper their excesses and ensure that they led godly lives; yet Ogilvy failed to lead by example. Far from being a calming influence, his machinations aroused yet more discord and left folk without restraining moral direction.

The repercussions of Sunday's quarrel whirled on. Many spoke out against the rector; some deserted the established church and took themselves off to sit at William Bartlett's feet. Ogilvy had a great deal to answer for, thought Hill. The wretched man would have folk flocking to Bartlett and those of Independent thought had been a thorn in Hill's side these many years past. He had battled to contain the dissenters, ensuring that their services were disrupted. He'd had their preachers fined. A few at least had been convinced of their error; though it might be that the fear of punishment was more persuasive than theological debate. Yet still the faction flourished.

It was but days after the incident in the churchyard that it began. The whispers. The mutterings. The sideways looks. The averted eyes. One by one, folk came forward to make wild claims about their neighbours. At such times, it was always the defenceless whose names were uttered. Those who lacked the eloquence to contradict the charges that were laid at their door; the weak, who had no one to speak up for them. Hill was as keen as the next man to rid Byddeforde of sorcery but it seemed that half the town had fallen victim to one curse or another. It was Hill's task to record each and every incredible accusation, claims that gathered momentum and became ever more extreme with each passing hour. He knew he must act. Someone must stand scapegoat as a sop to the rising discontent. Hill shuffled the sheets of parchment that lay upon his desk. He studied the names. One stood out amongst the others. He summoned the constables and set them to their task.

The cornerstones of the old chantry house were crumbling. It stood, forlorn, on the far side of the bridge, away from the town. It was no longer the scene of fervent prayers for those who wished to shorten their time in purgatory. That belonged to the old ways, the ways long gone. Now the dilapidated building did service as the town lock-up and any prayers that were uttered within its walls were for a different kind of salvation. Amidst the Saturday morning Byddeforde bustle, the arrest of one old woman drew little attention at first. Temperance Lloyd, her arms pinioned by a burly constable on either side, stumbled as she was hustled along the quay. As they passed the new grammar school, first one, then another pointed a finger, nudged their neighbour and started after the trio. By the time they were halfway across the bridge a small crowd had gathered.

"Well, would you believe it. Not before time. Allus said she had it coming to her."

"She's been taken afore o' course. You recall that business with old Maister Herbert back along."

"Then there was Ann Fellow. Goody Lloyd should never have escaped the noose that time. The custom house has a melancholy air now Ann has been taken."

"'Tis true, Mistress Fellow has been downhearted these past two years."

"Well, 'tis hard to lose a child when they have grown into your heart. I remember Ann as a little maid, running down the quay, proper comely she was."

"This time they say 'tis Mistress Thomas who has been overlooked."

"Well, mayhap Goody Lloyd'll not wriggle out of that one so easy."

Emboldened by the strength of numbers, they began jeering, hurling insults and the occasional missile. The growing throng reached the door of the lock-up. One of the constables produced a key from the pocket that hung on his belt. Folk surged forward, eager to be able to say that they had witnessed a witch being brought to justice. Whilst his colleague cursed softly and struggled with the key, the other constable drew his stave to ward off the most tenacious onlookers. Temperance gnawed on her knuckle but appeared unconcerned. Oblivious to the noise of the crowd, she pushed her straggly hair back from her face and with a far-away look in her eyes, she gazed up the river, her head on one side. She nodded sagely, as if she was responding to an unheard conversation. The lock rasped and the door of the former chantry house sagged forward on reluctant hinges. The constables bundled Temperance inside and turned the key. The crowd stared at the nail-studded door, uncertain what to do next. A few stones, thrown in frustration, scarred the wooden panels. The sensation-seekers had been deprived of their quarry. Gradually, they drifted away, still muttering self-righteously, conveniently forgetting the times that they had run to Goody Lloyd for a potion or a poultice.

***

John Hill jumped involuntarily as Tom Eastchurch banged his fist on the desk. He had little regard for the enraged man, who was an adherent of the dissenting faction that Hill sought to eradicate, yet he must hear the fellow out. The townsfolk had become increasingly bad tempered of late and it was Hill who was bearing the brunt of their antagonism.

"You, sir, must allow us to question the witch."

Spittle landed on John's desk as Eastchurch expostulated.

He sighed; his records would have to wait. The fellow was right to demand satisfaction, after all, it was he who had laid the charges. Who knows, mayhap an encounter between the accuser and the accused would bring forth a confession. Hill did not want to see Goody Lloyd go free a third time. He nodded. Anything to assuage Eastchurch's fury and allow Hill to resume less unpleasant tasks.

"Calm yourself Master Eastchurch," he said. "You are entitled to put your questions to she whom you have charged with this offence."

It seemed that his acquiescence was not enough. Mistress Eastchurch too was determined to have her say.

"We must force her to lift the curse," she said. "My sister is complaining of a pricking in her knee. I have seen it with my own eyes, that I have. Nine pricks, as if they had been made by a thorn. We must demand to know if the witch has made a poppet of wax, or of clay."

John rose reluctantly from his seat and reached for his hat. "The mayor has arranged for a searching this morning," he said. "If we go across now, we can gain admittance."

"Indeed, our neighbour Mistress Wakely is one of the matrons who will search for the devil's marks," said Mistress Eastchurch. "She has been tending poor Grace these six weeks past. None knows better than she how my dear sister has suffered."

***

There was scant space in the stuffy cell. When the Eastchurches arrived, accompanied by John Hill, Temperance was rearranging her ragged shift and pulling a soiled petticoat over her head.

Annie Wakely bustled forward. "We found them Master Hill," she said, with a smirk of triumph. "The teats where she suckles her familiar."

This at least was progress, thought John. If he could just secure a conviction, the heightened emotions in Byddeforde might settle once more.

He addressed Mistress Wakely, "So she has a common token by which all witches be known?"

"Yes, two teats in her secret parts. She could not hide them from us."

Annie turned to Temperance, "Tell them," she said. "You tell them what you told us. Tell them how you suckled a black man there just two days past."

Temperance inclined her head in what might be taken for a nod.

Not satisfied with this, Annie addressed Temperance again, "Dost thou know of any bird that might flutter in a window?"

Temperance paused, as if she was waiting for an answer to come to her. After a few moments, she spoke in a firm voice, not looking at Annie but fixing her eyes on a space above the heads of the onlookers.

"I know what it is of which you speak. I was at Master Eastchurch's door. Indeed, I didst spy a maggoty-pie. I knew it to be the black man and that he had taken upon himself the shape and form of a bird."

"Never mind that," said Eliza Eastchurch, pushing Annie aside in her eagerness to confront Temperance.

"A poppet. Did you fashion a poppet to torment my sister, Mistress Thomas?"

Temperance smiled sweetly.

"A poppet Mistress? Nay. No poppet. Not for this one. I pricked some leather nine times that I did but never did I shape a likeness of Mistress Thomas."

Hill looked around the dingy room for somewhere to set out his quill and ink. He needed to scribe down her speech. Each word the old woman uttered would tighten the noose around her neck.

"Mistress Thomas was pinched and pricked to the heart, with pains in her head, her arms, her hands and thighs," said Tom Eastchurch. "'Twas as if her skin was being flayed from her. You left my house that day, nigh on ten of the clock it were. You met a darkly man nearby. I saw it with mine own eyes. 'Twas then you laid your spell on my wife's sister."

Temperance spoke softly, almost as if she was talking to herself.

"An arseworm he, no more than the length of my arm, with broad eyes and a mouth like a toad. And yes, his clothes were black."

The Following Day

John Hill watched as Grace Thomas stepped forward at the mayor's behest. She stumbled a little but did not seem overawed by the presence of the dignitaries in the town hall. At her side was her sister, Eliza Eastchurch. John took a fresh quill and prepared to note down Mistress Thomas' deposition.

"I was taken with pains in my head and all my limbs," she began. "Pains which did last for several months. When the pains abated somewhat, I was able to go abroad and take the air. But in the night, they returned and I was unable to rest. Last September I was going up the High Street and met Goody Lloyd."

At this point, Grace Thomas cast a resentful glance at the old woman who stood to next to Hill's desk, a constable at her side.

"As soon as Goody Lloyd was apprehended and held within the gaol my pains lessened. I verily believe that the said Temperance Lloyd hath done much harm and hurt to my body, by pricking and tormenting in the manner I have told."

They all took their turn. Casting stone upon stone. Each wishing to outdo those who had already spoken. Master and Mistress Eastchurch, Annie Wakely, then they called upon Goody Lloyd to step forward. Hill fervently hoped that she would not remain mute. They needed a confession. That way she would not slip through their grasp as she had afore. She must not retract the admission of guilt that she had made in the lock-up. The town was baying for blood and would not be quietened else.

Thomas Gist the mayor spoke first, reading from the notes that Hill had penned the previous day. "Temperance Lloyd. You have been brought before us by some of the constables of this borough, upon the complaint of Tom Eastchurch, gentleman of Byddeforde and are charged upon suspicion of having used some magical art, sorcery or witchcraft upon the body of Grace Thomas, spinster of Byddeforde. Upon being asked where last you had discourse or familiarity with the devil in the likeness of a black man, you saith that it was in a certain street or lane of Byddeforde called Higher Gunstone Lane and that then and there he did tempt and solicit you to go with him to the house of Tom Eastchurch, to torment the body of Grace Thomas."

Gist referred back to the parchment in his hand. "At first you did refuse to do so but by temptation and persuasion of the devil, you did go to the house of Tom Eastchurch and ascend the stairs after the black man. You have confessed that you went into the chamber and there found Grace Thomas and Annie Wakely, rubbing the arms of the said Grace Thomas and that afterwards you did see something in the form of a grey or bragget cat and that the cat did go into Tom Eastchurch's shop."

Hill looked at Goody Lloyd. The words were damning. Why did the woman seem unmoved by her predicament?

"You further confessed," Gist intoned, "to returning to Tom Eastchurch's shop the following day, invisible, unseen by any person and that you did meet with this bragget cat and the cat didst leap back within the shop."

John held his breath. This was it. What would the woman say? If she withdrew her words now, the confession of the previous day would count for little.

"I didst see Mistress Thomas in a very sad condition." Temperance said to the silent, waiting, crowd. "Yet the black man did bid me to plague her again. Whilst Master and Mistress Eastchurch were from home, with the aid and help of the black man, I did torment Grace Thomas. I did pinch and prick her in the belly and the breast, for the space of two or three hours. I had almost drawn her from her bed, with the intention of putting her life from her. For the black man had promised I should not be discovered. I gave suckle then to that black man. I did kneel down to him in the street as I was returning to my house."

John scribbled furiously. He could copy up his notes in a fine hand later.

"Of what stature was this black man?" asked Gist. "What of his appearance?"

"He was but an arms-length high sir. He hopped and leapt in front of me and a mighty pain within my head did come upon me. Afterwards, as I lay on the wayside, to still the hurt, he did suckle from me again. Then he vanished clear away from my sight."

John wondered if this would suffice. Temperance had thwarted justice when she had been accused before. Alderman Davie took up the questioning. He was pressing her further now, asking about that occasion and seeking the names of others she had bewitched.

"What of the time, some twelve years since, when you were accused, indicted and arraigned for witchcraft upon the body of Walter Herbert, late of Byddeforde?"

asked Davie. "When you were acquitted at the trial for your life at the Castle of Exeter."

The room was silent. Temperance smiled. John wondered if it was only he who found that smile disconcerting. The words poured from her like beer from a cask that had been broached.

"I did indeed, by the persuasion of the black man, prick Walter Herbert to death."

The Following Day

As much as he disliked the man, John was thankful that Goody Lloyd had been taken to be further questioned by the rector. The Eastchurches had not been satisfied with Temperance's explanation regarding the leather and it seemed they were right to demand that she be interrogated further.

"What of a poppet?" asked the rector. "Did you leave a poppet to wish ill upon Mistress Thomas?"

"I did leave a poppet," replied Temperance "but I didst not prick it."

This was new, thought John. Yesterday she had claimed that there was no poppet.

"In what part of the house or bed did you leave the poppet?"

"That I cannot say sir, for the devil would tear me to pieces were I to disclose it."

"How long since the devil did tempt you to do evil?"

"About twelve years ago I was tempted to do evil to Walter Herbert and the devil did vow I would live well henceforth."

From the look of her, the devil had reneged on that promise thought John. Yet still she unnerved him. There was some small comfort to be gained from being within the cool stones of the church. Although John was not wholly convinced that this feeble looking old woman could harness the power of the devil, there was that creeping sense of unease. It was as well to take every precaution.

"And did you lie with the devil?" Ogilvy asked.

Hill observed that the rector seemed to be in an agitated state. Ogilvy's breathing was quickening and he was running his tongue round his lips and leering at Goody Lloyd, as he might at a whore in a stew. The woman though, seemed oblivious to everything but her confession. Would she mention the other accusation? John wondered. When, these two years past, she was accused before the then mayor and justices of the town for practicing witchcraft upon the body of Ann Fellow. Then too she had gone free, although the proofs against her on that occasion were not so clear and conspicuous. Then four women had searched her and found nought.

"Yes. The devil came to me in the guise of a black man, I did do some bodily hurt to Ann Fellow and shortly after, Ann did depart this life."

She had, by her own admission, added to her crimes, confessing that she had overlooked both Walter Herbert and Ann Fellow. It seemed that there was still more to sweeten the ear of her listeners.

"I was the cause of Mistress Dallyn's death, she who was wife to Symon Dallyn the mariner. I did prick her in one of her eyes but I did so secretly and I was never discovered or punished for the same."

No one spoke. They looked at one another. What next?

"I did bewitch unto death Lydia Burman"

Ogilvy was the first to recover his composure, "Why did you do so?"

"She bore witness against me when I was on trial for my life."

"You must recite the Creed," cried Reverend Ogilvy.

For the first time that day, the old woman appeared ill at ease.

"Come now," said the rector. "The Creed and the Lord's Prayer. For none who are in the devil's power can do so."

Temperance folded her arms across her chest and squeezed her eyes shut.

"Our father, what art in heaven," she gabbled. She paused. "Hallowed be thy name."

Whereas earlier her speech had been firm, now it was as if she was forcing words past gritted teeth.

"Thy kingdom come."

She was hesitating, her words were mumbled, jumbled. She's mis-remembering it, thought John. Now for the Creed.

"He suffered," she hissed, "suffered, was crucified, died and was buried."

"He shall come again to judge the quick and the dead," said Temperance, having stumbled her way through the first lines of the Creed. "I believe in. I believe in ……"

She paused, looking up as if seeking inspiration.

"The communion of saints, the forgiveness of sins, the resurrection of the body."

Was it desperation that John glimpsed in the old woman's eyes? Desperation, or fear? Ogilvy was triumphant. He ran his finger along a passage in the leather clad Bible. He proclaimed the verse in ringing tones, "thou shalt not suffer a witch to live." They were justified by God in all this.

Two Weeks Later

There was no end to it. Once again, John was at the Town Hall, acting as scribe as Mayor Gist and Alderman Davie listened to yet more deponents giving accounts of ill-wishing. Not Goody Lloyd this time but two other women who reeked of poverty. The elder, Susanna Edwards, looked resigned to her fate. The other, Mary Trembles, was shaking uncontrollably and seemed scarcely able to lift her eyes from the floor. Before them stood Joseph Barnes. Beside him was his wife, a pale woman with black smudges beneath her eyes. She leant heavily on her husband and spoke in whispers, as if each utterance required supreme effort.

"It is she, that Mary Trembles," murmured Mistress Barnes. "She is to blame for my hurts."

At this, Trembles uttered a strangled sob and began to twist her apron round her hands.

"It was Mary Trembles," Barnes agreed. "She be the cause of my wife's pains and the prickings. Came to our door Trembles did with a white pot in her hand, as if she was going to the bakehouse. We refused her charity."

Next came the blacksmith, a broad-shouldered man, yet he seemed in awe of his surroundings. He cast anxious glances at the two women who were at the front of the room.

"Her," he said, pointing at Susanna Edwards. "I heard her say that the devil had carnal knowledge of her body and he had sucked her breast. She said that she and that there Mary Trembles had appeared hand in hand, invisible like, in the house of Mistress Barnes."

"To be clear," asked Alderman Davie, "you saw Susanna Edwards and Mary Trembles enter Master Barnes' house," he paused, "errrr, invisible like?"

John pondered the contradictory nature of the man's statement but he wrote it down nonetheless.

Urged on by her husband, Mistress Jones pushed herself forward impatiently.

"As soon as ever I heard they'd been taken up for conjurations, I went to see Susanna Edwards and Mary Trembles in gaol," she said. "I felt it 'twas my duty so to do. I asked Susanna Edwards how she became a witch and she said she had not confessed afore but she would do so now."

At this Susanna looked shamefaced. Very different from Goody Lloyd these two, thought John.

"She admitted to a familiarity with the devil and to bewitching Charity Barnes and Dorcas Coleman," went on Mistress Jones, "and she said Mary Trembles was her servant and would do her bidding. I heard Mary Trembles say she did prick Charity Barnes."

Susanna Edwards was brought forward and questioned next. John continued to record the proceedings. Black words etched on to parchment for posterity.

"Susanna Edwards," said Gist. "You have told Mistress Jones that you have had congress with the devil."

"I was out gathering wood," said Susanna quietly, "and a gentleman did draw nigh. I had hopes of gaining a piece of money from him."

"Where did you meet him, the gentleman?"

"'Twas in Parsonage Close."

The morning dragged on. John stretched his fingers, stiff from grasping the quill overlong. One deposition was very much like another. Susanna was confessing now, as Temperance had just two weeks earlier. Admitting to bewitching Mistress Barnes, with Mary Trembles at her side. A cry went up from the younger woman. Like Susanna, she was clad in a gaol-begrimed shift. Her petticoat was ripped and her bodice was fastened awry. She wore neither coif nor shawl.

"Oh, thou rogue," screamed Mary Trembles, casting accusatory looks at Susanna. The woman had all the appearance of a lack-wit, yet she realised that Susanna's words had condemned her.

"I will now confess all, for 'tis thou who hast made me a witch and thou art one thyself."

"I did not think thou would have the wit to discover it," Susanna retorted.

Gist turned to Mary, "Mary Trembles, you have been brought before us, accused of practicing witchcraft upon the body of Mistress Charity Barnes, wife of Joseph Barnes, yeoman of Byddeforde. How long hath you been practicing witchcraft?"

"About three years last past sir. Susanna Edwards did promise me that if I would do her bidding then I should do very well, that I should not want for meat, nor money, nor clothes. I had naught sir. I had been put from my home, so I didst make this bargain. I did as she bid."

"And did you ever lie with the devil?"

"Once sir. He came to me like a lion. He did suck me. He did suck me so hard that I did cry out from the pain."

Mary was sobbing now but Gist paid no heed.

"And did you torment Mistress Barnes?"

"We wus starvin' sir. The pickings have been poor of late. We were of a mind to beg for bread. Susanna Edwards, she did lead me to Master Barnes' door. We could get no meat nor bread there for the servant denied us. We were set fair to leave when Susanna bade me return. She thought mayhap, though there be no bread, we might beg a farthing's worth of tobacco. I came away with naught and when I told Susanna of this she was greatly angered and she took me by the hand and said we must go within the house unseen and prick Mistress Barnes unto death."

"And have you ill-wished Mistress Barnes even unto death."

"I would have sir but I could do naught else, for the devil bade me do so. I was on my way to the common bake-house with a white pie dish, thinking to warm the vittals, for we'd scarce tasted meat for many a day. I spilt some meat sir and I was that distraught I was turned from my purpose. I did not do the devil's bidding. That's why I be here. He will no longer succour me."

Still this is not the finish of it, thought John, resignedly. Now they returned to Susanna.

"Ofttimes the devil comes to me in spirit," said Susanna. "I did prick at Mistress Coleman at his bidding. These two years gone, I did suckle the devil at my breast.

In Stambridge Lane, up towards Abbotsham it were. In the shape of a boy he came to me. Mortal cold he be, yet I must bend to his will. He drew the blood from my breast he did."

Susanna began moaning softly. Her hands flickered over her body and she began to stroke her arms, her face, her thighs. She closed her eyes and tilted her head back, as her hands rubbed harder. John watched, mesmerised, as she reached between her legs for her privities and cried, "Thou devil, thou art now tormenting some person or another."

As she did so, there was a crash and Anthony Jones fell to the ground yelling, "Wife I am now bewitched by this devil."

Susanna screamed, "Well enough I'll fit thee," but soon all attention was diverted from the accused women, as Master Jones thrashed and shook and quaked and foamed upon the floor. John had seen folk taken in a fit afore but this was worse than any he had witnessed dancing to St. Vitus' tune.

Two days Later

John Hill broke the red wax seal and fingered the parchment in front of him. The distinctive signature of the mayor, Thomas Gist, was penned in thick ink at the bottom. He sighed. Not more. He had thought the town would have been satisfied when Lloyd, Edwards and Trembles were arraigned but it seems they were still not yet sated. The days were sultry, passions were ofttimes enflamed when there was little respite from the relentless sun. It seemed that it was not enough to send three women to the Assizes accused of witchcraft, here were two more accusations. He read the mayor's letter avidly. Polly Beare and Elizabeth Caddy. These were respectable women, very different from those who now languished in Exeter gaol. Who laid the accusations this time? Would it never end?

Martha's Story
2020

Martha had spent another sleepless night avidly checking her phone for the latest messages. Was Hunter seeing these? Surely, he would have blocked people, taken down his social media accounts. Yet Martha knew how difficult that was. Even when the bullies were making their most hateful comments about her, Martha had been unable to refrain from reading the posts. Hunter was probably the same. He must be feeling dreadful. There had been a wave of #BeKind messages earlier in the year, when a high-profile suicide hit the headlines but it seemed that the fashion for being kind soon waned. It was all too easy to post memes and gifs exhorting each other to be kind but to actually be kind, to take the trouble to reach out, to care, that took more effort.

By 5am Martha had given up all hope of sleep, next door's cockerel was already driving her nuts with its crowing. She turned to her phone yet again. Surely, she could do something more positive than just be thankful that she was not in the bullies' current line of fire. She could not get Hunter out of her mind, how he might be feeling, where his despair might take him. She'd do it, no one need know, she'd send him a direct message, nothing much and definitely nothing public. She'd just say Hi, so that he had something to read that was not hate. It didn't take long for Martha to find Hunter on social media, he'd been tagged in some school athletics posts, in the days when he was adulated for his sporting achievements. He was still that same person, thought Martha. How easily the coin flips and popularity turns to infamy.

Martha's finger hesitated above the button that would send her message, irretrievably, on to Hunter's phone. She'd agonised over what to say. In the end she'd begun, "Hi Hunter, not sure if you remember me, we were in the same maths set last year." After all, why should he know who on earth she was, no one ever took any notice of her, unless it was to make some scornful remark. That was the easy bit. After much deleting and re-writing, she settled for continuing, "just thought you could do with a friendly hello right now. Not to worry about replying if you don't feel up to it. Martha." Oh send it, she told herself. It isn't like you've put it where anyone else can see it. Martha knew she would never forgive herself if Hunter did something stupid and she hadn't made contact. 'Something stupid', go on, say it, think it. Suicide. Supposing Hunter killed himself and she had been too pathetic to even send one message. Her finger made contact with the screen of the phone. There. It was done. Now she would worry. If there was a reply, what would he say? It wasn't like they'd exchanged more than a few words in the past. What if there was no reply though? What would that mean? That could be infinitely more scary. If Hunter did respond, the worst he could do was tell her to piss off. Or maybe he would block her. No reply could signify anything.

Martha got out of bed and closed the window. It seemed a shame to shut out the air of the warm summer's daybreak but the pitch of the cockerel's crow made her want to scream. She flung herself down on the bed and buried her head in the pillow. Her phone told her that it was still only 5.45, at least if she couldn't sleep, she could try to rest now the cockerel's sounds were muffled. Her bleeping phone signalled an incoming message. Who on earth would be awake at this hour. It was probably spam but she'd better look, just in case.

"Hi Martha. Yes I remember you. Thanks for the message. You are the only person from school who has been in touch apart from Zainab. It helps. Hunter."

Zainab. Of course, that was the name of the Muslim girl in maths. Martha was angry with herself for not seeing beyond the hijab, for labelling Zainab, without taking the trouble to get to know her.

***

Martha peered at the computer screen, trying to decipher the seventeenth century handwriting. She was early, it could be another half an hour before Joan arrived. She'd wanted to make a start but maybe she'd have to leave this until she had help. There was a movement behind her as someone entered the library's computer room. It was rare that anyone else came to use the machines while she was there. The stifling summer was dragging on. The news spoke of record-breaking temperatures and more sinisterly, of irreversible climate change. It seemed that people had not yet tired of the sun. Or perhaps the lingering fears of COVID-19 contributed to a reluctance to use a public keyboard, thought Martha. She was aware of the pot of anti-bacterial wipes that stood at each workstation, of the laminated signs that exhorted people to wash their hands before sitting at a desk and the instructions to clean the keyboard after use.

She looked up. The newcomer was instantly recognisable as Zainab. Martha felt a flash of shame. It was the hijab that was familiar, not the girl's shyly smiling face.

Martha smiled back, raised her hand and said, "Hi."

Somehow that did not seem enough, so she added, "Are you doing the school enrichment project thing too?"

"No," replied Zainab. "Our router is down at home, so I am just checking some stuff. I need to print it out, so my phone's no good for that. I'm not on the enrichment programme. I'm doing a weird A Level mixture, so I didn't really fit into the science or the humanities project group."

There was a pause. Both girls were aware that this was not the only way in which Zainab did not fit into school life.

Martha broke the awkward silence, "What are you doing next year?" she asked.

"Politics, maths and psychology," Zainab replied. "What about you?"

"I'm doing psychology too," said Martha. "We'll be together for that, there's only one set. I'm doing English and history as well."

"Oh, so you'll have Mr Mortimer for history then," said Zainab. "I've got him for politics. I think he's a brilliant teacher."

"Yes, he's great," said Martha. "He's helped me loads with this project."

It was weird to be having a conversation where you admitted to liking a teacher but with Zainab it didn't seem embarrassing.

"What's the project about?" asked Zainab. Then, apologetically, "Oh, I'm sorry, perhaps I'm interrupting. It's just that I don't seem to chat to people much at school."

"No. It's fine," said Martha. "I'm early. The person who I need to help me with the next bit won't be here for a while." She paused, "I don't talk to many people at school either."

"I've seen you in maths," said Zainab. "What did you think of the exam? I am really worried about my result, especially as I want to do maths next year. I ran out of time on paper two."

"I'm hoping I've scraped at least a 5," said Martha. "We'll know in three days. Are you going up to school to collect your results?"

"Yes. I was going to go really early, when there might not be so many people about. Or do you think everyone will want their results as soon as possible? Maybe it would be better to wait until the afternoon."

Martha could understand Zainab's wish to avoid as many of their fellow students as possible.

"I can't see most of them getting out of bed in time to get there when the office opens," she said. "I'm going in first thing."

She paused. There were words in her head. Should she say them out loud? No. That wasn't the question. She knew she should voice her thoughts but could she? Oh, go on, she told herself. After all, messaging Hunter turned out ok and they'd exchanged several tentative texts since her first approach.

"We could meet up and go in together," she said. "That's if you want to of course and you don't have other plans."

"Oh yes, that would be great," said Zainab eagerly. "I'll give you my phone number so we can arrange to meet."

The girls exchanged numbers and Martha hesitantly began to tell Zainab about her project. By the time Joan arrived, they were deep in conversation.

"Oh, I'll let you get on," said Zainab. "Your research sounds really interesting. I'd love to read it when you've finished, if that's ok with you."

"Well, if you really want to. I didn't imagine anyone would be interested in it but me. I'll text you about meeting up on Thursday," Martha said, as Joan wheeled up another chair.

Zainab booted up her computer and Martha showed Joan the baptism register that she'd been trying to read.

"I'm not doing very well with this," she said.

"Who are you looking for?" asked Joan

"Elizabeth Caddy. There were Caddys in my village but I'm not sure if she's one. There seem to be lots of Elizabeth Caddys."

"How does she fit in to the story?"

"Well she was accused alongside the other three, her and someone called Polly Beare but no one ever talks about them. I suppose, because they got off, no one is interested in their story."

"Except for you," smiled Joan. "Well, let's see what we can do to bring Elizabeth, Caddy I think you said, back to life.

Chapter 10
Elizabeth's Story
July 1682

The door of the grammar school slammed shut, signalling the end of tuition for another day. The pupils, no longer boys but not yet men, stood idly in the summer's heat. In search of a diversion, four of the lads walked along the riverbank, jostling and scuffling as youths will when seeking supremacy amongst their fellows. They were an assorted bunch. Benedict Dunscombe, their acknowledged leader, already sporting the shadow of a moustache, his greasy hair inexpertly tied back at the nape of his neck. Philip Weekes, tall and skinny, with gangling limbs and bony wrists that protruded from his outgrown shirt. Edmund Smale, a stocky lad, with a pock-marked face and sandy hair. The youngest, Robert Wren, with unbroken voice and childlike mien, was there by sufferance. He was not yet fully accepted as part of their coterie.

The boys paused outside a substantial house. The dwelling stood back from the lane. With glazed windows and a slate roof, it signalled respectability, affluence, privilege. To one side was a thatched outbuilding, a brew house perhaps, or a laundry. A horse could be heard whinnying but there was no sign of life.

"That's it," whispered Benedict. "That's where she lives."

"What, Mistress Caddy?" asked Edmund. "Her they say is a witch?"

"Yes, my father has dealings with Master Caddy. That's where they live, no doubt."

"'Tis hard to countenance. Yet Mistress Weekes be certain sure, 'twas Mistress Caddy that overlooked her. That's right, baint it Philip," Edmund looked to Philip for confirmation.

"Oh yes, mother has no doubt that Mistress Caddy is the cause of her affliction," replied Philip Weekes, self-importantly.

"I've never seen a witch," remarked Robert.

"What, never seen a witch?" said Benedict, scathingly. "Did you not see Goody Lloyd these days past, when they dragged her off to gaol?"

Benedict knew perfectly well that he was the only one of the friends who had witnessed this momentous event. He had bragged about it ever since, his account becoming more fanciful with each retelling. It didn't hurt to put Robert in his place now and again.

Robert shook his head, ruefully.

"They do say that if you take straw from the thatch of any that be suspected of witchcraft and burn it, she will come running," remarked Edmund.

The boys eyed each other speculatively.

"But the roof is slate," said Robert quietly.

He was ignored. The boys moved round the side of the house towards the outbuilding.

Benedict eyed the thatch speculatively, "I am sure this would do just as well," he said. "It doesn't need to be the actual house, does it? This still belongs to the witch after all. I'd do it myself of course but it needs someone of height."

All eyes turned to Philip.

"Even I'll not reach the thatch from the ground," he said. "There's no sign of a mounting block or aught I could stand upon."

Benedict took command, as he so often did, "Edmund here can bend over and Philip can climb upon his back."

Edmund, a lumbering youth, who struggled to keep up with his lessons, looked doubtful.

"Are they from home do you think? Might there be a serving maid who will see us?"

"The servants will be about their business, won't they. They won't be watching out for the likes of us," said Benedict. "Go on, I durst you," he continued.

A dare was a dare. Philip and Edmund knew that they had little option but to acquiesce.

"There be no one about," said Benedict, encouragingly. "Robert here'll go back and stand guard by the gate lest anyone should pass by."

Robert hesitated. He did not want to miss the fun. He sighed, knowing that he must do as he was bid if he were to gain favour from these older lads, whom he strove to emulate. Obediently, he waited by the gate whilst the others stood under the eaves of the thatched outbuilding. Edmund bent his back as Philip pulled his latchets from his feet. Many a lad went barefoot when the weather allowed but grammar school pupils were expected to be respectably dressed. In any case, the Weekes family were comfortably off, gentlefolk forsooth and Philip would not dream of going unshod. Gingerly, he climbed aloft, helped by his eager friends.

"Reach it down," cried Benedict. "You can surely pull a handful of straw from there."

Philip stretched upwards, wobbling as he did so. The thatch was new and firmly laid. Philip managed to loosen a few strands from under the eaves.

"Have a care," moaned Edmund, as Philip scrambled down, with little regard for his friend's welfare.

Eagerly, the boys ran back to the road.

"Quick," gasped Benedict, grabbing Robert by the arm, "We'll go up to Ford Woods."

The weather was overly warm for haste but soon they lay panting in the trees' shade, the few precious straws clutched in Philip's sweaty hand.

"Have you a tinder?" asked Edmund, looking at Benedict, who could usually be relied upon to have such useful items about his person.

Benedict was known to smoke an illicit pipe of tobacco on occasion. Something that he could now accomplish without coughing, much to the admiration of his friends. He pulled a tinder box from the pocket that hung on his belt. The boys smiled at each other conspiratorially, although Robert looked less than serene. He did not like to point out that Mistress Caddy was no doubt on her way to Exeter gaol, ready to stand trial at the Assizes and would not be appearing however much straw they burnt. None of the others seemed to have taken this into account. In any case, as much as he wanted to see a witch, Robert wondered if it was wise to attempt to summon one. After all, look what had happened to Philip's mother. Added to this, Master Caddy was a man of some importance within the town, his belt was something to be afeared of, if naught else.

Benedict struck the tinder. After a few attempts, the spark found its mark and the straw began to smoulder. Despite the day's heat, a chill descended on the wood.

Two days Earlier

Elizabeth Caddy shifted in the creaking side-saddle and stopped, allowing her horse to pull grass from the side of the road. A servant accompanied her. After all, a woman of rank never rode out alone. He halted his mule a respectful distance away from his mistress. It had been a hot summer, parching the soil and withering anything that attempted to grow. It will be a poor harvest again this year, thought Elizabeth. The town's beggars would become ever more vociferous, accosting respectable folk in their homes, pestering them in the street. She sighed. No doubt the poor rates would be raised once more. After a few moments, Elizabeth gathered up her reins and urged her mount onwards. There was a trough at Moorhillhead, she would allow the mare to drink its fill there. She was returning from Buckland Brewer, where she had spent a few days visiting the kinsfolk of her husband Ralph. It was by virtue of Ralph's family connections that they had been able to obtain the lease of their Byddeforde home. A pleasant residence, with many attributes that were deemed essential to a man of influence such as dear Ralph was becoming. It was through his Buckland cousins that the Caddys could claim acquaintance with John Davie, whose country seat was at Orleigh, an impressive residence that she would soon pass.

Yes, life in Byddeforde was good, thought Elizabeth. Here she was, elegantly clad, mounted on a fine mare, with servants to do her bidding. Ralph was prospering, she could count many of the town's elite amongst her associates. Take Polly Beare, a most respectable woman, kin to the physician no less; she had become an especial friend of late. Elizabeth was looking forward to meeting Polly that afternoon and exchanging the latest gossip. There had been much of import taking place in Byddeforde in recent days. More squabbling between those who sought to worship in different ways and then the news that there were sorceresses in their midst. Of course, there were ofttimes fallings out between folk. She herself had those whom she found uncongenial. Mistress Weekes, for one. The woman had taken offence at some trivial remark of Elizabeth's and had retorted in a most uncalled for manner. Mistress Weekes' cutting speech was a minor irritation but disquieting, nonetheless. Now, Mistress Weekes refused to acknowledge Elizabeth, if they passed in the street. Odious woman. Might her ill-words choke her, thought Elizabeth. With good fortune, some indisposition would afflict Mistress Weekes and Elizabeth would be spared her presence when partaking of a dish of tea with the gentlewomen of the town. Elizabeth shrugged, she should not let such pettiness trouble her. It was of no account, what harm could Mistress Weekes do?

Elizabeth was thankful when the journey was over; the sun's rays made riding uncomfortable. She felt a sense of pride as she turned into the lane to her home. With the assistance of the servant, she dismounted and he led the beasts off to the stable. A flustered maid rushed out of the door.

"Oh, Mistress," the girl gasped. "The Master will be that glad you be 'ome. He's that discommoded an' all."

Servants today need to acquire more decorum, thought Elizabeth, exasperated.

"Calm yourself, Abigail," she said. "Anyone would think that some catastrophe had befallen us."

"But Mistress," said Abigail, "Master Hill be here, him that be the Town Clerk."

"I am well aware of Master Hill's position," Elizabeth replied. "He is a regular caller; no doubt he has some business with your Master."

"No Mistress," responded Abigail, emboldened by the enormity of the situation. "You don't understand. Master Hill be here with the constables. 'Tis you they've come for. They say," Abigail dropped her voice to a whisper, "there's naught to it o' course but they do say you be a witch."

Later that Day

Polly Beare twisted in front of the spotted looking-glass. Merely having such a modish object on her wall gave Polly pleasure. She smoothed down her black gown and admired the striped satin petticoat beneath. It had been greatly coveted by her gossips. She hoped that her stylish appearance might encourage Henry to hasten the day of their marriage. Henry Paul was prospering, much sought after to work on the many new buildings that were appearing in the town. He could no longer claim insufficient wealth as a reason to delay their nuptials. Polly knew that her sister, Phoebe, thought poorly of Henry, accusing him of trifling with Polly's affections. Henry's name had been associated with several women since his widowerhood but Polly was confident that she could bring him to the mark. Now that she had such a fetching new outfit, their imminent encounter might be just the occasion.

Polly was approaching forty but still comely and after all, Henry was well past the first flush of youth. Whatever Phoebe might say about him being seen on the arm of some much younger women of dubious character, Polly knew that Henry would not entertain the notion of taking a flighty young thing as a wife. Polly prided herself that she was a suitable spouse for one such as Henry. She was well connected, a woman of some means and respected within the town. Here she was, waiting for her dear friend Mistress Caddy to call. It was not everyone in Byddeforde that associated with such as Mistress Caddy, who had dined with the Davies at Orleigh no less.

Polly bent forward towards the looking-glass and examined an invisible blemish on her cheek. Her flesh remined firm, thanks to concoctions of ladies' mantle and her hair retained its glossy sheen, without yet a hint of grey. Polly gave silent thanks to her downtrodden companion, Moll Fry, who dutifully sponged Polly's hair with sage juice on a regular basis. Yes, there were ways of cheating time's ravages, secret, whispered ways of gaining a man's regard. Moll had her uses. Being country bred Moll's knowledge of herbs and simples was greater than Polly's own. Moll was unremarkable. She could slip unnoticed through the towns byways and acquire many a useful potion that could aid a woman of riper years. Of course, Polly could not possibly procure such things on her own behalf, she would be the talk of the town in no time. Yes indeed, it was worth suffering Moll's whines and her irritating, overdone deference.

It was some years since Moll had come to live with Polly as her companion. It did not do for a well brought up woman, such as Polly, to live alone. In truth, Moll was little more than a servant but she was the daughter of a substantial farmer out to Putford and as such, had to be granted a status that was commensurate with her position. Polly pitied Moll. Unprepossessing in both appearance and demeanour and inconveniently unmarried at thirty, there had been little prospect for Moll beyond languishing in her father's farmhouse and waiting to become a burden on her eldest brother, when her father died. Yes, thought Polly, if were not for me rescuing poor Moll and bringing her to town, what a sad life she would have led. Polly did not in any way perceive it as ironic, that she should disparage Moll for her spinsterhood whilst she herself had not yet ensnared Henry. Today was surely the day that Henry could be persuaded to set a date for their union. Once Elizabeth arrived, a necessary chaperone, they would walk into town and meet Henry as arranged. Elizabeth would discreetly withdraw to a suitable distance and then.... Polly twisted the gold rings on her fingers. Surely soon she would be able to add a wedding band.

The clock chimed the hour. How fortunate she was to have a timepiece of her own within the house, thought Polly. Three of the clock already, Elizabeth was very late. Whatever could have detained her?

The Next Day

John Hill regarded the bold young woman who stood in front of him. Much as he deplored the town's Independent faction, Hill had no time for those who bedecked themselves with fripperies and furbelows. Vanity was a sin and this lady, he used the word advisedly, had all the markings of a trollop. A higher-class trollop 'twas true but a trollop none the less. Mistress Beare, whom she was denouncing, was little better, with her fingers bedecked with gold and her gaudy petticoat. Polly Beare was however clearly a woman of some status, despite her somewhat ostentatious appearance. Hill's sympathies lay with her, yet he was obliged to hear the other woman out. His patience was wearing thin. There had been altogether too many of these accusations of late. Yet he could do naught but listen to the flamboyant creature before him.

"So, to be clear," he said resignedly, reaching for his quill. "'Tis your contention that Mistress Beare here," he gestured towards Polly, "is guilty of conjurations."

Ignoring Polly Beare's indignant intake of breath. The woman shrieked, "'Tis more than a contention. Bewitched my Henry she did, no doubt. Tried to turn his head from me, when we was set fair to wed afore long."

Polly snorted derisively, she was not going to stand for this.

"Good sir," Polly addressed Master Hill. "Do you honestly believe that a respectable mason such as Master Paul could entertain taking such a… such a creature to wife?"

Hill had to agree that Mistress Beare had a point but the other woman was having none of it.

"He'd not look twice at an old maid such as yourself, not without unnatural aids. You've cast a spell upon him that's what 'tis. It can be no other."

"Hardly," replied Polly, conveniently putting from her mind the herbs that Moll had stirred into Henry's ale on more than one occasion. "Master Paul can see the worth of a woman such as I. One with a position in the town, one with friends of influence. You are nothing but an ale-house haunter, a fortune hunter."

In her indignation, Polly's voice rose in both pitch and volume, "a whore!"

"Have a care, Mistress Beare," cautioned Hill. "We do not want this to become an occasion for slander."

"And that's not all," the young woman wagged her finger under Hill's nose. He recoiled from the sickly smell of her perfume. "Mistress Beare consorts with others she does. All do know that witches do not work alone. I's seed her I 'ave, with her nose in the air, thinkin' she can look down on the like o' us. Her and Mistress Caddy both, in it together they be and my poor Henry be proper mazed with it all. She's turned his head with her devil's ways. I'd lay any coin that she's been frequenting with that there Goody Lloyd an' all. She who be taken this week just gone."

"Indeed, I have not," said Polly. "Why on earth would a respectable woman, such as myself, associate with the likes of Goody Lloyd?"

The two women continued to bat accusations and refutations back and forth. Hill struggled to note them down. He regretted not asking his clerk to be present. There was no real substance to the case. The younger woman was crossed in love and seeking revenge, no more. Until recently, this would have led to no more than name-calling. It was only of late than any would have thought to make a case of witchcraft from such an incident. What was the town coming to? He would summon Master Paul, who was well-known within the town, fair set to be a burgess one day. That would be an end to the matter. It was true, there had been some tattle that Master Paul had been seen in one or two of the town's less salubrious ale houses. Nonetheless, all could see that Polly Beare was a far more suitable consort for the up and coming mason, than this scarlet-clad harridan. Hill shuddered as he regarded the woman. Her low-cut bodice was revealing far too much flesh and he observed with horror, it appeared that she might even have painted her face.

"I will ponder on the matter," Hill said, decisively. "Seek more evidence. Mistress Beare, I see no need to detain you at this point. You are free to go."

"I should think so too," expostulated Polly. "'Tis scandal enough that you are holding Mistress Caddy for no good reason. What times we live in when the matrons of Byddeforde cannot go about their business without censure."

***

John Hill rubbed his eyes. It was enough that he had had to cope with Mistress Beare's indignation and the ridiculous accusations of whatever the other woman was called. He realised that he had not even noted her name. That was remiss. Now he must deal with the claims against Mistress Caddy that were being brought by Mistress Weekes, who would no doubt be supported by her brash husband. He could in all conscience dismiss the wild accusations against Mistress Beare but Mistress Caddy was a different matter, not least because her accusers were prominent in the town. Why these two? mused Hill. He could understand that Susanna Edwards, Mary Trembles and Temperance Lloyd might find themselves before the authorities. They were poor, disreputable women of no account. What had Elizabeth Caddy and Polly Beare done to enrage their neighbours? Of course, both came from families with taints of papistry and memories were long, perhaps that was it. He could delay no longer. He rang the bell on his desk. His servant entered, with eyes lowered deferentially.

"Summon my clerk," requested Hill, "and send word to the constable that he should bring Mistress Caddy across from the lock-up, forthwith. Are Master and Mistress Weekes still waiting?"

The servant nodded, "Indeed, sir."

Hill sighed, "You'd best send them in."

Mistress Weekes entered the chamber on her husband's arm. Without seeking permission, Master Weekes drew up a chair and solicitously settled his wife upon it.

"This has been such an ordeal for my wife," he said by way of explanation.

"I am mindful of that sir," replied Hill, "but I must question your wife as to the nature of her complaint if we are to proceed in this matter. Pray be seated."

Robert Weekes settled himself on a carved oak chair, taking care not to crease his heavily embroidered justacorp. It was far too warm for such a garment but Weekes cared more for fashion than comfort. Mistress Weekes took a fan from her reticule and twisted her fingers through her luxuriant curls that owed more to artifice than nature.

"Mistress Weekes," began Hill, "we are here to ascertain the nature of your complaint against Mistress Caddy."

"Where is the woman?" asked Master Weekes. "Surely she should be here to answer for her crimes. She must be persuaded to lift the curse."

"Be assured sir, that Mistress Caddy has been sent for. The constable is, at this moment, bringing her from the place where she is being held."

Hill was conscious that appeasing Master and Mistress Weekes was a very different matter from satisfying his earlier complainant, a woman of so little account that he could not even recall her name.

"Mistress Weekes, for the record, perhaps you could outline the charge that you are bringing against Mistress Caddy," Hill nodded to the clerk in the corner, poised with quill and parchment. This allegation would be meticulously recorded. Hill was not going to make his earlier mistake again.

"Never mind charges," cut in Robert Weekes. "My wife has already made her allegations. We are here to demand to know what is being done. Has this woman been searched? Has she confessed? Have watchers been appointed, lest she summon her imps? Have they swept the floor of the cell where she is held, for fear that the devil should appear in the form of a spider?"

"Master Weekes," said Hill. "I can assure you that all that is required is indeed being done. I do however need to have my clerk set down your wife's evidence."

"Very well," said Weekes reluctantly, as he produced an embroidered kerchief from his sleeve and wiped his brow ostentatiously.

"Mistress Weekes, would you please recount your complaint against Mistress Caddy."

"Well," began Mistress Weekes, "'twas a few weeks since, that Mistress Caddy and I had words. She spoke most sharply to me, without justification."

"About what matter, Mistress Weekes?"

"All I did was make some mild remark about the many delinquents in our midst and how the papist leanings of the Duke of York did not bode well for the future of our country. She became quite indignant and to my mind, seemed to defend the papist cause. Has she no mind for the trouble that Catholics have caused us in the past?"

"I think we can dispense with the details," said Hill, regretting that he had asked for elaboration.

He had no wish to let the meeting turn into a religious debate. It seemed that the Weekes were not aware of the Caddy family's Catholic leanings. Granted, the Byddeforde Caddys now seemed to be conscientious Anglican worshippers but one never knew.

"Pray tell me why you believe yourself to have been overlooked."

"I have been sorely afflicted, ever since Mistress Caddy and I had our falling out. Ofttimes I can scarcely walk and I have pains and prickings in my limbs. Moreover 'tis as if my throat has been stopped. There's times when I can neither swallow nor draw breath."

Mistress Weekes' well-being did not look compromised to Hill and any restriction in her throat did not seem to be affecting her ability to speak but he could not gainsay her. That was the trouble with these witchcraft claims. It was confoundedly tricky to prove matters one way or another. There was a knock on the door and the constable escorted Mistress Caddy into the room.

Despite her confinement, Elizabeth had retained her composure. Her husband had ensured that she received comforts in gaol that were not granted to more lowly prisoners.

"Mistress Caddy," said Hill. "Mistress Weekes asserts that you have used diabolical arts and have ill-wished her. What say you?"

"Indeed sir, I have no notion why she should say such a thing," said Elizabeth firmly. "It is true that we have not been on the best of terms of late but one cannot maintain an intimate acquaintanceship with all and 'tis natural to find the company of some more congenial than others. I have no reason to wish Mistress Weekes, or indeed any other, harm."

"I hear what you say Mistress Caddy, yet Mistress Weekes is convinced otherwise. I am at a loss to know how to resolve this matter."

Elizabeth Caddy stiffened her spine, "You have my word Master Hill, that I am not guilty of malfeasance."

Mistress Weekes sprang from her chair, ignoring her husband's warning frown and giving no indication that she was in any physical discomfort, "And I give you my word that I am bewitched," she shouted.

Hill got to his feet. He always felt at a disadvantage when he was seated and those that he was questioning were standing.

"Good dames," he said, "this is not a matter upon which I can pass judgement. I have heard your accounts. It will be for the Assizes to declare the truth of the matter. Mistress Caddy, I have no recourse but to detain you until such time as you can be taken to Exeter to await trial. In the meantime Mistress Weekes, should you wish to pursue this claim, I suggest that you frame your complaint in more precise terms."

The constable took Elizabeth gingerly by the arm. He was not accustomed to having ladies of quality under his care. He was uncertain how to deal with someone of rank. Elizabeth swept out of the room with all the dignity that she could muster, avoiding the Weekes' gaze. Once through the door, her shoulders slumped and her fingers plucked at the sides of her petticoat. The constable could not bring himself to treat this unusual captive as he would a common criminal. As he gently escorted her back across the bridge, Elizabeth lowered her head, reluctant to exchange glances with any curious passers-by. The constable was a garrulous soul, free with his gossip. He had already shared with Elizabeth the news that her friend Polly had also been brought before the Town Clerk but that she had not been detained. In truth, Elizabeth had expected that the ridiculous charges against her would similarly be dismissed. She was innocent, she had caused Mistresses Weekes no hurt. She cast her mind back to her last hours of freedom, to her journey home from Buckland. No, she had nothing with which to reproach herself.

Martha's Story
2020

Martha approached her grandmother's house. She was hesitant. She used to love coming here but now, now dementia was inexorably erasing the grandmother she knew, it was difficult, scary. Gran was forgetful, understandably; Martha could cope with that. Although it was upsetting when Gran got confused and said 'Hebe', when she meant 'Martha'. Recently, she had become more unpredictable, angry even and Martha didn't know how to react. She was glad that Hebe would be there waiting for her. Awful though it was, she was afraid to be on her own with her grandmother now. Martha pushed the door; she knew that it wouldn't be locked.

"It's only me," she called.

"We're in the conservatory," Hebe replied. "How did it go?"

Martha fingered the piece of paper in her pocket. She took a deep breath and walked into the sunny conservatory. She looked enquiringly at her mother. Was this a day when she could hug her Gran, or would it be best to just sit down? Hebe nodded and Martha gave her Gran a kiss.

"Hi, Gran. I see you've been feeding the birds again."

Sparrows, chaffinches and a fat woodpigeon were scrambling for the bread and seed on the bird table, whilst blue tits swung on the fat-ball holder. Martha remembered her Gran teaching her the names of all the birds. Even before she'd learned to read, she'd been able to identify the common ones from the pictures in Gran's bird book.

"So, come on," said Hebe. "What did you get?"

"Five 9s, three 8s and two 7s," said Martha, secretly pleased with her good GCSE results.

She had met Zainab as arranged and they'd gone into school together. Despite the early hour, the atrium was a heaving mass of anxious sixteen-year-olds. Even those who had professed not to care, the likes of Jeremy and Tyrone, looked worried. Probably because their parents were outside in their cars, waiting impatiently, fingers tapping on hot steering wheels, glancing at the other parents, hoping that their child had outshone his peers. Most of the other pupils were too busy celebrating or commiserating to take much notice of Martha and Zainab but a few looked askance at the new alliance of two of the school's misfits. It had been good to have someone her own age to share her success with. Not a friend exactly, not yet but maybe soon.

Hebe was congratulating her and breaking open the elderflower cordial. Gran sat quietly watching her beloved birds. Martha decided that it was now or never. She hadn't just come to broadcast the news of her exam results.

"Gran," she said, "could I look at your old photo album please? You know, the one with you when you were a baby and your parents' wedding and stuff."

Gran said nothing.

"Just get it," said Hebe. "She'll be fine, she's having one of her silent spells."

Martha took the book from the bottom shelf of the bookcase with care. She cleared the mugs off the coffee table and laid the album where both she and her Gran could see it. The sepia images stood out against the black pages. Many were labelled in a thick white pen. Martha pointed to a severe looking couple in a photographer's studio.

"Look, it says Grandmother and Grandfather Renouf," she said.

She knew better than to ask a direct question. That would confuse and frustrate Gran if she couldn't remember the answer. She just had to hope that Gran would start talking.

Nothing.

"It's an unusual name," Martha ventured.

"It sounds French," said Hebe.

"It's not French at all," said Gran, indignation stinging her into speech. "They lived in Southampton but it's a Guernsey name. Don't they teach you anything nowadays?"

Wow, thought Martha. The Channel Islands. I wonder if Joan knows anything about researching family history there. She got her notebook out of her bag. If this formidable Victorian couple were Gran's grandparents, then they were her great great grandparents, what a brilliant start to her family history.

"This is my father of course," said Gran, pointing to another picture. "He was born just after Grandpa Renouf came back from the Great War. His medals. I had his medals. Find them."

Hebe was on her feet.

"Yes, I'll find them," she soothed. "It might just take me a minute."

"Or more," she mouthed at Martha. Martha could tell that Hebe had no idea where to begin the search.

273

"You talk to Martha about some of the other photos while I get them."

"They'll have been stolen," Gran was saying. "Some of those carers that come in, make off with anything they would."

"They'll not have been stolen," Hebe sighed. "They'll be where they always are."

"On top of the wardrobe," said Gran unexpectedly. "In that old suitcase but they'll have been stolen, like some other things I could mention."

At least now Hebe had somewhere to start looking, thought Martha and the chances were that Gran had remembered that snippet correctly. She hurriedly turned the page, hoping to divert her grandmother's attention.

"Great aunt Fanny," Gran said. "There was something not quite right about her. They put her in an asylum."

She turned worried eyes on Martha. Gran's face was so familiar. She had been a constant presence in Martha's childhood. Gran had read her endless stories, celebrated Martha's achievements and offered comfort when things went wrong. Now it was Gran who sought reassurance.

"Don't let them put me in a home," she pleaded. "I couldn't bear to be away from my birds and my garden and all my things. I'd be surrounded by old people. I'll die inside if you put me in there."

Martha made non-committal noises and smiled weakly. She couldn't make promises she might not be able to keep. It was so unfair. Gran wasn't really even that old. Other people in their seventies went off on world tours, did Zumba, or took pottery classes. Gran struggled to do even the simple things that she used to enjoy. Playing board games, reading an eclectic range of books, watching television quiz shows, taking solitary walks along the coastal footpath, they were all beyond her now.

***

Martha was looking forward to getting home and organising all the information that she had found. The medals had indeed been in the suitcase on top of the wardrobe, along with ration books, wedding invitations and a few invaluable birth, marriage and death certificates. Martha hadn't dared to ask if she could take these treasures home. If her Gran saw that the case was missing, she would forget that she'd given it to Martha and be accusing the carers of stealing it. It had been easy enough though to copy all the documents and some of the photos using her phone. Excitedly, Martha realised that she already had information stretching back to the mid-nineteenth century and Joan had promised to help her with census returns and things. There were far more documents available for the 1800s than there were for the 1600s. As much as she was enjoying her project, Martha was impatient for it to be finished so she could work on her own family history. This was personal. This was her story. Her ancestors' lives might turn out to be every bit as fascinating as those she'd been researching. Perhaps she'd text Zainab and tell her about her exciting finds. Now she'd got Gran talking a bit maybe she'd try recording her, as Joan had suggested.

Chapter 11
Roger's Story
August 1682

The jolting of the carriage unsettled its three occupants; one alert, one pensive, the other seemingly able to doze despite the discomfort. The Exeter road was rutted with the passing of numerous conveyances and baked hard by rainless days. Roger North was impatient, eager to get to their destination. There was a great deal that he wished to record in his journal. He was a few weeks short of his thirtieth birthday and already he had achieved much. A successful lawyer, well-connected, unencumbered, as yet, by wife or child; there was time enough for that. Yes, Roger had plenty about which he could congratulate himself. His older brother, Francis, seemed lost in thought, his brow was furrowed, his expression grave. Francis was the senior by some fifteen years. It had been he who had encouraged Roger to complete his legal training at Middle Temple, something for which Roger was particularly grateful. Momentarily, Roger wondered if he would grow old more gracefully than Francis. Both men were fashionably good-looking, with full lips and a long visage. Roger pulled at a luxuriant, chestnut curl, he had no need of a wig, yet poor Francis was already losing his hair.

He turned his mind to more serious matters. For Francis this journey was no jaunt. The summer Assize circuit had been lengthy and Roger knew that his brother was already weary of his task. Not for him the leisure that Roger had the freedom to enjoy. Francis was to preside over the Assizes at Exeter, whereas Roger could attend the proceedings as a mere observer if he wished. Or he could forego the courtroom altogether and indulge in the attractions of the city.

Roger regarded the third occupant of the carriage, Francis' fellow justice, Thomas Raymond. The older man was laid back in the corner, legs splayed, snoring gently. Roger was grateful for some respite. Raymond's need for incessant conversation was irksome. In the last few hours they had been subjected to the tedious recounting of the fellow's past courtroom triumphs. He had been condescending in the extreme, despite Francis being the senior justice. It was pleasant to be able to watch the passing countryside in silence. This was not Roger's first visit to Exeter. He recognised the approaching bridge at the bottom of Castle Lane. He breathed a sigh of relief; their journey's end was nigh. Francis would be eager for a comfortable chair and a quiet evening. There were cases of great import before the justices on the morrow. Roger was concerned on his brother's behalf. It would not be easy to steer an objective course. Passions were enflamed; there would be a sinister tone to the proceedings. This would be no ordinary sitting of the Assizes. The grave charges that had been brought were an iron mantle laying heavily upon Francis.

Roger did not wish to interrupt his brother's reverie. Francis North, preoccupied with his contemplations, ran a finger under his tight neckband. The summer's heat was oppressive. Darkening clouds were gathering on the horizon; no doubt there would be a storm afore nightfall. Exeter's great castle surveyed them from above, stony-faced and ruddy in the remnants of the late afternoon sun. The curious light cast blinding beams. The daunting walls were silhouetted against the glow. Time was, a garrison had been stationed here but since the late war, the only combatants to enter under the archway were those who would face each other in court. Roger could see that Francis was sobered by the responsibility. The gift of freedom was his to grant or to deny. God-like, he could liberate or condemn. The prospect of presiding over the Assizes did not normally trouble Francis but this time, this time there was an unease. His disquiet was palpable. What was to come?

The carriage lurched, finally awakening Raymond from his slumbers. It took Roger a moment to realise that the eerie shrieking that set his teeth on edge was coming from one of the horses. It would be a misfortune were an axle to have broken when they had but a short distance left to travel. It was a common occurrence on the poor roads of the south-west of course. So much so that many travellers preferred to ride, or sail and farmers abandoned carts in favour of sledges drawn by horse or oxen. Roger put his head out of the window. The axle was sound but inexplicably, the carriage had halted on the bridge. It could go no further. Francis exhaled resignedly but Raymond began to bluster.

"We are cursed," he said, his face reddening. "Cursed I tell you. Have a mind for those we have been sent to try. It will be witchcraft this, mark my words."

Roger exchanged glances with Francis. Raymond was a nincompoop, no better than a rustic. How could a someone of learning be so credulous? A man of law should not countenance such superstitious notions. Despite his dislike of Raymond, Roger tried to be fair. He supposed that there was some small justification for the prejudices of the man. He had, after all, grown up in the eastern counties. Young men were impressionable and as a youth, Raymond had been much exposed to the machinations of the likes of Hopkins and Stearne. Men who had wreaked a bitter campaign against witches during the war. Yes, hundreds had faced the gallows at the hands of Hopkins, the self-styled Witchfinder General. Although the North brothers had also spent their formative years in East Anglia, matters had taken a different turn by then. Their home had not lain under the constricting influence of puritan thought. The Norths moved in court circles, had welcomed the Restoration, whilst Raymond exuded all the trappings of barely concealed antimonarchism. Only that morning, he had expressed his dissatisfaction with the king with all vehemence of a fanatic.

During the journey, Raymond had spoken, at interminable length, of his memories of the Essex witch persecutions, voicing his approval of the outcome. No doubt, past experiences influenced the man's current irrational and intractable stance. It was worrying, nonetheless. This obsession with hounding those who practiced the dark arts did not bode well for Raymond's impartiality. Here he was, on the eve of a witchcraft trial, railing against all manner of unnatural occurrences. Next, the man would be claiming that the horses were the witches' familiars, thought Roger, ruefully. When matters calmed down and they were once again on their way, Francis would surely caution his colleague against pre-judging the case.

***

Francis returned from his third visit to the privy and settled himself beside his brother in a private room at the back of the Bell Tavern. Roger looked up expectantly.

"You seem increasingly discommoded brother. I cautioned you 'gainst the mackerel. Mayhap it was on the turn. Or was it all those miles in that jumble-gut carriage? You can scarce be running back and forth to the privy in the midst of a trial."

"Indeed. I had not wanted to cast matters of import over to a man such as Raymond but this indisposition has led me to resolve that I shall confine myself to hearing the civil cases. I must leave the criminal indictments to him."

"But you are the senior justice, Francis," said Roger, "a man of rank, Chief Justice of the Court of Common Pleas no less. I know that you are gravely concerned about the outcome of the witchcraft accusations. After today, I fear that Raymond will stir up trouble with his claims of sorcery. The news of the mishap with the carriage will be round the city afore daybreak. Ridiculous. The carriage became wedged, naught more."

"I had hoped to damp down such thoughts," said Francis, "but country folk will believe aught. It seems many have made the journey from Byddeforde. They expect a conviction. I fear there will be disorder if the verdict displeases them. Yet justice must be done."

"Have you done right to abrogate your duty? You only have to be out in the city's streets to see that the populace is in high dudgeon."

Francis glanced at the rain-lashed windows. "This storm has invaded their very bones. Men grow ever more unsettled when thunder and lightning rent the skies. As you say, I cannot preside over a lengthy trial whilst I am unwell. I have done what is necessary Roger. Raymond is a justice of many years' standing. We must have faith in his judgement, despite what we might feel about the man. I confess though, I am now wondering if I have placed too great a burden on one who is a sycophant, ever eager to follow a course of action that will endear him to those of rank."

Roger leaned back in his chair, a pewter mug of spiced ale in his hand. He shared his brother's unease.

"You have delegated Raymond a hard task brother. I fear that the man has more concern for his own popularity than he does for justice. The country is fully possessed against these women. This city is ringing with tales of their preternatural exploits. The unrest engendered by such tattle overfloweth."

Francis nodded. "Such cases never pass off without incident. In their fear, folk band together and will not be swayed by reason. It brings to mind that case I heard at the Somerset Assizes. Then too it was a matter of error and ignorance, brought about by mere malice. That young girl, why is it always young girls who cry witch at the slightest opportunity, eh? A poor woman was near condemned to death because the girl claimed she had been over-looked and was spitting pins. It was all artifice but the devious child had duped most of her listeners."

"'Twas maybe more that she was uttering what folk wanted to hear. Her claims suited their needs," said Roger, thoughtfully.

"'Tis ever thus. Men will twist aught to further their cause," agreed Francis. "There was a great outcry and fury on that occasion, when the girl was shown to be a fraud and the woman she'd denunciated went free but it was the just outcome. Yet even then the passions were not equal to what I have seen here in Exeter this night. The whole city is afire with the matter. Every pot-boy and scullery maid has their opinion. It is of no account that they know little of what has occurred in Byddeforde these past months."

"Ofttimes disquiet stalks the streets when temperatures soar and storms abound. The heaviness of the air unsettles the humours. Folks' brains do addle in the heat. We can but pray that the crowd's mood will quieten, brother and that Raymond lays his prejudices aside."

"Indeed," said Francis. "You've only to recall that pother over Titus Oates, with his fabricated nonsense that the papists were plotting to kill the king, to understand how a whispered word can spread like the pox, gathering in venom as it goes. Ere long, hysteria floods the country and violence is ne'er far behind. Rumour all too rapidly becomes fact and none will pause to ponder on the truth of the matter afore spreading it further."

"That was a time when wise men behaved like stark fools. Men will forever be set one against another over matters of faith brother. The Oates affair may have been something that was wrought from naught but men swung for it and we will suffer the consequences for many a year."

***

The words spun across the courtroom and eddied into the minds of the listeners. Truth? Lies? The witnesses spoke with conviction, respectability adding to the veracity of their words. Roger tried to capture every nuance of the occasion so that he could report back to Francis. He could not help but feel that Francis might regret allowing these cases to come before Raymond. There was Raymond, self-important, bellicose, jovial even. The man was a fool of course, a toady, ever keen to flatter and appease. He was clearly impressed by status, gratified that wealthy merchants and those who held mayoral office, were amongst those who had brought these women before the Assizes. It did not bode well for a fair trail. It was out of Francis' hands now.

There had been four unfortunate women on the list of those indicted for witchcraft. Four poor souls who had, at best, fallen foul of their neighbours, at worst been perpetrators of maleficent deeds. One, Caddy, had an air of faded gentility that set her apart from her fellow accused. The evidence against her was flimsy. The principal accusation was brought by a Mistress Weekes, an impassioned woman who was forceful in her delivery but whose account did not stand up to the slightest scrutiny. It was a wonder that the allegation against Caddy had been referred thus far. Mistress Weekes' husband was a man of some standing of course, it was difficult to ignore the entreaties of a woman of rank. Thankfully though, the Grand Jury had swiftly realised that there was little enough to warrant taking Mistress Caddy's case further and she had been released without appearing before Raymond. Although this would not be popular with the baying crowd, for whom only blood would suffice, Francis would be relived, thought Roger.

Of course, indictments for witchcraft were always problematic. Of a necessity, the evidence was circumstantial, based largely upon rumour and common fame. It was as well that the number of accusations being brought to trial had dwindled over recent years. One could not witness bewitchment, merely the manifestations of it in those who claimed to have been overlooked. Justices at all levels of the proceedings struggled with accusations that were difficult to substantiate or refute. Fear made even the most level-headed of officials see evil where there was none. It was all too easy to bow to the pressures of the most vociferous; the inarticulate had no voice.

With a zealot's gleam, Raymond turned to the three remaining women who had been brought before him. Evidence, such as it was, was brought. The usual fare for such a trial, complaints of pinchings, fits, congress with the devil and the like. The women were downtrodden, dishevelled, disorientated. At first, they seemed scarcely capable of coherent speech. Under Raymond's unremitting questioning, they muttered, they stuttered, they said little that would either exonerate or condemn. Then, just as Roger felt that the trial was heading for an acquittal, with little of substance to merit a conviction, the mood changed. Goody Lloyd was the first to speak. Her monosyllables were replaced with a babble of words as assuredly, inexplicably, she began to confess. She stood before them and in bold tones admitted not just to the death of Walter Herbert but also to bewitching Jane Dallyn and Lydia Burman, whose names had not even been mentioned in the depositions. What had prompted the woman to speak thus? Roger wondered. If she had remained silent, she might have saved herself. She had, after all, gone free on two previous occasions.

"I have had congress with the devil," Lloyd was saying, all traces of her earlier bewilderment gone. "He has come to me in woeful shapes. He has taken my blood and caused me to do harm. A bragget cat did enter Master Eastchurch's shop. 'Twas in that form that the devil was beside me when I did torment Grace Thomas in her chamber. He urged me to kill her and when I did not, he beat me about the head and back. He did leave the mark of his fist upon me. I did not kill her but I did bruise her thus."

At this point the woman put her hands to her sides, palms inwards and mimed a squeezing action.

"I did bruise her until the blood ran from her mouth."

There was an audible intake of breath in the courtroom. Goody Lloyd looked round, unabashed. It was as if she relished the stir that she had created.

"I have been in league with the devil these twenty years or more. I have lain carnally with him for nine nights together. He did suck upon my paps to provoke me into lechery."

"And you didst entice others to do likewise did you not?" said Raymond.

It was a leading question but it went unchallenged. It was as Francis had feared, thought Roger, Raymond cared more for his reputation than he did for justice. He was determined to secure conviction at all costs.

Unhesitatingly, Lloyd continued, without a glance at her fellow accused, women whom she was about to condemn. "I did instigate Mistress Edwards and Mistress Trembles in the damnable arts these three years past. I acquainted them with many wonderful, unlawful tricks. They grew to be most proficient, trying their hand 'gainst man and beast to the injury of both. The devil used to be with them by night in several shapes. Sometimes like a hound that hunted before them but without doubt, it was souls that he sought."

Now the foolish woman was speaking of causing a vessel to be sunk and of cursing a boy, so that he did fall from the topmost mast of a ship and break his neck.

Why mention that? None of the witnesses had spoken of ships. The account was becoming ever more fanciful. Roger could see that the onlookers were drawn in by the old woman's words. The pathetic specimen of humanity that was Temperance Lloyd, a woman so ancient as to be upon the point of death, was holding the attention of all present. Hypnotic, mesmerising, the words dripped from her toothless gums. Her speech was strong now, whereas earlier it had been almost impossible to hear her indistinct mumblings. It was as if the woman was possessed. No, not possessed, Roger shook himself. He needed another explanation for what he saw before him but he could find none.

Susanna Edwards was Raymond's quarry now. Quieter than Lloyd, more hesitant 'twas true but it was as if she had been infected by the other woman's new-found spirit. She too seemed set upon a course that could have no other outcome but death.

"They say I be a witch good sir, though in truth I know not what that be. I be that troubled with melancholy and waking dreams," Susanna stated.

And so it went on, confessions of guilt, confirmation of all that had been brought in the indictments and more.

Only the youngest of the three remained over-awed by the proceedings. Mary Trembles had broken down sobbing, cowed by Raymond's unrelenting questioning. The woman's confusion seemed genuine. She was no more capable of lucid speech that Roger was of flying from the window. Three times, Raymond asked the distraught woman to repeat herself, to speak up so that she might be heard. She kept casting her gaze upon

Temperance and Susanna, as if seeking guidance. None came.

Finally. Finally. In a cracked whisper, "The devil didst suckle from me, him with the saucer eyes."

***

"How went the trial?" asked Francis.

"It was as you feared brother," replied Roger. "The four women were brought to the Assizes with as much noise and fury of the rabble set against them as could be showed on any occasion."

"I was not expecting that they would be condemned, or three of them at least. If one went free why not the others?"

"She was of a different cut, Caddy was," said Roger. "A dame of respectable mien. The others were the most downtrodden, despicable, miserable creatures I ever saw. They confessed, brother. I'll own I was not anticipating that. Once they had condemned themselves out of their own mouths there was little Raymond could do, even had he wished for a different outcome, which it is clear he did not. The man lacked the dexterity of mind and strength of spirit to gainsay the vast tide of feeling that there was against the women. He was hot for a conviction from the outset. It mattered little what the plaintiffs said. In the end it was all of no account. They owned they were guilty and in truth their confessions did exceed the testimonies against them and those same testimonies were very full and fanciful."

"Full and fanciful Roger? What mean you by that?"

"All that you might expect in such a trial, dead pigs, cats entering through windows, prickings and the like."

"A dead pig is but a dead pig. A cat coming in a window is an everyday occurrence. How does this equate with bewitchment?"

"As we said last night brother, folk are eager to twist everything to their cause. Indeed, there could be no favourable conclusion to this affair."

"Justice would have been the favourable conclusion," replied Francis, soberly. "My thoughts are in turmoil. What prompted these confessions? And you say they admitted to more than they were indicted for! These decrepit creatures, reeking of poverty, outcast by their town; are these poor unfortunates so weary of their lives? Is their situation so burdensome that they seek the noose? Why would they admit aught? There were those who spake against them 'tis true. They had indeed been vilified but who were those who accused them? Those whose fear made them fanciful, those warped by bereavement or pain. Much of the evidence against these poor souls was but the whimsical ramblings of the delusional and the easily swayed. Surely these confessions were the product of ignorance, poverty and irrationality. Anyone with sense could detect the insubstantiality of the evidence and that the women were feeble minded. 'Tis a misfortune that this guilty verdict has been returned. Why were the confessions not dismissed as inventions born out of melancholy, or the delusions that come with age? Why were they not acquitted and carried to the parish to which they were chargeable? It is their deficiencies that have constrained them to wish for death."

As Francis paused for breath, Roger replied, "I can offer no thought upon the matter Francis. Remember the plaintiffs were folk of import. Mayhap undue pressure had been brought upon the women, who can say? I wish you had been there for yourself."

"It will be my deepest regret that I was not. And as for undue pressure, there are always those who will do aught to get an admittance of guilt. In truth 'tis difficult to secure a conviction without. All else is mere tales."

"Do not rebuke yourself brother. I doubt that you could have brought in a different verdict. There is little that can be done if those on trial own themselves culpable."

Francis banged his fist on the table in exasperation. "I abhor cases such as this when the populace have condemned before the evidence has come before the justices. 'Tis public outcry that has sent these women to the gallows, not the law. I would not speak of this in company but you know brother that I have grave doubts about matters of bewitchment. Conjurations are but figments of over-active imaginations. Can folk really harness the devil's power as is claimed? These pitiful women, could they ill-wish their fellow man with effect?"

"The alleged victims spoke with conviction," replied Roger. "Though, as is ever the case in such trials, there was scant solid evidence. It was clear that many were persuaded of the potency of the witches' work. Though 'twas as you surmise. Those that were standing trial were so dull of thought that they could scarce tell fantasy from reality. At first, they said little, mere gruntings, scarce acknowledging that they had been addressed. But then 'twas as if a curtain lifted and the one, Temperance Lloyd came forth with strange tales. I believe she knew what she was saying. 'Twas as if Edwards followed suit and there was little Mary Trembles could do but admit that she had known the devil."

"You know, if I had my time again, I own that I might have been a man of science, a member of the Royal Society mayhap," said Francis. "I have little truck with the old ways, the ways of superstition. Such ideas are being eroded, at least in the opinions of men of education. Yet the human mind is malleable, open to persuasion. Even powerful men might be swayed by the convictions of their peers and these plaintiffs were, in the main, simple country folk, for all their self-importance."

"There's naught to be done," said Roger. "They drew upon the vulgar traditions, speaking of familiars, diabolical sucklings and the like. 'Twas what the crowd craved. They were appeased."

"I fervently hope that this will not take hold," said Francis. "I would not want to see the return of the days of the Witchfinder. I had hoped we had put such tyrannies behind us. These puritans, those who would seek to once again depose the king, they too are of that ilk. They must not be allowed a foothold." Francis paused to ponder the matter. "I regret that mercy cannot be shown," he continued. "We cannot grant reprieve without appearing to deny the very being of witches. I might be sceptical on these matters but witchcraft is enshrined in the law of the land." He shook his head, frustrated by his impotence. "These women must now face the noose. Our hands are bound as surely as the ropes that will tether those unfortunates and lead them to their fate."

Martha's Story
2020

Martha's phone bleeped, signalling an incoming message. Hunter.

"Hi M really glad you messaged. Everyone is still on about the party thing not sure how much more I can take. Might as well just say it was me."

She sighed. Messages directed against Hunter had dwindled during the flurry of commiserations and congratulations following the issuing of the exam results. In the last few days though, there had been a lack of new gossip and the comments had resurfaced. Even the reports of celebratory beach barbeques had not eclipsed the speculation about Hunter's sexual preferences and his role in summoning the police to the party. This was now regarded as a matter of fact, yet Martha believed Hunter when he said that it was nothing to do with him.

"But it wasn't you. Why would you say it was?"

"It would shut them up. Things can't get much worse. At least then it would blow over."

Martha could understand why Hunter might feel that appeasing his accusers would make them seek a new quarry but she knew it wasn't the answer.

"Hunter you can't. Don't give them the satisfaction. Maybe someone will own up, you can't stay hiding forever."

"Can't face people. Not spoken to anyone since it all kicked off. Going crazy here."

Martha debated what emoji she could send that would convey sympathy. A smiley face seemed wrong. A heart would be stupid. She went for the hug symbol.

"Thanks your messages really help. Don't know where I'd be without you & Zainab."

"Don't admit to something you didn't do though. They will forget in time."

Forget. Yes, the bullies might eventually stop targeting Hunter; after all they had moved on from taunting Martha. That was just diverting the issue not putting an end to it; they'd find a new victim. There would always be those who bolstered themselves up by picking on the vulnerable. Being part of the gang was comforting. Yet belonging, by its very nature, meant that there were those who would be excluded, ridiculed, condemned.

Martha wished she could talk some sense into Hunter. The 'Lynch Hunter' WhatsApp group had disappeared, taken down by its instigator maybe, or perhaps it had been removed by the social media watchdogs. The anti-Hunter messages would tail off eventually, if he could just bring himself not to react. There was little sport in baiting someone who did not respond. The last thing Hunter should do was fuel all the hate with a public confession. Why would he say he'd done something when he hadn't? Somehow Martha needed to persuade him to let the matter drop. Messages were all very well but it was difficult to get someone to see reason when you had to type everything out. Maybe they could Facetime. That would be easier. Should she suggest it? She'd never asked a boy to Facetime before. Not that this was quite like asking any other boy. Hunter knew that she knew he was gay. There was no chance that he'd think she was coming on to him.

"Can we Facetime? Easier to talk."

***

Martha was putting the finishing touches to her project. School started again next week and she would need to hand it in. Normally, the prospect of a new term sent Martha's anxiety levels rocketing. This time though, there were glimmers of anticipation threaded through the unease. Not that she wasn't apprehensive; after all there was the whole new world of the sixth form to negotiate. Yet this term was different; the dread was tempered by excitement. She could look forward to specialising in subjects that she enjoyed, to seeing what Mr Mortimer thought of her account of seventeenth century Bideford, to having Zainab to sit with in psychology class and at break. The spectre of Kayleigh, Jeremy and Tyrone still loomed but it was muted like a sea mist that would be burnt off when the sun rose. It no longer consumed her.

It was a shame that Hunter would not be returning to school but he had always planned to study sports science at college instead. Sadly, the summer's events were not yet forgotten. The gossip ricocheted from one social media account to another. When groups gathered on street corners, in the park or on the beach, whispers crescendoed into roars. Hunter was in a bad place right now, crippled by the thoughtless comments carelessly uttered by those he had thought were his friends. Martha wished she could be more supportive but it was difficult to know how best to help. Although they Facetimed regularly now, either just the two of them, or with Zainab as well, Hunter refused to leave his house to meet them in town. He still had moments when he wanted to take the blame for calling the police on the night of the party. It troubled Martha that he might be pressurised into admitting to something that he didn't do.

Martha debated whether she should go round to Hunter's but he lived opposite the park gates. His front door was clearly visible from the area where the gangs congregated. She would be seen. No. It would be too much. An insidious spark of self-reproach rose up in Martha's throat. Sour-tasting, crushing, paralysing. She told herself that Hunter needed her, that she should be able to shrug off her fears but her anxiety was insurmountable.

Chapter 12
Temperance's Story
25 August 1682

I squeeze my eyes tight shut against the light. Darkness is my kin. Yet I am glad that the sun shines down this day; thankful to feel its warmth one last time, as I journey to my destiny. 'Twas deathly dark, that room where we were held. Pitiful women within the dank stones, amidst rats, amidst our own waste, amidst the chill of death. Women begging. Pleading. Praying. Women waiting in fear. Well, poor Mary was mighty afeared; Susanna little better. On their knees in the filth they were, beseeching to a deity they neither know nor believe in. But I, not I. No, I did wait in triumph, eager for what this day must bring.

The voices, always the voices, since I was little more than a maid. They've guided my life, the voices. Unbidden they come to me and I canst turn from them.

Gifts I have had aplenty for following their bidding these past years. For many a month I have known that my end was nigh. Few women see as many summers as I. It is indeed my time. When they assaulted me with their questions, I grasped the opportunity to infect the minds of those who derided me, who spake against me, who refused me charity. I could not deny the chance that I had been granted and my words gave them reason to fear. Scorn me they might, yet scuttle to me they ofttimes did, no matter what they said of me in company. Sneak to me under darkness's anonymity to seek a potion, they might. Mayhap they wanted to catch a lover, or to keep their master's eye from roving. Or they sought to rid themselves of an unwanted child. Yes. Then they had a need of me. But now, now, 'tis attention that they seek; that and their neighbours' acclamation. I matter nought. I am but a token, a token whereby they can affirm their respectability and their authority.

They are taking us part way on horseback. Mayhap old women's stumbling steps be too slow for the likes o' they. Look at them now, keen for all this to be done, so that they might get on with their narrow little lives. I have seen to it though, done enough to plant that gnawing worm of doubt within their minds. For many a year they'll wonder. When matters do go awry, I'll give them pause. They will think on me then and question. Was it mere happenstance, or was it a curse that I have laid? I will be at peace but that haunting dread, that terror, that uncertainty, that will plague their dreams and taint their lives.

I am unaccustomed to horseflesh. No ambling mare or donkey has aided my path in times past. This poor beast does their bidding every bit as much as I. He knows not where he leads me. He sways. I slip. My ancient legs cannot grip his sides. I lurch back into the saddle. They've fastened my hands to the pommel, so as I will not fall. If I did so, would they see it as a portent? Onlookers line the streets. They jeer. They scoff. A rough clod of earth hits my cheek. I do not flinch.

I can hear Mary's wails above the crowd's cacophony. I foresaw she would be thus; she allus lacked resolve. Weak-minded that one. Susanna though, I thought she had more about her but it seems I misjudged her resilience. They struggled to get her upon her horse, a patient beast with swaying back but Susanna would have none of it. Screamed, begged she did. She wrenched herssen from the guards' grasp and lay howling upon the wayside. Thrashing as if she'd been taken in a fit, despite her advancing years. Ne'er have I seen a body in such a takin'. What did she expect? She'd proclaimed her guilt. This would allus be how it transpired. To no avail, her tantrums. Dragged her up they did, slung her across the saddle like she were no more'n a sack o' straw. Now she be travelling all the way like that. Face in the horse's flank, head bob-bobbing on the one side, scrawny, naked legs upon the other. Fool that she is, now all will doubt her power. But I. I smile, I nod in acknowledgement of the anonymous faces that seek salacious gratification from our plight. I do not bow to their needs. Not I. I am invincible, they shall not see me weaken. I waited, I did, in court, waited until they thought nothing of me. Then I started. Told them of my powers, I did. I omitted naught, going back and back, speaking of those who have suffered at my hand. Left them wondering. How many more? What of their neighbour, their friend, they themselves? Had they been touched?

The others are pulled from their mounts but when they loosen my hands, I shrug off their attempts to assist me and slide to the mounting block unaided. We are to walk the final yards, Susanna, then Mary, then me. The press of the crowd is too much for the guards to hold back. I hear the occasional cheer amongst the catcalling and the insults. A ripe plum is pushed within my hand. I draw upon its succulence. The juice runs down my chin, staining my flesh blood-red. We are nearing the gallows now. Heavitree they call it and that oaken beam is indeed heavy, heavy with the weight of men's lives that have ended here.

They are here our arresters, our accusers, the sightseers, those who have come to gloat. It seems our trial was not enough. They wish us to put on a show for the onlookers. Master Hann, he that calls hissen Reverend. He is pulling Mary forward first. Like as not she'll say naught. She was ever a mite simple and these past days have addled her wits still further. What's to be gained from more questions? Look at ee now, thinks hissen so important he do. The crowd has hushed to hear his speech. Only a child's cry, a dog's bark and Mary's wailing; that's all I hear. I want to harken to the birdsong; I want to dream messen far from here. I don't wish that matters were different. No. I have long been set upon this path, there can be no other. Yet I might yearn for one more moment's solitude, one more glimpse of the cot that I called home.

"Mary Trembles, what have you to say as to the crime you are now to die for?"

Will she answer? Yes. It seems that she has found her tongue. But what's to be said now? Nought she can say will alter matters.

"I have spoken as much as I can speak already and can speak no more," Mary says.

Hann will ne'er be content with that. He wants to hear her speak out. He wants tales of diabolical congress. I can hear his words, ranting as he is. What will Mary say?

"In what shape did the devil come to you?"

"The devil came to me once, I think, like a lion," she replies.

Ah. Her fear has loosed her tongue.

"Did he offer any violence to you?"

"No, not at all but he did frighten me, thou he did naught to me. I cried to God and asked what he wanted from me and he vanished."

"Did he give thee any gift or didst thou make him any promise?"

"No."

Well that will not placate Hann. He'll not desist until she has spake the words he wants.

"Did he come to make use of thy body?"

The man's lascivious thoughts are plain to see. Look at him now, eyes bulging, tongue running round his lips, sweat upon his brow. He'd shake the words from her if he could.

"Never in my life," she says.

Come on Mary, 'tis as good as done. Utter the words he wants to hear. But Hann has moved on.

"Have you a secret teat?"

"None."

Does she think she can deny all now and go free like Mistress Caddy? She's more of a fool than I thought.

"Mary Trembles, was not the devil there, in that gaol, with Susanna, under her petticoat, when I was once in prison with you both?"

Now he speaks of the time when he questioned her in Byddeforde. What benefit to mention this now? Mary knows not how to answer.

Hann will not be quietened, "Susanna Edwards told me the devil was there but is now fled and that it was the devil that halted my way when I was going to Taunton with my son, he who is now a minister."

Ah. So the thread of uncertainty be growing in Hann's mind then. 'Twill be like a canker, eating at his composure. He will know no peace henceforth. I cannot help but smile. This. This was ever my intention.

"Thou speakest now as a dying woman and as the Psalmist says, 'I will confess my iniquities and acknowledge all my sin.'"

He prates of the Bible. I sense his desperation. Mary is ever afeard when folk do bandy about what they hold out as the word of God.

"We find that Mary Magdalene had seven devils and she came to Christ and obtained mercy. If thou breaks thy league with the devil and make a covenant with God, thou too may obtain mercy. If thou hast anything to speak, speak thy mind."

Mercy! The man preaches mercy! We all know that there can be no mercy here. The crowd have come to see us die and canting of mercy will provoke them sorely. 'Tis a spectacle they want and they'll have no truck with such talk of lenience. 'Tis all a jaunt to them. The food sellers, the jugglers, the fiddler with his flea-ridden monkey and us, us as just another side-show. But Mary, will Mary sense hope where there is none? I am close enough to hear her words but those at the back of the crowd must wonder at the delay.

"I have spoke the truth and can speak no more," she says. "Master Hann, I desire that they also may come forth and confess, as I have done."

What's this Mary? You wish Susanna and I to confess? Well, we spoke out in that fashion in court yesterday. That's made Hann think. He turns to me now. I am not so addle-pated that he will trip me with his fine words. I shall say as I like. The voices. The voices will speak for me and confusion upon all who seek to entrap me. What will I say? Mayhap today I shall deny all.

"Temperance Lloyd, have you made any contract with the devil?"

"None."

"Did he ever take any of thy blood?"

"No."

"How did he appear to thee at first, or where? In the street? In what shape?"

Ah, he will talk of devils then. I can make him fear my power.

"In a woeful shape."

"Had he ever any carnal knowledge of thee?"

"No, never."

"What did he do when he came to thee?"

"He caused me to go and do harm."

And I'll do harm to you sir. That I will. The crowd are getting restless. Mary is still weeping. Her face is blotched and red, as if she already has the noose around her neck.

"And did you go?"

So he wants tales of harms I have done. I'll give him tales. 'Tis as well to spark the interest of the crowd. 'Twill be my final opportunity. Give 'em summat to remember. Give 'em summat to fear.

"I did hurt a woman afore, against my conscience. The devil carried me up to her door, which was open." I pause. "The woman's name was Mistress Grace Thomas."

"What caused you to do her harm? What malice had you against her? Did she do you harm?"

None you fool, none. 'Twas the voices. Why will they not understand?

"How many did you destroy and hurt?"

Many, too many, those that I cannot number in my head. Back over a score of years or more. But I've done good too. I've healed. I've tended. That should count for summat. I'm getting tired now. I cannot recount all the names. Let us be done with all this.

"None but she."

"Did you know any mariners that you or your associates destroyed by overturning of ships and boats?"

In court I did own to this but 'tis time to twist the truth.

"No. I never hurt any ship, nor barque, nor boat in my life.'"

"Was it you or Susanna that did bewitch the children?"

Susanna? How am I to know what she has done? He looks to lay her crimes at my door, does he?

"I sold an apple and the child took an apple from me and the mother took the apple from the child, for which I was very angry. Mistress Fellow, she did rail at me that time. The child died but 'twas the smallpox, that did fer en."

"Temperance, how did you come in to hurt Mistress Grace Thomas? Did you pass through the keyhole of the door, or was the door ajar?"

So, he has got nowhere with these other matters. Now he returns to Mistress Thomas.

"The devil did lead me upstairs and the door was open and this is all the hurt I did."

"How do you know it was the devil?"

One can allus tell the devil for all he comes in many guises. Surely one who calls hissen a man o' God should know that.

"I knew it by his eyes."

"Had you no discourse or treaty with him?"

"No. He said I should go along with him to destroy a woman and I told him I would not. He said he would make me and then the devil beat me about the head."

"Why had you not called upon God?"

God. God. What use is it to call upon God? He abandoned me long since. Look at Mary. Look at Susanna, praying even now. What good will it do?

"He would not let me do it," I say.

'Tis hot, mortal hot. We've been standing overlong without a tree to shade us. My head is spinning now. What must I say?

"You say you never hurt ships nor boats. Did you ever ride over an arm of the sea on a cow?"

What nonsense folk do speak. How to turn this man from me? I fear they will not let me sit and if I do not sit, I might fall. Questions. Allus questions. I do not stand here accused alone.

"No master, 'twas she."

I wave my hand towards Susanna. That's it, I'll see that the fault be not mine alone. I'll turn his mind to another. She's done naught but blubber and mutter psalms. We will see what she has to say.

"'Tis a grevious lie. You are the cause of bringing me to my death," Susanna sobs.

So that's the way of it. She will cast the blame upon me now. Me who did teach her much, who did tease her powers from her. Now she turns to Hann, she does. As if he will have sympathy. Her finger points in my direction.

Susanna is whining now, I hear her speak, "Goody Lloyd said, when she was first brought to gaol, that if she was to be hanged, I would hang alongside her. She said I should ride on a cow before her, which I never did."

I did. I did speak thus. Out fate was ever intertwined. There was ne'er a doubt that Mistress Caddy would go free. I could foretell that. It would always be we three. There's a neatness to it, giving them three to swing from the scaffold together. But Hann has not done with Susanna yet.

"Susanna Edwards, did you see the shape of a bullock? At the time of your first examination you said it was like a short black man, about the length of your arm."

"He was black sir."

"Are you willing to have any prayers?"

Susanna nods and Hann is rattling words he feels might comfort us. The crowd are impatient. The buzz of their talk irritates me. I can scarce hear what Hann says. 'Tis not for my benefit anyroad. No God-filled mutterings can ease my path. Susanna and Mary are upon their knees. I will fall to my knees too, 'twill be more restful thus. But I'll have none of their prayers. Not now. Not ever. They cannot have dominion over my deepest thoughts.

Susanna is pleading for a psalm to be sung. What know we of psalms? Why does she show her weakness thus? Singing now she is, or what passes for the same. The crowd are taking up the words.

"I waited patiently for the Lord; and he inclined unto me and heard my cry. He brought me up also out of an horrible pit, out of the miry clay."

I have long been in this pit. The pit of my imaginings. The pit that gives me my art. The voices hold me here. I do not look for escape.

"And he hath put a new song in my mouth, even praise unto our God: many shall see it, and fear and shall trust in the Lord."

Let them sing. I will put no song in my mouth. Not for me this show of piety. But fear. Oh yes there will be fear. Not mine though, Not mine. The crowd are moved by this. Their song grows ever louder but it will not invade my mind. It will not. I will not let it drown the voices that speak to me.

"For innumerable evils have compassed me about: mine iniquities have taken hold upon me, so that I am not able to look up; they are more than the hairs of mine head: therefore my heart faileth me," they sing.

A song for the scaffold this, in truth but I will have none of it.

"But I am poor and needy; yet the Lord thinketh upon me. Thou art my help and my deliverer, make no tarrying, O my God."

They've finished. The crowd have fallen silent. They are pushing us towards the platform. We mount the ladder now, Mary Trembles first, then Susanna Edwards. I am the last. Yet, no, I am the first. I am all. Susanna's noose is placed around her neck. The hangman is asking if she has any last words before he lowers the hood. She speaks and again she carps of God. If I had saliva in my throat I would spit in the dust but my mouth is dry, dry as chaff.

"Lord Jesus speed me, though my sins be red as scarlet, the Lord Jesus can make them white as snow. The Lord help my soul."

Sins as red as scarlet? There be sinners here 'tis true but who be those sinners? That's the matter to ponder on. The hood is lowered. The stool is kicked from beneath her feet. The crowd gasp. Her body jerks and writhes, on and on. Not for us the luxury of hangers-on within the crowd; those who might pull upon our legs to hasten our end. So Susanna will dance and dance as her bowels loosen and her bladder empties on the ground. I say no friends, yet I have glimpsed those in the crowd who might have been close to Susanna in a life that has long-since been forgotten. Yes, I caught sight of Bess Gard as we passed her by, her two sons beside her and an infant in her arms. Sickly too that one. He had the mark of death upon him. Strange that so many of her children have been taken, or mayhap not so strange. Who would have thought that she would have come to watch her mother die? There was no place for Susanna in Bess Gard's life. Not once Bess had put on airs and married above her station. Moved on, Bess did, rejecting her past. Susanna had not exchanged words with her for many a year, for all they did live in the same town. That Bess, she'd cross the street and turn away if her mother was nigh. But she was here. Here today. In sadness or in triumph? Prompted by duty or by guilt? I know not. Did Susanna spy her daughter amongst those who came to witness her end? I trust not. I be that glad I have had no child who might spurn me.

Mary screams and screams. It's her turn now. She looks to me. Does she think I can, by some diabolical power, save her? Or does she blame me for her end?

"Lord Jesus receive my soul. Lord Jesus speed me."

That's it. Her final words. Now they come for me. They expect me to ask for mercy. Shall I? Shall I not? I will not beg but 'twill do no harm to give a dainty speech.

"Jesus Christ speed me well. Lord forgive all my sins. Lord Jesus Christ be merciful to my poor soul."

Will that appease them? 'Twas mere words, for form's sake. Now the sheriff will have his say. Will this never be done? The heat weakens me.

"You are looked on as the woman that hath debauched the other two. Did you ever lie with devils?"

How many more times? I could say yay. I could say nay. What difference will it make? Let's deny it; 'twill be speedier thus.

"No."

"Did you know of their coming to gaol?"

"No."

"Have you anything to say to satisfy the world?"

Why should I satisfy a world that has done naught for me?

"I forgive them, as I desire the Lord Jesus Christ will forgive me."

But I don't. I do not forgive, nor do I forget and nor shall they. Mayhap I should not have spake of forgiveness. Will they let me talk of devils once more?

"The greatest thing I did was to Mistress Grace Thomas. The devil met me in the street and bid me kill her," I say.

"In what shape or colour was he?"

"In black like a bullock."

That's what they need to hear. Darkness. Devils. That will turn their minds.

"How did you know you did it? How went you in? Through the keyhole or through the door?"

"At the door."

On and on he goes; keyholes, doors, what matters it? We've had all this already. To what end? The noose dangles afore me. All this prattle is for naught. First Hann, now the sheriff. Let's be done with it.

"Did you ever lie with the devil?"

I'll not speak of the fleshly arts. I'll not give them the satisfaction of hearing how I did lie with men. And not just men. No. I owned to it in court but this is a time for denial. Confuse them. Turn my words so they will doubt what is true and what is fancy.

"No. I did not lie with any devil."

"Did the devil never promise you anything?"

"No, never."

"Then you have served a very bad master, who gave you nothing."

So, they will say he is my master then.

"Well, consider, you are departing this world; do you believe there is a God?"

Now is the time for the religious cant, it seems. I can give a pretty gallows homily. They can scribe it down those pamphleteers. Oh yes, there's those who will recall my name long after my persecutors are but dust.

"Yes."

I am drawing nearer now. I have no regrets. It is the time for death's oblivion.

"Do you believe in Jesus Christ?"

"Yes and I pray Jesus Christ to pardon all my sins."

The rope. The rope is rough upon my chin. They offer me the hood. I shake my head. I will gaze into their eyes until mine do close a final time. The crowd fall silent. Their faces are a blur but I feel their uncertainty. I sense their fear.

Epilogue
Martha's Story
Autumn 2020

In the crowded school hall, Martha sat between Zainab and Lucie. There was a buzz of conversation, as they waited for the annual awards ceremony to begin. At the back, sat their parents. Martha tried to ignore Hebe's frantic waving. Her mother was oblivious to the stir that her unconventional appearance attracted and now to wave, as if Martha was in the infants, it was mortifying. As space was limited, each student was allocated just two seats in the audience. Gran would not have coped with the crowd so, after much thought, Martha had invited Joan to take her second ticket. The two were still meeting regularly as Joan was helping Martha with her family tree. It had taken Martha a while to pluck up the courage to ask Joan to be her guest. Would she think it was stupid? Would Joan not want to come and not know how to refuse? When Martha finally blurted out the

311

invitation, in an embarrassed rush, Joan had been visibly touched and eager to accept.

After just a few weeks, Martha was beginning to enjoy life in the sixth form. Mr Mortimer had been very pleased with her project and suggested that she might continue to work on it as an extended project qualification. Martha had got to know Lucie when she found that they had English classes together and now Lucie often joined Martha and Zainab in the sixth form common room at lunch times. There were still sideways glances and snide remarks from a few other students but it was easier to ignore these when there were three of you. Having friends to confide in was a new experience for Martha. Hunter had gone to college in Exeter to study Sports Science. He was enjoying the course but finding the social side of college life difficult. The bullies had crushed him and Martha was concerned for his mental health. He'd stopped training with the county athletics squad, spending his evenings and weekends at home, afraid that he might be spotted if he went into town. He still refused to meet up with Martha and Zainab.

Zainab was looking nervous. They were all to be given their exam certificates but Martha knew that Zainab was secretly hoping that she might also get the maths prize. Martha's own anxiety stemmed from a different cause. The prize-giving held no qualms, she had no expectations beyond her GCSE certificate but she'd made plans with Zainab for after the ceremony and this was the source of her disquiet. The headmaster walked up to the lectern and a hush descended on the hall. As their names were called, students filed across the stage to receive their certificates from the chair of governors. Zainab's name was read out as the recipient of the maths award. Martha was still clapping and smiling as Zainab returned to her seat. No one seemed to be going up for the next prize. Martha had been so excited for Zainab that she'd missed the announcement. Lucie dug her in the ribs.

"It's you," she said. "Go on. You've won the history prize."

Martha went bright red, pushed her glasses up her nose and got to her feet.

"This is for hard work and achievement at GCSE and an outstanding submission as part of the enrichment project," the headmaster said, shaking Martha by the hand.

The chair of governors handed her a small cup. Martha's name was engraved on one of the shields that were fixed to the base. Taking the cup and muttering her thanks, Martha walked across the stage, desperately hoping that she would not stumble on the steps. She walked back to her seat, past Kayleigh, past Jeremy, past others who had taunted her. She fixed her eyes on Zainab and Lucie and smiled.

***

The girls stood in the school car park, clutching their certificates and awards. Hebe opened the door of the battered Nissan Micra.

"Are you coming Martha?" she asked. "I'm off to Gran's for a couple of hours before we go home."

"Zainab and I have something important that we must do. Please could you take my certificate and cup and I'll pop up to Gran's when we're done?"

Thunderclouds were gathering in the sultry September evening sky. Before nightfall they would unleash a storm on the intolerant town. Martha and Zainab walked along by the hedge that bordered the park. They were approaching the gates. They could already hear the shouts from the group of boys that were loitering by the park's entrance. As they'd feared, here were Jeremy, Tyrone and their gang with girls, including Kayleigh and Skye, simpering on the edges of the crowd. Jeremy swigged the last of his drink and lobbed the empty can into the garden of the house opposite the park gates.

"Bloody paedo," someone yelled.

There were a few half-hearted cat-calls of support. Martha and Zainab did not go undetected, nor were they ignored. Their progress slowed and then stopped, as the gang surged forward blocking the path.

Kayleigh shrieked and pointed, "Look, it's the freak and her terrorist mate."

Sycophantic laughter drowned a comment from Skye. Martha felt her cheeks redden and tears prick her eyes. Momentarily, she felt her resolve weaken, then she glanced at Zainab. With a deep breath, Martha took Zainab firmly by the hand. Together, the girls walked up the steps and knocked on Hunter's door.

Sins as Red as Scarlet

A song by Dan Britton
www.chrisconway.org/dan.html

Sins as red as scarlet
That's what they say I've done
But I'm just an ordinary woman
I've never hurt anyone
Witch, pariah, dangerous liar
I just want to be left alone
Now I wait here in front of the jeering crowd
For my Lord to carry me home
Sins as red as scarlet
since the day I was born
When you're not the same as the others
You just get treated with scorn
Sorceress, crone, driven from my home
Just because I practiced my craft
Now I stand with the noose around my neck
While the lynchmob heckle and laugh
Sins as red as scarlet
Now the ending is near
Narrow minds have sealed my fate
Full of hatred and fear
They raise their hand to what they don't understand
The charges against me were lies
Now I swing at the end of the Hangman's rope
As the darkness covers my eyes

About the Author

Janet Few inhabits the past. You may find her lurking in her four-hundred-year-old North Devon cottage, or spot her thinly disguised as the formidable Mistress Agnes. This alter ego is a goodwife of a certain age, who leads a somewhat chaotic life during the mid-seventeenth century. One way or another, most of Janet's time is spent working to inspire others with a love of history, heritage and the written word.

In a vain effort to support her incurable book buying habit, in the past, Janet has been known to pull the odd pint or two, sell hamsters and support very special schoolchildren. Somewhere along the way, she acquired a doctorate in community history "for fun". Janet has an international reputation as a family historian, giving presentations across the English-speaking world. She has written several non-fiction history books and *Sins as Red as Scarlet* is her second published novel. The first, *Barefoot on the Cobbles*, is based on another North Devon tragedy.

Any time that Janet can carve from her history-obsessed existence, is spent embarrassing her descendants, travelling and trying to make her garden behave itself. Janet is fascinated by human behaviour, past and present, real and fictional. She loves the wonderful Devon landscape and leading her grandchildren astray.

If you have enjoyed reading this book, it would make a decidedly eccentric author very happy if you were to leave a few words on the reviewing platform of your choice.

Keep in touch with Janet Few via her website and blog thehistoryinterpreter.wordpress.com
or by following her on Twitter @janetfew

By the Same Author
Fiction

Barefoot on the Cobbles: a Devon Tragedy (Blue Poppy Publishing 2018) Winner of a Chill with a Book Award.

What People have said about Barefoot on the Cobbles

"Impeccably researched." "Clovelly is described with such vividness that it is itself a character in the novel. Few's gift lies in how she imbues her writing with a sense of period in the smallest details."

From a review by Katherine Mezzacappa, for the Historical Novel Society

"The creative energy of a dedicated historian bursts through the facts and research in a beautifully written narrative about real people. Janet's novel speaks on so many levels: a riveting holiday read for everyone, grounded in serious academic research married to a living empathy for the people about whom she writes. ... In just sixteen pages of chapter eight Janet takes us into one of the most poignant and empathic commentaries of WW1 that I have ever read."

S.C. Goodreads

"I would highly recommend this book to anyone who enjoys historical fiction with a gritty edge and multi-faceted characters."

C.A.

"I have never cared *so much* about so many people in one story, not just Daisy and her parents Polly and Albert, all of them! Each character is skilfully drawn, the joys and woes of their lives are vividly portrayed; we see and hear them going about their daily business."

Devon Family History Society magazine

"A lovely story, more so as it was true. So descriptive you could imagine yourself transported back in time."

Chill with a Book Reader

"I could hardly put it down! So impressed by the detail, the believable characters, the villages and the research I know was put in. Had to pause after the battlefield chapter - so much realism – the author immediately paints a picture of the devastation, the thoughts of the soldiers and the dreary daily routines required when they moved positions. A sad and gripping tale to the end."

R.S.

"This book brings alive my home. Awakens the past and inspires the future. Loved every single word. Many many thanks."

Clovelly resident

The following is the introductory chapter from Barefoot on the Cobbles. A list of non-fiction titles follows thereafter.

Barefoot of the Cobbles: a Devon Tragedy
January 1919

The magistrate was saying something but with throat tightening and heat rising, Polly struggled to focus. He repeated his question but she was transfixed, unable to answer. Images and incidents from the past kaleidoscoped before her eyes. She saw her childhood home in the secluded Devon valley, her courtship with Alb, her firstborn being put into her arms. Her daughter, Daisy, skipping barefoot down the Clovelly cobblestones, living, loving, laughing. Daisy, bone thin and dying. Daisy, whose passing had somehow, in a way that Polly couldn't comprehend, led to her being here in this crowded, claustrophobic courtroom, with every eye upon her. She must compose herself, pay attention, escape from this nightmare. All she wanted to do was dream of the past, both good and bad times but somehow more certain, safer, predictable. Times before everything began to spiral terrifyingly out of control.

Mr Lefroy, the solicitor, had assured her that she wouldn't hang; this was a manslaughter charge not murder. Nonetheless, phantom gallows had haunted Polly's restless nights. Even when she calmed and the hangman's noose receded, there was still prison. Prison meant Holloway. Polly's hazy and fragmented impression of Holloway was gleaned from the terror-ridden stories of suffragettes' force-feeding, that the pre-war newspapers had revelled in. Or would they say she was mad? Echoes of insanity had touched her in the past. There were barely acknowledged tales of people she knew who had been locked away. When compared to the prospect of prison, the asylum at Exminster was somehow more familiar but no less formidable.

Polly knew she must concentrate, breathe slowly, think about what she should say. Mr Lefroy had explained that all she needed to do was to keep calm and tell the truth; so difficult in this alien environment with all these well-to-do folk looking on. Faces. Faces whirled and blurred in front of her. There was Alb, shuffling in his chair and running his finger round the restricting collar that she had helped him to fasten only this morning. He looked lost and bewildered, unfamiliar without his beloved trilby hat. Faces of the villagers, reproachful and remote. Mr Collins, her accuser, cold and confident. Mrs Stanbury, gossiping neighbour, once a friend maybe but now here as a witness for the prosecution. Then, overlaying all of these, the vision of Daisy. Daisy looking like a young lady in her new hat, proudly setting off for her first job beyond the security of the village. Daisy fighting, screaming, twisting her head away from the spoon that held the broth that might save her. Daisy dying. Was it really her fault, as they were saying? Polly wondered. Could she have done any more? She was a mother; mothers should protect their children. She had tried, she really had, struggled in vain to shield them all from harm. The enormity of her many failures consumed her. There was Bertie, not quite the full shilling, Violet and her troubles, the worry over Leonard while he'd been away at sea during the war. Nelson, poor little Nelson and now, Daisy. If she and Albert were sent to prison, what would happen to young Mark and her two little flowers, Lily and Rosie, hardly more than babies in her eyes? Violet was scarcely old enough to look after them all and would the children be allowed to stay in the cottage? There would be nothing but the workhouse, forbidding and final, a fortress of despair.

***

At the back of the courtroom, in the seats reserved for the press, sat Richard Ottley. He had been expecting it to be merely another day in court; yet more hours of listening to melodramatic tales of insignificant people's lives. His forty years as a journalist had exposed him to tragedy, to violence and to despair. He'd seen defendants who were angry, who were terrified, who were blatantly lying. It was all one to him. Empathy was long-buried, part of his nature no more. He was there to record, to report, to remain impartial and aloof. There was something though about this case, these defendants, these witnesses, that had caught his jaded attention. The evidence unfolded, the confident tones of the officials interspersed with the hesitant whispers of those for whom court was an intimidating experience. Ottley found himself uncharacteristically caught up in the events and emotions that were being laid before him. He looked at the magistrates, the counsel, the prosecutors. His gaze swung from the accusers to the accused. How had they all been drawn inexorably, inevitably, to this day, to this courtroom, into this horrific situation? Were there clues in what had gone before; harbingers of this dreadful moment? What events, what actions, what hurts, in the tangled web of their pasts had brought them, inescapably, to this appalling instant?

Non-Fiction

Remember Then: women's memories of 1946-1969 and how to write your own (Family History Partnership 2015)

'I have laughed and cried reading all the memories. It just transports me back to that period.'

Coffers, Clysters, Comfrey and Coifs: the lives of our seventeenth century ancestors (Family History Partnership 2012) available from Blue Poppy Publishing.

'Whether you like to read a book cover to cover, or dip into random chapters, this book presents a rich flavour and a well-balanced portrait of seventeenth century life.'

The Family Historian's Enquire Within (Family History Partnership 2014)
Shortlisted for a Chartered Institute of Library and Information Professionals award.

'If you only have one Family History reference book on your shelf, this is the one you need.'

Ten Steps to a One-Place Study (Blue Poppy Publishing 2020).

'An essential purchase if you're considering starting a One-Place Study - or if you simply want to know more about what it would entail.' Peter Calver - Lost Cousins.

A request from Blue Poppy Publishing

We sincerely hope you enjoyed this book as much as we enjoyed producing it. On behalf of the author, we would encourage you to write a review of this book. Every author writes for different reasons but, when we publish our work, what we desire most of all is for it to be read. As much as it may seem like a small thing, every review, especially those on goodreads.com and on Amazon helps towards getting the book noticed by potential new readers. We especially appreciate sincere reviews with a few words of explanation as to what you enjoyed and even what you did not enjoy about the book. Something which one reader may not have enjoyed might in fact be the very thing another reader is looking for. Thank you.

You can find out more about Blue Poppy Publishing, including our other authors and titles, as well as how we help aspiring authors to self-publish their work, by visiting our website at bluepoppypublishing.co.uk.